MW01114001

The Were Queen

A novel of the Seven Deadly Veils, Book Eight

Diana Marik

Praise for Diana Marik's Veilverse

The Were Queen

"Marik excels at building the tension throughout the story to the final conclusion." —Goodreads Reviewer

"I loved the characters in this book. There's lots of action to keep readers turning the pages." —Amazon Reviewer

Veil of Honor

"Marik has done it again, written an 'I don't want to stop reading even to go to sleep' novel with Veil of Honor. Her Seven Deadly Veils series remains one of my all-time favorite vampire series." —Amazon Reviewer

"I can never get enough of the sexy, honorable Remare and the chemistry between him and Miranda. Lord Valadon remains a true and honorable leader." —Goodreads Reviewer

Veil of Orion

"Orion and Bas' love story ignites in this book. Marik really turns up the heat showing us the unbridled passion between Orion and Bastien." —Goodreads Reviewer

"Be prepared for lots of steam, laughs, fun, and anxious moments. Bas and Orion's attraction to each other and their chemistry is off the charts." —Amazon Reviewer

Veil of Destiny

"Danger, deception, loyalty, love, romance, and history are all seamlessly woven together which is what Ms. Marik does very well. A captivating storyline, as with each book in the series, some secrets are revealed and some left hidden, leaves you with a thought-provoking plot and desiring the next book in the intriguing series." —LM Reigel Reviews

"The relationship between Remare and Miranda has really grown into something very special. Ms. Marik's detail when it comes to weaving in the history of art, books, and possible origins of Elementals is fascinating. What a web of intrigue Ms. Marik continues to weave!"   —Goodreads Reviewer

"The sixth book in Marik's Seven Deadly Veils series (if you include the novella), Miranda's relationship with Remare has grown and strengthened, like her powers. Miranda meets other elementals who give Miranda an insight on her powers, their origins and possibly her future. Filled with spectacular imagery, Miranda's journey is bumpy, but the resolution is satisfying, as if Marik had veiled Miranda's past, this book blows everything open."   —Amazon Reviewer

Veil of Secrets

"The characters are well-developed and fascinating. The series plot is growing and expanding; the action, suspense and romance are woven perfectly together!"
—LM Reigel Reviews

"Ms. Marik has created an interesting, intricate vampire world. All paranormal fans need to read this series filled with strong, sophisticated, fun, sexy characters."
—Amazon Reviewer

"A fantastic installment in this intriguing series. Superb! A delicious plot! Once again all her richly developed characters pop in the spotlight teasing with juicy clues behind the veil. When it's pulled back be prepared for some shocking revelations."   —Goodreads Reviewer

Veil of Darkness

"The chemistry between Miranda and Remare is extraordinary. Marik holds nothing back in this action-packed romance, which delivers all of the danger, darkness and sensuality that readers crave; this is one series not to be missed." TOP PICK!   —RT Book Reviews

"Smoking hot chemistry! A wonderful suspense and action novel complete with a sizzling romance. Very addicting!"
—L.M. Reigel Reviews

"Another fantastic read in this series. An amazing journey. The characters come to life on the pages pulling you into their world." —PNR/UF Book Lover's Haven

Veil of Mists

"I am obsessed with this series. Diana Marik has created a high intensity series that grabs you and doesn't let go."
—Lisa Reigel Reviews

"Danger and deception know no bounds in this riveting second installment of the *Seven Deadly Veils* series. Complex liaisons deliver the action and suspense paranormal fans crave. The passion and sensuality exceed expectations."
—RT Book Reviews

"Completely captivating! I LOVE this series and can't get enough of RRRemare. So much happening in this book...deception at its finest! Just when you think you have it figured out, everything changes. Definitely couldn't put this book down and one hell of a ride."
—Paranormal/Urban Fantasy Book Lovers Haven

The Blue Veil

"Marik's compelling delivery commands readers' attention; the easy, seamless passion and intensity between characters is a welcome companion to a perfect balance of action and suspense." —RT Book Reviews

"The characters are edgy and intriguing. The plot is suspenseful and sexy. I'm drawn into this series and fascinated by this world that Ms. Marik has created."
—Comfy Chair Books

"I am so Team Remare. This novella just keeps us hooked."
—Sik Reviews

"Just one word...Remare. Love that dark and dangerous vampire."

Veil of Shadows

"The suspense is as dramatic and intense as the action, and paired with Marik's steamy sex scenes, will leave readers satisfied on many levels. Off-the-chart chemistry."

"I flipping LOVED this book. I was drawn immediately to the main characters of *Veil of Shadows*. The characters are edgy, sexy, and intriguing. Her writing style drew me in and kept me fascinated; the suspense kept me on the edge waiting to see what would happen next. *Veil of Shadows* is fast paced and action packed. I highly recommend this book to fans of paranormal romance and romantic urban fantasy."

"Ms. Marik has made this new paranormal world come alive and leave me begging for more."

"I absolutely LOVED it! With so many awesome characters, can't decide who I love the most! Refreshing story that completely captivated me. I simply couldn't put it down until the last page."

Dedication

To all the Poets and Musicians who inspire us.
You make the world a better place.
Keep on keeping on.

Acknowledgments

A special thank you to my readers who continue to encourage me. I cannot tell you how much your kind words have meant to me and how much I appreciate you taking the time to let me know how much you've enjoyed my novels. Thank you, also, to my fabulous editor, Jessica Bimberg, who has been with me from the very beginning and kept me on the right track, and to Kris Norris for creating my wonderful book covers.

Chapter One

"She's a beauty, isn't she?"

Lizandra Wells, The Were Queen, stood on the precipice near Summit Rock in New York City's Central Park and ran her eyes over Black Star Clan's latest money-making venture. Her chin lifting with pride and her spine straightening to her impressive height, she inhaled the spicy scents drifting upward. "Andouille sausage sauteed with garlic and onions." *Mmmm.* Liz moaned sensually as a smile brightened her face. "*LAWE'S CAJUN GRILL.* I love it! The restaurant should bring in a fair amount of revenue for our clan."

"Hell, yeah!" Tia, one of Liz's personal guards and closest friends, gazed down in the clearing where their people were gathering for the ribbon-cutting ceremony. "Lawe is originally from New Orleans, and with all his family's recipes, he makes the most mouth-watering Cajun and Creole meals. Everyone says so." She licked her lips and purred. "I can almost taste the jambalaya. If the humans can have their Boathouse Restaurant on the east side of the park, we can have ours here on the west side."

Liz nodded. Along with the rock-climbing recreation area, the miniature golf attraction, and now, the open-air restaurant, Cyrus Lasker, her current alpha, aka *The White Wolf*, had proven his worth by designing and constructing projects that generated income to benefit their pack. A low growl of approval escaped her mouth; to say he was talented was a woeful understatement. With his shimmering blond hair and a physique resembling a Viking warrior, no other Were was built as huge or powerful as he, not in their clan or any other she'd ever seen or even heard of.

"It's a good idea." Ever watchful, Tia continued to scan the area. "In the warmer months, we can now hang out in the bar area of the restaurant, instead of being confined down below."

Down below was Werehaven, Black Star Clan's underground compound that housed a massive dance floor, two bars, private rooms, and Liz's favorite, Songhaven, where she often played piano and held concerts for her people. Music was as integral to her as being queen.

But Tia was right, the werewolves needed more outdoor areas to socialize and congregate. Being indoors for too long strained the composure of her people—something that was already being tested by the resentment of a rival clan, The Red Claws, who claimed Riverside Park, the territory that ran along the Hudson River, as their home base. A menacing snarl escaped her lips. Their constant skirmishes were wearing thin.

Fights between the more aggressive males within her clan had already broken out. *Like I don't have enough to worry about.* Thank God, Gavin McCray had been there. Her beta had always been able to mollify potentially explosive situations. *Always.*

Tia raised a brow as she tracked Liz's gaze. "I notice you can't take your eyes off of Gavin. Our *Red Wolf's* almost as muscular as Cyrus. But hot dayum! That red hair of his looks like something you'd want to run your fingers through. I bet it's real silky-like, smooth, and shiny like the rest of him." Grinning like a fool, she let out a sexy, naughty laugh that would make any dirty old man proud. "Any regrets?"

"Hmmp!" Liz scoffed as she tried to squelch her emotions concerning Gavin. Something that was growing harder and harder to do. Tia had been a confidante of hers for years and knew her very well. Too well. "As if you don't already know."

Tia's voice went high as she quickly turned toward her, making her gold earrings dangle. "I *know* you once told me he was the love of your life."

He was and still...

Sharon, one of the restaurant's waitresses, whose hair was as red as Liz's beta's, put her hand on Gavin's arm. Smiling, she leaned in to whisper something in his ear. Liz barely suppressed her lethally long nails from becoming claws, her beast yearning to break free. After Gavin relayed the information to Lawe, both males threw their heads back and chuckled. The sight of them laughing stirred up old memories, old emotions.

Of all the wolves in their pack, Gavin was still the handsomest. And that was saying a lot since the Black Stars had some of the most gorgeous men around. "That's true. But love doesn't get the bills paid. Cyrus has been good for the clan. Look at all he's built." Liz pointed to the fire pit near the restaurant and then to the massive gazebo where the Weres hung out on rainy days. "His projects have generated a nice amount of much-needed funds."

"I know that," Tia shrugged, "but money doesn't keep you warm at night."

"No, it doesn't, but it lets you sleep peacefully."

"And you didn't sleep peacefully with Gavin?"

Her growl returned. "You already know the answer to that." *Regrets?* Yes, Lizandra had a few, but she was a queen, and queens didn't have the luxury of making decisions based on personal preferences. Queens made resolutions that were in the best interest of the clan, even if that meant sacrificing their own happiness.

An image of an evening long ago surfaced in her mind. It was after the Lunar Run—their most sacred night when the moon was full and the Weres shed their human form and transitioned into wolves. After completing the exhilarating course around the myriad trails of the park, Gavin had come to her in her private rooms.

Presently, and before she could stifle it, her body shivered at the memory. She'd never forgotten the heated look in his eyes that would not be denied as he stood before her in all his glory. He was fucking magnificent, his body undulating with every breath. Frustrated at the time spent apart from each other, they had made love all night long, becoming completely lost in their passions. Both had woken with a soreness neither one of them complained about.

While they'd been involved, there had been many nights like that. As if hearing her thoughts, Gavin smiled and nodded in her direction, then drank from his water bottle, one droplet sliding seductively down his throat and chest. Something stirred deep in her belly, something she quickly squashed. No one had ever made her feel the way he did, and as Were Queen, she had her choice of all the hot men in the clan, but none ever made her purr the way Gavin did...not even Cyrus.

And that was certainly not from a lack of trying.

But a war was now seemingly inevitable. It had been brewing for some time. And, after the Commissioner of Clans had ruled in Black Star's favor, yet again, Edgar Renworth, pack master of the Red Claws, was not to be denied. His persistent quest to gain rights to Central Park had never abated. He knew the worth of the city's predominant park and salivated at the financial potential.

When legal channels had failed, he turned to other more dubious means of persuasion, even trying to seduce her with promises of marriage to unite their clans. *As if!*

After her refusal, his hit squads ramped up their torment of members of Black Star by increasing their attacks on or near her territory. Some men just didn't like being told no. *Too fucking damn bad!* If he wanted a war, she'd oblige him.

That's why she'd made Cyrus her alpha. No one could beat him in a fight. Much to the chagrin and wrath of Gavin, who had been her alpha for years.

Tia kept her gaze on McCray. "He hasn't been the same since you demoted him to beta."

"I'm aware." Gavin had made his displeasure known on more than one occasion. "But, in these trying times, we all need to make sacrifices."

"Some more than others." Tia's eyes softened. "He still loves you, y'know."

Liz exhaled loudly. This was a conversation she'd had more than once and was tired of it. There was no good to come from dwelling on it. What was past, was past. "Enough. Let's go down there and join the others." Scampering down the hill, they reached the clearing by the restaurant and were quickly requested to pose for pictures. Lawe on one side, his wide grin showing off his pearly whites as well as a few gold teeth, and Cyrus on the other side.

"This is a dream come true for me. I've always wanted my own place." Lawe beamed at her, his Cajun accent always more prominent when he was excited. His muscles rippled under his navy tank, and his ebony skin glistened where the sun met his flesh. "My cousin, Remy, has his own bar and grill down in New Orleans. And, now, I have mine. I've been sending him pictures of LCG all afternoon. Best Cajun and Creole food in all of Manhattan."

"Absolutely the best." Liz smiled back at him as she and Tia took their seats at one of the outdoor tables. She particularly liked the way the place was designed with the circular bar in the center of the restaurant and the tables along the left and right wings. The floor-to-ceiling hurricane-safe windows were retractable to let in the cool air in summer and close in the wintry months. Not that the cold bothered the Weres much. They naturally ran hot, but they tried to accommodate their human customers whose patronage they desired.

Decades ago, when the vampires and Weres came out, so to speak, and one of Liz's relatives had discovered the underground cave that would become Werehaven, the City Council had proclaimed that Central Park belonged to all peoples during the day. Anyone could visit and enjoy the sites. But, as soon as the sun set and night fell, the park belonged to the Weres. Walls were heightened and gates secured to prevent curious humans from entering.

Any non-Were foolish enough to still be in the park after hours was immediately escorted off the grounds. Unless, of course, they had special permission from the queen to be there. But that was rarely given.

Since the humans had lucrative ventures—such as the zoo, ice skating rink, the carousel, and the restaurants—the Weres had petitioned for similar prospects for their people. After several negotiations with Brent and Quint, the clan's financial advisor and lawyer, respectively, the city legislators agreed. Of course, taxes and fees would be collected to benefit the city's treasury.

Cyrus, dressed in a white T-shirt that showed off his rippling biceps and jeans that clung nicely to his ass, sat across from her; excitement was etched in his face as he placed their meals of Crawfish Etouffee down. His grin never failed to stimulate as evidenced by the sighs of the females, and even a few males, who sat close by. "A glorious day, wouldn't you say?"

Liz inhaled the marvelous, spicy scent and groaned. "That smells heavenly."

"You know, there's a spot of land over there," he pointed with his fork, "that would be perfect for a concert area. You could give outdoor music performances, if you wanted."

That was Cyrus, all right, always thinking, always coming up with new ways of making money. "I'll think about it. Not sure about the acoustics, though. I like my own Songhaven."

"For certain." Cyrus took a bite of his meal and moaned his satisfaction. "And I love your music. I was just considering options. Something to think about, maybe in the future."

Liz nodded as her gaze swept to where Lawe was talking to Gavin. Shirtless, his tanned skin glistened with the summer's heat. He'd just put the finishing touches on the façade of the restaurant. Not only an excellent chiropractor, Gavin was also one of the best carpenters in the clan. His tool belt made his jeans hang low, and she couldn't help but admire the muscles in his back. Muscles she'd run her nails down many times.

Her attention was diverted when Brent and Quint joined them at the table. Talk about handsome, both were stunning. "All the necessary paperwork has been completed and filed with the proper authorities," Quint offered as he grabbed a roll from the bread basket and dunked it in the pineapple habanero sauce, then took a bite.

Liz nodded as she swallowed a delicious morsel. "Good to know."

Brent's focus landed on Cyrus. "I must say, your projects have certainly paid off. Can't wait to see what you come up with next."

One of Liz's most trusted confidantes who she'd known for years, Brent was not as brawny as some of the other Weres, but his eyes flashed with keen intelligence. And he was fast, faster than any of the other Weres, including his lover and life partner, Quint. Together, they made an incredible team, especially when they acted as scouts during their runs. No one could catch them.

Cyrus wiped his mouth on his napkin. "We were just discussing that. I had an idea for a band shell, something similar to what the humans have. Thought it would be entertaining if Liz ever felt like performing outdoors."

Liz's voice held a tone of finality. "A consideration to be discussed at another time. Today is to celebrate Lawe's opening."

"Here, here." Gavin approached with a tray full of chilled beers he set down on the table. His whiskey-colored eyes met hers, lingered there, then he lifted his bottle. "To an amazing future." He turned toward Lawe. "A toast to a great chef and an even better friend."

Lawe grinned and raised his drink. "True dat."

They all stood, and Liz belted out: "To Lawe, may *The Cajun Grill* be all you want it to be."

"To Lawe!" they all shouted out as they clinked their bottles.

Lawe saluted them from the bar and said, "Thank you. You can bet your asses it will be, and then some."

***

Later that evening, the Were Queen strolled through her rooms in Werehaven while the others were up above celebrating, because Liz wanted some alone time. She had much on her mind, not the least was the disturbing news Brent had hinted at when he accompanied her down the trails leading to their compound.

Liz stared at the pictures of her family on the shelf—some still living, others in heaven—and hoped they were proud of her. She knew they were, even though they'd never gone through the challenges she was now facing.

No, they'd had to survive far more severe circumstances.

She stared at the African masks hanging on the wall. Some of her ancestors were from the Caribbean via Africa. No doubt that was where her height came from. Other progenitors were originally from Ireland—which would account for her aquamarine eyes. She stroked some of the figurines that Gavin had brought her back from Dublin—a place she'd yet to visit. They once planned on vacationing there together, but that had never happened.

Liz's gaze lifted to regard the wall hangings and intricate designs on the pottery she'd brought back from Mexico. Her heritage was also of Spanish and Native American descent. Not a bad lineage, she thought. Pretty damned impressive. Pride had her smiling. *Try fitting all that on a census form.*

When she'd been younger, she tried for a modeling career to help pay her way through college and med school. But the white agencies thought her skin tone not fair enough; when she tried the Black ones, she was told she wasn't dark enough. "Can't please everyone," she muttered.

"You always talk to yourself?"

Liz turned to see Gavin leaning leisurely against the doorframe with his arms crossed over his chest. His grin and the glint in his eyes hinted at humor. "I knocked, but I don't think you heard me."

Liz admired his form as he stood nonchalantly waiting for her reply. "I do when I believe no one else is around. What's up?"

"Everyone's in a celebratory mood above." He flicked his eyes to the ceiling. "I'd have thought you could hear all the dancing and partying down here. People have been asking for you, wondering where you are."

She shrugged. "I just wanted a break. There's just so much celebrating a person can do."

"Is that right? I seem to remember a woman who loved to dance. Kept me up most of the night singing and dancing." His gaze drifted to her lips. "She used to smile more often."

"Back then, she didn't have to worry about an impending war with another clan."

Gavin stepped farther into the room, shutting the door behind him. "Any news?"

Liz dropped down onto her couch and rubbed her forehead. "Nothing good, I'm afraid."

Her heart skipped a beat as Gavin sat beside her and sighed. After the silence stretched on, he rubbed his palms together. "You used to confide in me. Have I lost your trust?"

She met his eyes and immediately wished she hadn't. There was so much raw emotion in them. Whatever had been between them still flickered, even though it had dimmed much over the time they'd been apart. She patted his thigh, relishing the brief contact. "Trust was never an issue between us."

He covered her hand with his and gently squeezed. "Then tell me what's troubling you. You know I can keep your confidence."

At the feel of his larger hand touching hers, something spiked in her, a warmth she hadn't felt in some time, a vulnerability she couldn't afford. Before she thought better of it, she blurted out, "There's talk that Renworth might be planning an offensive."

His eyes narrowed. "Where's this news coming from?"

"Brent has his spies out, one in Renworth's inner court who owes Brent big time for his help with his financial woes. Brent's waiting to hear back from him. They've been stepping up their training sessions, their contests becoming more vicious, more bloody."

Gavin showed no surprise at the news. Both of them knew just how violent Renworth could be. Gavin had tangled with the Red Claws on more than one occasion. The corner of his mouth quirked up. "Maybe you should have accepted Renworth's marriage offer."

Liz huffed as she waved her hand dismissively. "Hell to that fucking no."

Gavin leaned back and blew out a breath. "In addition to building the restaurant, Lawe and I have been holding our own training exercises. So has Cyrus. Our people are in great shape; if he attacks us, we'll defend our territory as we've always done."

"It's just that...we have so many young ones. It doesn't seem fair to them."

"Their youth may be a good thing. They have heart and are strong fighters."

Liz reluctantly let go of his hand. "Not sure we've ever faced anything this volatile. Renworth doesn't have a merciful bone in his body. His people outnumber our own. It concerns me."

"He may have more warriors, that doesn't necessarily mean his army is stronger than ours. We defend our territory; we have reason and cause. People protecting their home fight with all they have. He only has greed motivating him."

She knew Gavin was trying to offer support. He always had. "Maybe, but some clans brawl because of their aggressive natures. They don't need cause. It's as if violence has been bred into them, just lying beneath the surface, waiting to erupt."

Gavin moved closer to rub her arm in a soothing gesture. "Have faith in me. I've trained our people, so have you. We're a strong clan, and your people love you; they'll fight with their hearts, as well as their brawn. Renworth doesn't have that level of loyalty. They only battle because they fear their pack master's wrath."

Liz closed her eyes. How long had it been since they sat this way and simply talked? Gavin's confidence seemed to imbue her with strength. "There's going to be blood on both sides. I can't stand the thought of losing any of our people." Her hand clasped his, this time, entwining their fingers.

So many emotions danced across his face. Not the least of which was sympathy. They'd been lovers for so long, he knew her better than anyone, even Tia. "In any war, there are always losses."

"Some of our people are so inexperienced. They may never recover. Not fully. I served in the army. I've seen what war does to people; sometimes, the damage is irreparable."

"That may be, but maybe it won't come to that." He gave her one of his most charming smiles. The one she loved most. "In any case, tonight, you belong up above. Your people miss you." He lifted her hand until they were both standing. As he led her to the door, she thought she heard him mutter, "I miss you, too."

Chapter Two

The party was in full swing when Liz and Gavin reached the outdoor celebration. Most of their people were dancing to the music, laughing, and saluted them as they approached.

Liz spotted Cyrus dancing with several women who were suggestively rubbing their bodies along his, their lust a palpable thing. Some in the clan loved him and his charismatic charm. Cyrus knew how to work a room better than anyone and had this way of influencing people around him. But, more than anything, Weres respected strength, and if there was any kind of conflict, they'd want Cyrus at their back and would do anything to garner his approval.

The music changed to Adele's "Rolling in the Deep," one of Liz's favorite songs she loved singing the most, especially when the entire clan joined in on the chorus. Their enthusiasm and excitement were infectious.

She and Gavin quickly joined the others on the makeshift dance floor. As Gavin grinned at her, her heart sped up, and she couldn't resist laughing when he started crooning to her. Gavin had many wonderful traits, but singing wasn't one of them.

As their bodies swayed to the music, she started singing, her voice crystal clear and loud enough to drown out the others. Forgetting her troubles for the moment, joy infused her, making her feel glad to be alive.

When the song ended, whoops and shouts of applause rang out in raucous approval. Their elation vibrating around them.

"Black Stars, forever!" she shouted above the rest. God, Liz loved her people. Feeling hot, she fanned herself. "I need a drink."

"I'll get us both one." Gavin departed to the bar to retrieve their drinks.

Liz sat at one of the tables, and it wasn't long before Brent joined her. "You looked good out there. Nice to hear you singing, again."

Her body still heated and wired from the excitement, Liz grinned as she took in the sight of her people dancing. "It felt good. God, I haven't sung that song in a long time."

"It suits you. So does Gavin."

Liz gave her favorite scout a once over. Brent smiled knowingly at her. She always had the sense Brent knew more than he actually said. His gaze held a rare perception few people possessed. "You've been talking to Tia."

Brent laughed. "Not really. But you should see yourself. You looked happy when you were with him."

She put her hand on her hip and cocked her head. "And I don't look happy with Cyrus?"

"Seriously?" He gazed in their alpha's direction. "No, not as much. Now, you look content."

"That's because I am. Really, Brent, I didn't think you took an interest in such things. I thought facts and figures were more your thing."

"They are." He winked her way. "But I'm neither blind nor deaf."

Liz peered into Brent's piercing blue eyes. "Something tells me I'm about to get another opinion on my love life."

Brent shrugged nonchalantly. "Your love life is your business."

"Mhmm." Liz tapped her long nails on the table. "Now, why do I think a 'but' is forthcoming?"

He returned her grin. "But...Gavin has always been a clan favorite. People respect and trust Gavin."

In defense of her alpha, she reared back. "And they don't trust Cyrus?"

"That's not what I'm saying. However, Gavin was with the clan for years before Cyrus joined us; of course, he has the favor of many. That's not to discount Cyrus' value. He's been very productive and was responsible for bringing in new people, as well as revenue. People respect money as much as they do strength."

Liz leaned forward. "Annnd...?"

Brent looked like he was about to say *but,* again, then changed his mind. "Some of our people will never trust Cyrus as much as they do Gavin."

Liz arched her brow. "And why's that?"

Brent turned toward where Gavin was up at the bar. "Gavin leads; Cyrus commands."

"He's alpha; he's supposed to."

Brent nodded. "True enough. But there are ways to elicit responses without...intimidation."

Liz waved that off. "Cyrus is larger than any Were I've ever met; of course, they'd be intimidated by his size."

Brent's eyes flicked to where Cyrus was dancing. "I'm not so sure it's size alone that has people feeling uneasy. But, be that as it may, that's not why I wanted to talk to you."

Liz lowered her voice, knowing full well that Were hearing was acute. "Have you heard any more from your agents?"

As if reading her mind, Brent flicked his eyes over the crowd. "Not here. Meet me by the overpass in a few minutes."

At that moment, Gavin returned with two beers and handed one to Liz. "Brent, I would have gotten you a drink, but I didn't see you here."

"That's quite all right. I'm going to track down Quint and see what's up with him." Brent rose and patted Gavin's shoulder. "The restaurant looks great. You and Lawe are to be commended."

Gavin turned to admire the restaurant's sign. "It was a group effort. We all worked to build it."

"But, from what I hear, you and Lawe did the most amount in constructing it." Brent's eyes slid back to hers. "Have a good night. Both of you."

After Brent turned and left, Gavin asked, "What's up with him? He's always so somber."

Liz finished swallowing a gulp of her beer. "Oh, you know Brent, always with his facts and figures. Something about investments for the future, diversifying our interests." She waved her hand in dismissal. "A discussion for another time."

Gavin shook his head and sat down across from her. "I don't know how he does it. That kind of work would bore me to tears, sitting behind a desk all day. I'd much rather work with my hands."

Liz hadn't forgotten just how talented those hands of his were. She tapped her bottle to his. "And you're so good with them." She smirked as she rose. "One thing Brent was right about—you and Lawe did an awesome job with the restaurant. It's amazing. You should be proud. Right now, I'm going to meet with someone. We'll talk another time. Thanks for the beer."

Sighing, Gavin watched her leave and finished his drink, then grabbed the empty bottles and made his way to his best friend.

"She shot you down, again, huh, my man?" Behind the bar, Lawe finished drying off a glass as Gavin leaned against the bar's edge.

Gavin gave him a look as he grabbed the towel from Lawe. Of all the Weres in Black Star Clan, Lawe had always been the one he was closest to. Over the years, they had worked out together, trained their people to fight, and always had each other's back.

And whenever either one of them needed someone to shoot the breeze with, the other always had been there to listen. "She didn't shoot anything down, so that would be a no." He swatted the towel at him. "Now, get your ass out on the dance floor. Tonight's your night. I'll take over the bartending duties."

"I'm going, I'm going." Lawe undid his apron and tossed it aside. "No need to tell me twice. But don't change the subject. You still want her."

Gavin rolled his eyes. "Is that what everyone thinks?"

Lawe scoffed as he tied back his long dreads with a leather strip. "Duh, you keep your eyes on her whenever you think no one's watching. Not blind here. If you're so hot for her, why not make a move, instead of sulking?"

"I'm not sulking."

Lawe placed his hands on his hips. "Oh, really? When was the last time you got any?"

"Well, there was that time..." Gavin squinted, trying to remember. "Then, at the holiday party, there was...what's her name?"

Lawe came around the bar to stand beside him and put a hand on his shoulder. "Don't bullshit a bullshitter. I'm just saying, you ain't ever going to get any if you don't make a move, so...make one."

"I will. All in good time." They watched as Liz sauntered through the crowd and made her way to one of the back trails. Uneasiness gripped him. "Lawe, do me a favor. Get one of our guys to follow Lizandra. I don't like the idea of her being alone on the paths."

"She'd kick your ass if she heard you say that. You know our queen can handle herself, probably better than anyone else here."

Yeah, he did know that. Still, his protective streak ran deep where she was concerned. He had half a mind to track her himself, but he hadn't been invited. "Humor me here."

"Okay, who do you want me to get to trail her?"

Gavin scanned the crowd, just as Quint came up to the bar. "Anyone see Brent? I've been looking for him."

Lawe winked at Gavin as he tugged on the blond lawyer's arm, a man they'd known for years and was part of their inner circle. When it came to scouting terrain, not only was he fast, he was stealthy and knew when to stay downwind. There were times when even Gavin had a hard time pinning down his exact whereabouts. "Quint, my man, I need a favor. Or, should I say, Gavin does."

"Sure, anything. Congrats, again, on the bar; it's fantastic." Quint ran his gaze appreciatively over the place. "What do you need?"

***

Liz looked up at the night sky and felt her skin prickle. Everything was so calm, deadly calm. She didn't trust it. She could detect different scents around her: lingering aromas from the restaurant, the natural fragrances of the woods, and exhaust fumes from the vehicles on Fifth Avenue.

There'd been another night like this, long ago, when she'd stood out here, not far from where she was now, with her best friend, Miranda. Both of them had been uneasy with the night, as if they could sense a change in the air. Feel as if something dangerous was coming, but having no idea what it was or when it would happen. God, Liz missed her friend. It had been some time since she'd heard from her and feared it would be even longer before she saw her, again.

A whiff of expensive cologne greeted her before Brent made his presence known. "There you are." He appeared out of the shadows.

Keeping her voice low as he had, she asked, "You really think this sort of secrecy is necessary? With our own people?"

"Secrecy is the source of safety. And, with my queen, I take no chances."

She nodded her approval. "Let's walk in the direction of the reservoir. Have you noticed how calm it is tonight? There's no wind, not even a hint of one."

Brent scanned the trail they were taking and sniffed the air. "Makes it harder to track someone without a scent being carried on the breeze. Did it bother you before, my comments about Gavin?"

"Unfortunately, you're not the only one who feels that way. Let me say this: My decisions are my own. I may not always voice why I do what I do, but know that the clan's best interests are always foremost in my mind."

Brent smiled as they continued walking, their steps silent in the dark. "There was never any doubt concerning that." He inhaled deeply. "Do you think we will have an early fall? Everyone loves the summer, but I've always been fond of autumn the best, all the intense colors of the falling leaves. Quint loves the yellow ones, but I've always been fond of the red ones, the blood red ones."

Liz scoffed. "You're a strange man."

He winked her way. "So I've been told. Many times."

"I wish it would rain. It hasn't rained in a long time. I love the way the park smells after a hard rain, so clean, so fresh and the flowers in bloom, their perfumes enticing." When they were far away enough from the others, she faced him. "So, spill it; what was so important you wanted to speak to me privately?"

Brent walked in front of her and perused the surrounding area. "My sources concur that Renworth seems to be mobilizing his people. He spares them no mercy in their training, as if he's preparing for war. My informants are becoming increasingly nervous. They say they've never seen him this ruthless, and we both know just how cold-hearted he can be. But, as bad as that news is, that's not why I wanted stealth tonight." He took a deep breath, then let it out.

"It was suggested by one of my agents that Renworth has seduced one of our own to his cause. One we would never suspect. One close to you."

Liz didn't flinch at this particular piece of unsavory news. "Any chance your source is just mind-fucking you?"

"No. I could smell a lie a mile away, no matter the weather. Just like you. He was quite honest and...afraid."

"This source give you a name?"

"No, but he was concerned about contacting me, anxious he might be found out, said transmissions would be few from now on." They stopped by one of the park benches away from the lamppost so that they were still in shadow. Brent faced her. "You show no surprise. Is this something you've suspected?"

"My instincts have always been strong. Something's been off." She rubbed one of her arms. "I'm just not sure what. Or, in this case, who."

"That's unfortunate. I was hoping you'd have some idea. It would be bad enough if it was one of the newer people. But it's hard to accept that one of our own would even consider siding with Renworth. We have a traitor in our midst."

"He's extremely wealthy, and as we both know, money buys friends." Liz's anger began to boil beneath her skin. "When the territories were first allocated by the Commissioner of Clans, the premise in mind was that the distribution of land would be equitable so there would be no fighting among the different clans."

"Little did they know how much greed would play a role decades later."

"Indeed." Liz felt her beast rising to the surface, even though it wasn't the full moon, yet. "Will you run with me, Brent? I need to burn off some of this energy." With her blood coursing through her veins, she always thought more clearly while running, gained better perspective.

"With pleasure."

They shed their clothes and folded them on the bench to retrieve later. As both of them were black-haired, they transformed into black wolves. They crouched down, low to the ground, and their snouts slowly protruded, as did their sharp claws. Fur erupted from their skin, and their bones stretched and bent into their lupine form.

Snarling and growling as they morphed, it almost appeared as if they would attack each other, but each knew to keep their howls low so not to alarm the clan. Their feral sounds were a melodious affirmation of their beastly natures.

Under the lamplight, their pelts shone brightly.

The Were Queen arched her back and then took off running. Liz's wolf was larger than that of Brent's, but he was the only one who could truly match her for speed as they loped through the wooded trails, jumping over fallen branches and flower beds, the need to stretch their animal muscles invigorating.

Neck and neck, they ran, enamored of the joy of setting their beasts free. Hearts pounding, senses heightened, awareness of their surroundings so much more acute than that of their human forms. They ran and ran, the ecstasy of feeling free and unfettered rousing in its simplicity, its perfection. Freedom at its supreme best. No human could ever know how it felt to be this liberated, this alive.

Feeling powerful, feeling strong, they rounded the reservoir near the northeast sector of the park and stopped to get a drink of the cool water. They bowed their heads down to lap up the refreshing liquid. When he finished drinking, Brent raised his head to offer her a wolf's version of a smile of solidarity in the exhilaration of running and the peacefulness of their surroundings.

United in desire, bound in lore.

She was about to return his grin, but something in the air alerted her. Her hackles rising, she sniffed the air. Instincts rose to a crescendo. It was then that a scent hit them, at once familiar and deadly: blood.

Chapter Three

Compulsion to discover the source drove Liz to rush quickly toward the northeastern gates, Brent right behind her, but when they heard the agonizing howl of a wolf in pain, they ran full-out, their paws clawing at the ground.

Just as they neared the entrance, Liz saw two of their most beloved packmates guarding the fallen body of one of their own. Maxine, the youngest and smallest of the wolves, but also a fierce warrior, was preparing to fight the gray wolf who had his fangs bared. And Sasha, who had once been victimized by the Red Claw Clan but had recovered remarkably well, was cradling the fallen victim.

Liz growled menacingly loud enough to get their attention, her muscles increasing, strengthening, readying herself to lunge. But, before she could reach them, without warning, another wolf appeared out of the shadows with incredible speed.

She barely had time to register the golden streak in his light brown pelt as he leaped high into the sky and clawed at the other wolf. Snarls and howls rent the air as they rolled and attacked each other. The ground vibrated with their hits as one fell the other.

The gray wolf fought fiercely, but the golden wolf was just too fast for him and bit deeply into his flank. The gray wolf yelped in pain and limped away. Turning back to catch a quick glimpse of her and Brent, the cowardly wolf snarled one last time then reared back and thrust his body high up over the fence.

The soft patter of paws faded into the distance.

Liz changed into her human form and went to the bloodied victim. Naked, she bent down close to him. As soon as she saw his dark curls, she knew who it was. "Oh, no. It's Granger."

After scanning the area, Brent transitioned and kneeled beside her. When the golden wolf nudged him, Brent ran a hand over his pelt as he shimmered and resumed his human appearance. "Couldn't stay away, huh?"

"You know me, I like to be in the thick of things." Panting hard, Quint offered his lover a wink.

Max huffed as she tried to collect her breath, her concern for her fallen packmate etched in her voice. "We were just coming home from the 92nd Street YMCA. Granger wanted to hear one of his favorite authors do a reading there. We did nothing to elicit this. The gray wolf attacked us without provocation."

Brent asked, "Are you two all right? Did he hurt you?"

Both Max and Sasha shook their heads.

Liz examined Granger's injuries. "He's got a gut wound that's still oozing." The wolves knew, once he transitioned into a wolf and back into human form, the gashes would heal. But, sometimes, when a Were lost too much blood or was severely injured, morphing was difficult. "Granger, you need to change. Do you hear me?"

Granger opened one eye and coughed. "I'm okay. I got in a few punches, but he took us from behind."

Liz ordered, "Change. Now."

Granger nodded and made the attempt, but she could tell his body was not obeying the demand. His muscles barely rippled to that of a werewolf, but not that of a wolf. The healing would be slower, but better than that of a human.

"Okay, we're gonna take you back to Werehaven. You're going to the medical wing. I want Gavin to look you over."

"I'm fine." Granger tried to stand on human legs, but his knees buckled. "Okaay. Just a little dizzy."

Brent slid his arms under Granger and lifted him. "I'll carry him there."

Liz checked the locked gates at the entrance. No outward signs of damage or tampering. She'd make it a point to have patrols sped up and surveillance enhanced at all entrances to the park.

After Brent and the girls took off at a brisk pace, Liz turned to Quint. "Any reason you were following us?"

He failed to hide the good-natured smirk he was trying to bank. "I suppose, if I said I just felt like going for a walk, you wouldn't believe me."

She arched a brow. "Try again." As queen, she didn't usually tolerate insolence from her pack, but Quint was a trusted friend.

Quint blew out a breath. "Gavin just wanted you protected. Don't be mad at him." He raised his arm at their wooded surroundings. "He's got a point. You shouldn't be out here alone."

"That's not his call. And I wasn't alone. Brent was with me." Not affected by their nudity—after all, Weres considered skin as natural as fur—she asked, "By the way, where are your clothes?"

"Same place you and Brent left yours. On the park bench. Fairly easy to track you by scent. You've worn the same lavender perfume since I can remember."

She shrugged. "I like it. Don't see a need for change."

"I didn't say you should. Just that it's familiar."

"Hmm." When they approached the bench with their clothes, they noticed Brent's were missing and realized one of the girls must have retrieved them on the way back to their compound. After they'd dressed, Liz and Quint double timed it back to Werehaven.

Once there, they found the restaurant locked up and only a few of their packmates skulking around. She returned their nods, assuring them she was fine. The sight of Granger's mangled body must have upset some of their people, who then probably sought refuge below.

After descending the stairs to their haven, Lizandra made her way to the medical area. She discovered Gavin attending to Granger. "How is he?"

After making eye contact, Gavin continued bandaging the cut across Granger's cheek. "A few cracked ribs, multiple lacerations. He needs rest, plenty of fluids. He's already healing, albeit slowly."

The loss of blood was the likely cause. "Does he need a hospital?"

Granger spoke up. "The better question would be, would he actually go if requested to do so?"

The Were Queen stood against the doorway with her arms crossed. "If I order your ass there, there will be no question about it."

Granger sighed. "Yes, ma'am."

After finishing with his cheek, Gavin inspected the bandages around Granger's ribs. "If he promises to stay here tonight and not sneak out, I think he should be fine by tomorrow or the day after."

Granger looked between her and Gavin and must have realized he really had no choice in the matter. He nodded. "Okay."

Liz moved closer to Granger's side and slid her hand over his. "Mind telling me what went down tonight?"

"It was like Max said, we were on our way here when we got jumped. I didn't have time to change, so I tried to fight off the guy with my fists."

Liz asked, "He didn't go after Max or Sasha?"

"I don't think so." Granger rubbed his forehead. "It happened so fast. One minute, we were just walking, and the next, I was being pommeled to the ground."

"You didn't sense anything, anyone following you, bad vibes of any kind?"

"No. Nothing like that." He shook his head. "We had a good time at the Y, we were laughing and joking about some of the things the author had said, and then, bam! I'm being knocked into the dirt."

"That's pretty much what Sasha and Max said when I questioned them." Gavin rolled up the tape and placed it in the cabinet with the other medical supplies.

A quiet knock had their heads turning toward the doorway to find Sasha and Max. "Can we come in, now?"

When Liz nodded, Max said, "We just wanted to check up on him."

"I want you to take Granger back to your room tonight. Make sure he stays there until tomorrow." Liz wasn't surprised when Sasha's eyes lit up. She'd suspected for some time that the feminine beauty had a thing for the handsome wolf. When she glanced at Max, her smile also conveyed her delight. "He's to rest. No strenuous activity at all. Understand?"

Both females enthusiastically nodded.

The corners of Granger's mouth rose. Good thing since he didn't get a vote in the matter. "Go, now. And get some sleep. All of you."

The girls helped Granger down off the exam table and wove their arms around him as they left. At the door, Granger turned and said, "Thank you."

When they were gone, Liz quietly closed the door behind her, never taking her eyes off Gavin. "I find it odd that three adult Weres couldn't detect the scent of another wolf in their midst."

He ran a hand through his hair. "I thought that strange, too, but with so many odors of the city hanging in the air, especially the exhaust fumes from Fifth Avenue, it's possible."

"Even with the other scents, he should have sensed the other wolf. I don't like this. I'm wondering, now, if the Red Claws have found a way to mask their scents."

Gavin finished washing his hands and dried them on the paper towel. "A dangerous possibility."

"Indeed." That was something she'd look into tomorrow. She circled the exam table, trailing her finger over it. "I hear you sent Quint to follow me."

"Don't start. After you saw what was done to Granger, you can hardly blame me for being concerned."

Hands on hips, Liz strolled gingerly around the room. "I understand your protective nature. I get it. But my decisions are not to be questioned. By anyone."

His lips quirked up on one side. "I didn't question anything. As one of your elite enforcers, it's my responsibility to make sure members of the clan are protected. All members." He grinned her way. "That includes you."

Not wrong there. But, damn, why did he have to look so damned handsome when he smiled? It made arguing with him that much more difficult. Her skin began to prickle; the chemistry between them still there, even after all this time.

Liz shook her head, burying those thoughts. She wouldn't quarrel with him tonight. She neither respected nor appreciated anyone who didn't question her from time to time. The last thing she'd ever want was a *"yes"* man. But there were limits. "As long as you don't negate or question my orders in front of any of the clan."

His eyes were heated with the passion they once shared. "I would never be so bold. You know that."

"I do. Tensions are running high now with the latest incidents. It has everyone a little on edge. Hardly a chance it was a rogue wolf. It was a Red Claw tonight, wasn't it?"

Gavin turned and retrieved a steel particle from the instrument table and handed it to her. "I dug out one of these metal shards from Granger's side. Look familiar?"

She'd seen these before. Not long ago, a member of the clan, Dori, who had been one of Renworth's moles, had instigated a fight with her. She'd embedded her claws in Liz's waist, leaving the fragment behind. After kicking her ass in the altercation, Liz had thrown Dori out of Werehaven. "Yes. Definitely Red Claws. But why go after Granger? He's so young, as are the girls."

"Easy targets. And they were at the farthest point from here."

Liz's mind was whirling with new ways to protect her people. "Tomorrow night, we're going to have a meeting. I want security increased, especially at the entrances. I think it's a good idea we had cameras placed at all entry points, maybe increase or change the routine of the patrols."

"I agree. Let's open it up to the clan. Consider all options."

"Yes. And I think it's time I met with Renworth."

Gavin's eyes widened. "Not alone."

"I didn't say that. But these skirmishes won't stop. He'll only increase them. What's next? He has one of his wolves murder one of ours? Enough blood has been spilled. I'll see if I can negotiate some sort of truce."

"I hope you do, but my gut tells me that's the last thing Renworth wants. It's not in his nature. Even in his business ventures, he's known for being ruthless."

"I know. But perhaps some neutral ground can be covered. I need time to think this through. Thank you for seeing to Granger." She sighed as she rubbed her neck. "I'm concerned about the scar on his face. He's such a handsome guy, almost pretty. As an actor, his looks matter to him more than most. His livelihood is dependent on it."

Gavin nodded. "It was deep, but it's healing. The scar is temporary, but I'll have another look at it tomorrow. You should get some rest."

"I will." She reached for the door and was about to glance back at him but then decided against it. She had much on her mind and needed to relax to sort it all out. Meeting with Renworth was a dangerous prospect but, most likely, a necessity. She thought about going to her rooms but knew sleep would evade her tonight. She needed to go someplace where she could relax, where she could clear her head.

Only one place came to mind.

Chapter Four

Edgar Renworth, the Red Claw King, stood with his arms crossed and stared out the window from high up in his castle in Riverside Park. From this vantage point, he could gaze past the Hudson River into New Jersey. With hardly any boats on the water, everything was so still, so calm. A man of action, he didn't trust it when things were too quiet. He much preferred when things were in motion.

Always, he needed challenges to keep his mind and body focused, some attainable goal to work towards, a course carefully plotted out.

"The scout you sent for is waiting outside." His second in command, Victor Gren, interrupted his thoughts. In his early forties now, with just a hint of gray showing at his temples, Gren was still a handsome man with his slender build and olive complexion, even though he didn't have the musculature many in his clan possessed.

But what was most striking about Gren were his penetrating brown eyes that indicated an intelligent mind. The man rarely blinked; an admirable trait considering some of the people he associated with. It was also one of the reasons that made Victor a great poker player. Renworth seldom lost at the game, but when he did, it was usually to Gren.

"Send him in, but before you do, any word from our Black Star friend?" Renworth's mouth watered at the prospect of one day taking over Central Park's clan. As wondrous as Riverside Park was, stretching across a sizable portion of New York's west side, it wasn't as strategically located as Central Park.

As a successful business man, he had many visions for the future, many ideas on how to increase his already formidable wealth. And, as with corporate spying to get a leg up on his competitors, he kept spies within his rival, the Black Star Clan.

"Not yet. I have Sinclair keeping an eye out for any transmissions. I'll alert you as soon as we hear anything."

"Good."

As Victor turned and left, Renworth appreciated his second's efficiency. There were few men he admired, and less that he actually liked. But Gren had been with him for over a decade and never once did he doubt his loyalty. And wasn't loyalty an important thing when considering your top people?

Another was ambition. Although Gren agreed with most of his business dealings, he wasn't ambitious enough to pose a threat to Renworth's position as clan leader, nor was he strong enough to challenge him in the fighting arena.

No one in his clan was, and he liked it that way.

"You sent for me?" his scout asked from the doorway. Robin was one of his best spies he sent out to periodically check Black Star's perimeter. Along with his deceptively good looks, Robin had a fierce attitude and enjoyed the arena games as much as he did.

Renworth motioned for him to enter. "I hear you got into a scuffle with some of Queen Lizandra's people tonight?"

"Hardly a scuffle. I was just having a bit of fun with one of the younger members at the north gate." He scoffed. "That is until the queen showed up with one of her enforcers."

"The queen was there with only one guard?" He frowned. That didn't make sense. From his reports, the queen always had her entourage with her at all times.

"Not just one. Another showed up. Gotta say," Robin rubbed at his shoulder, "he had some punch to him."

"What happened then?"

"Well, with the queen, her two enforcers, and the two females who were with the youth, I decided not to push my luck and retreated."

"Injuries?"

"The other enforcer got a few scratches, but the youth? He got gutted by one of my claws." His scout sneered. "Not a kill strike, but I'm sure it hurt like hell."

"How long were you tracking them for?"

Robin shrugged. "A couple of blocks."

"And he didn't scent you?"

"Nope, so either the scent blocker worked really well, or the young one was too enamored of the females to pay attention."

Renworth had paid good money to steal the formula that hid the scent of his people. It would be a valued tool in his arsenal when the time was right. "Maybe both. Okay, go get cleaned up. I'll send you out on patrols, again, when I need you."

Robin nodded then turned and left.

Renworth sank down in his desk chair, which resembled a throne with its wood carvings, and rested one foot on his desk as he swiveled back and forth. How strange that Lizandra would be so far from her stronghold with only one or two enforcers. Unless she had more guards hidden where Robin couldn't see them. More than likely.

Now, Queen Lizandra was an enticing female. Statuesque, good bone structure, high cheekbones, and those amazing aquamarine eyes. Normally, a mixed-heritage woman wouldn't attract him, but he found himself growing hard at the thought of taking that female. If she would only agree to his proposal to unite the clans, it would make things so much easier.

But no. Typical of her gender, she was stubborn, refusing to see the perfection of his plans. She would learn soon enough that Edgar Renworth didn't take no for an answer. He never would have gotten to his position of power if he had.

Still, with her craftiness and how she trained her Weres, he had a certain amount of respect for her. What wonderful offspring they would produce. Idols among their kind. Strong, powerful, the elite. Did he mind that children of his would have mixed blood? Hmm, not really. He already sired five of his own. All disciplined, loyal to him.

Well, except for one.

His eldest, Drayton.

He reached for the scotch and poured himself a tumbler full and slowly sipped the liquid down, relishing the smooth burn. After his first wife's death, Dray had moved to Houston and never returned, despite Renworth's demands. No matter how many times he tried to explain that his mother had died from injuries suffered in a car crash, Dray refused to believe him.

Always, suspicion marred his eyes, preferring to believe the rumors that Renworth had Julienne killed because she'd cheated on him with another. Stubborn son of a bitch. He sneered. Even if the rumors at the time had been true.

Of all his wives, he'd loved Dray's mother the most. Pity she hadn't returned the emotion. He still kept her portrait displayed in the castle. Some thought it was a sentimental gesture; others believed it was a warning to anyone who thought to betray him. Maybe it was both.

His other wives had served their purpose, giving him the strong sons and daughters he needed to establish his dynasty.

Over the years, he'd tried to make peace with Dray, but his son had made it clear he wanted no part of him. Even legally changing his last name to his mother's maiden name, Beaumont. As if deserting the clan hadn't been insult enough.

Renworth downed the last of his scotch. But all that was past. So be it. He had a future to plan for, even if that meant making war on the Black Star Clan.

And, for that, he would have to ready his troops.

***

Before heading to her oasis to relax, Lizandra thought she'd check on Granger. Make sure he was all right. When she got to the room Max shared with Sasha, she thought about knocking but didn't want to wake Granger if he was already asleep.

Or...there was a possibility that Sasha and Max were entertaining him. But, surely, they wouldn't be foolish enough to engage in anything strenuous tonight, especially since she'd warned them off such indulgences, or would they?

After some vigorous training sessions, she'd unexpectedly walked in on other members of her clan while in the throes of passion. The exhilaration of the one often carried over into the other.

Deciding on stealth, she slowly opened the door to take a peek. Granger was out cold in the middle of the bed. God, how sweet and serene he looked. He really was a looker. Young, but oh so handsome. On one side was Max with her arm protectively over him, and on the other side was Sasha, who had one of the California twins wrapped around her.

Liz could never tell the two blonds, Drew and Daniel, apart. Strange that only one of the twins was here. They were usually together wherever they went, but she didn't see how a fifth could fit on the bed. Two females, two males, made sense. Although puppy piles rarely had a fixed number; they were designed to give comfort and weren't based on gender.

She slowly closed the door and turned down the hall.

Her sanctuary called to her. She could think of nothing more relaxing than a good soak in one of the hot tubs. She heard the music playing before she even entered the cave where the walls were decorated with scenes from her beloved Caribbean and decorated with strings of tiny lights. Josh Groban was crooning, one of Brent's favorites. She inhaled deeply and caught his scent, along with Quint's. "Not surprised to find you guys here tonight."

Straddled over Brent's lap with their lower bodies submerged in the water, Quint whipped his head around and smiled. "Should we leave or did you want company?"

She laughed. "By all means, stay. What do we have, now, seven or eight Jacuzzis? This area belongs to all my enforcers. The elite ones, anyway." After turning the dial on for her favorite tub, selecting a towel from the rack to cushion her head, she disrobed and slid into the oasis of swirling warm water. A sensuous moan escaped her lips. "Now, this is what I'm talking about. Pure heaven."

"That's what I told Quint when I suggested we come here." Brent brushed his lips over his lover's. "Though anywhere with Quint is heaven."

Quint smiled as he wrapped his arms around Brent's neck. "Ah, you say the sweetest things."

Brent nipped at his lower lip then turned to her. "After his encounter with one of the Red Claws tonight, I thought a good soaking was in order, but if you'd rather be alone, we can leave."

Liz purred in ecstasy as she sank lower into the water. "Not at all. I just came from checking on Granger. He's resting well. Has the girls keeping him company. And one of the twins."

"Really? I didn't think they batted for our team," Quint joked as he slid to Brent's side.

"As far as I know, neither of the twins do. The one had his body curled around Sasha."

Brent asked, "What did Gavin say about Granger?"

"He'll heal. Some of the lacerations were deeper than others, a few broken ribs that will mend. I hate that they targeted one of our younger people."

"Easy target." Brent shrugged. "I suspect Renworth has his scouts checking out our boundaries. Although, I'm surprised one of theirs attacked ours when there were three of them."

Liz scowled. "The Red Claws may not see some of the females as worthy opponents."

Quint snorted. "They've never seen Max in full battle mode. I swear she fights dirtier than anyone else I've ever seen."

"Oh, yes." They all agreed.

Liz inwardly grinned. She'd been the one to teach Max how to make up for her lack of height. After a while, she said, "Tomorrow, I'm calling for a general meeting. These attacks have got to stop."

Quint shook his head, as if in disbelief. "You would think with all our complaints to the Commissioner of Clans, Renworth would have backed off by now."

"Renworth respects no one else besides himself." Brent growled. "He won't be satisfied until it's all-out war between us."

There it was, Liz thought. What they were all thinking, but only Brent would voice. "Maybe not. I'm going to meet with him. On neutral ground. Perhaps there is a way to negotiate a truce."

"The only way a truce could be reached is if you agree to hand over a piece of the park to him." Brent stared her in the eye. "Dear queen of mine, tell me you're not even considering such a drastic action."

Quint agreed. "Give one parcel of land to that hyena, and he won't stop until he has it all."

Liz was considering several options to avert a war, but she wouldn't tell them that at this moment. "There are other things that might cease the hostilities between clans."

Brent raised his brow. "Such as?"

She never got the chance to answer as Gavin did so for her. "Such as accepting his offer of marriage."

Two sets of eyes widened as Gavin stripped and stepped into the tub adjacent to hers. Brent's jaw finally decided to work. "Surely, you jest?"

Liz nearly laughed. "As if. Remember how his first wife, Julienne, died? Car accident, my ass." Try as she might not to stare at Gavin's naked body, she found she couldn't take her eyes off him. *Fucking perfect.*

At their questioning glances, she said, "It was long ago. Rumors swirled she was going to leave him for another. He decided he had other plans for her. His other wives didn't last quite as long but settled for whatever their pre-nups suggested. Wise moves on their parts."

Gavin stroked the water over his arms. "Glad to see you're not considering something so extreme."

Her eyes never left his as the steam warmed the air around them. "Glad to see we're on the same page."

Brent and Quint must have picked up on the vibe between them, because Brent rose from the water, wrapped a towel around his hips, and said, "I think if I stay in the water any longer my skin will start to shrivel."

Quint followed suit. No doubt out of respect for the alpha he'd always admired and followed without question. "Can't have that, though I can't ever remember *any* part of you ever shriveling." He winked her way.

Brent smirked as he wrapped an arm around Quint. "If you two will pardon us, a warm bed awaits." Before he left, he went to the music system and hit a few buttons. His eyes glinted as he gave them a final salute.

Liz nodded in farewell, as did Gavin. A moment, later Duran Duran's "Hungry Like the Wolf" started playing.

She grinned at Brent's choice of music. *Apropos!* Even though they'd broken up long ago, the hunger never abated, not completely. *Not ever.*

Alone with her former lover, the heat from the warm water seemed to increase as they stared at each other. She lifted one arm in the air to watch the water trickle down in rivulets. "How's Lawe doing? I'm sure he's ecstatic about his new restaurant, even if tonight got marred by Granger's injury."

"He's fine, hanging out with Tia and a few of the others, and looking forward to many more nights of celebration. It was a wise move to invest in The Cajun Grill."

Try as she might, Liz couldn't peel her eyes away from him. "Good to hear."

Gavin slid both arms across the water, the water sliding seductively over his skin. "The clan is concerned about Red Claws' latest invitation to battle."

"Yes, I'm sure. I plan to have a meeting with all our elites tomorrow night to discuss options."

"Now, why do I get the feeling you've already made up your mind about your next step?"

"As queen, it's my responsibility to keep guard over my pack. And make the best decisions concerning their welfare."

"Care to share your thoughts?"

She was imagining sharing a lot more than just her thoughts. So many memories started flowing through her mind, some more pleasant than others. Each one becoming more sensual and erotic than the last. "Not at the moment. Tonight, I just want one moment of bliss. There'll be plenty of time to discuss strategies and tactics tomorrow."

He seemed to be studying her, as if he was reading her mind. "All right, then. Mind telling me why you disappeared with Brent tonight?"

She wanted to remind him, as queen, she didn't answer to anyone. But, for too many years, they had shared everything, and she felt she owed him some sort of explanation. "Brent fears war is becoming more and more inevitable. I tend to agree."

Gavin moved closer to the rim of his tub. "What did he tell you?"

"You and I both know what a prick Renworth can be. He's training his people hard. Brutally so. Every indication is that he's readying his troops for an offensive."

"How many?"

She didn't want to discuss this tonight. Not that she was squeamish or delicate. She was neither, but she knew what his reaction would be. Now was not the time for emotion, only cool, clear-headed logic. "I suspect all of them."

Gavin scoffed and shook his head. "Jesus, he'll come after you with everything he's got. He won't show any mercy."

"I wouldn't expect any. It's not in his nature." As her traitorous body disobeyed her best intents, she glided through the water closer to him, the vibe between them ever so strong. "But, before it comes to that, perhaps negotiations can assuage his desires." As soon as she uttered her last word, she realized her mistake.

"And your desires? What do you want most, Lizandra?" Gavin's lips beckoned as his tongue darted out to lick along his bottom one. Hunger flamed in his eyes.

She'd seen the heated looks he'd given her over their time apart and had been able to ignore, but why it was becoming harder to evade she didn't know. She'd like to blame it on the full moon but knew that wasn't happening, yet. No, it was because her own hunger was pulsing stronger—something she needed to suppress. She rose to leave, and he grasped her arm.

"No! Don't do that. Don't try to avoid me. I've seen the way you look at me when you think I'm not looking." He sniffed the air. "You think I can't smell your arousal."

She peered down to where his fingers were digging into her arm and then looked back up at him. "You no longer have the right to make any demands of me."

His lips quirked up at the sides. "Demands. That's an interesting word. Your eyes betray you Liz. Even now, your own body is making overtures. Desires I suspect Cyrus can't fulfill."

Her temper flared. "Leave Cyrus out of this! He's been good for the clan."

"Yes, I know. He's insinuated himself very well into clan business." Gavin released her arm but then propelled himself into her hot tub. Her heart started beating fiercely. "But he doesn't satisfy you." He lifted her so that their bodies were aligned without an inch separating them. "Not the way I can."

Before she could command his obedience, his lips were on hers, igniting flames that danced wildly in the pit of her stomach. The rising heat between them became smoldering as he deepened the kiss, his muscular arms holding her close enough to him she could feel his erection along her hip. She was succumbing too easily to a desire she had long held at bay.

But this was not the time to give in to such basic yearnings. She tore her lips away. "I will not deny what's between us. But I'm with Cyrus, and as queen, my decisions are final."

"Are they, now?" he panted. "Is that what you tell yourself at night?"

Gavin knew her all too well. And that was why she'd kept her distance. "You can't keep doing this, Gavin. Accept my choices; you have little recourse in the matter."

"No, I don't, but you have. Don't think for a moment I don't know why you made Cyrus alpha." He rose out of the water, his body taut with muscle. Male perfection.

Her mouth watered at the rigid organ between his thighs that taunted her. She swallowed audibly as her skin prickled. How much longer could she resist him? She shook her head. They were due for a talk, a talk they should have had long before now. One in which she would tell him, in no uncertain terms, that her decisions were final, and his attempts to resurrect what once was were futile.

The clan needed Cyrus. And the clan came first.

And always would.

Chapter Five

In their rooms, Brent was seated at his desk with his laptop when he heard Quint's voice as he stood in the doorway to their bedroom. "Still can't sleep?"

"My mind won't shut down. Too many things vying for my attention."

After years of being together, Quint knew him well enough to guess what was on his mind. "You think Renworth is going to launch an offensive."

"I do. The man is inexorable. He won't stop." Brent leaned back against his chair and pinched the bridge of his nose. "I've worked with men like him in the past. His sense of entitlement is as large as his ego. He firmly believes he has a right to our lands. Lizandra wants to negotiate with him, and I won't disparage her attempt, but I fear it will amount to little."

Quint strode over to him and squeezed his shoulder. "Then, war is inevitable."

Covering his hand with one of his own, Brent gazed up at Quint and nodded.

"We've been expecting this. I think we've known all along and just hoped it wouldn't happen." Dressed only in his black silk pajama bottoms, Quint walked to the bar in the corner.

Brent admired his long, lean body. For a slender man, Quint was powerfully built and more than capable of holding his own in fights. His speed alone gave him an advantage— as the gray wolf discovered too late. "What are you doing?"

"Making you a martini. It will help you sleep."

Brent rubbed his tired eyes. "I'm sorry I woke you."

Quint brought his drink to him and leaned up against the desk. "Drink."

"Thanks." He took a sip. "But you needn't have made it; I'd have come to bed, eventually."

"And tossed and turned all night." Quint smiled as he rubbed his bicep over the clan tattoo of a black star. Not only had they gotten tattoos in the same place, they'd each had the other's name inscribed, as well as the words, "*Forever Mine*" underneath the star. "Maybe, now, you'll actually get some sleep."

Brent swallowed more of his drink. "Maybe."

"You worry too much. If it does come to war, we've all been properly prepared by Gavin. He's had us running drills like crazy. Between him and Cyrus orchestrating our workout routines, we're in the best shape possible."

Brent agreed. "Yes, Gavin has always kept us in ultimate fighting mode."

"And Cyrus? You never liked him much since he joined Black Star Clan."

He finished his drink and placed the empty glass on the desk. The accountant in him would not abate. "Something about him just doesn't add up. I don't know what it is, maybe the way he carries himself, so damn sure of himself, or the way he smirks when he thinks all eyes are elsewhere."

"He's huge. Men like that always have an air of confidence about them. Why wouldn't they? There's no one to keep them in check."

"There's *always* someone bigger, better, or more badass."

"Oh, really? I've never seen a Were bigger than Cyrus. If it does come to war with the Red Claws, we'll certainly need him."

"True."

"What is it, Brent?" Quint made circling moves with his index finger before tapping it against Brent's forehead. "I can see the wheels turning."

"Cyrus is just so...different from Gavin." He exhaled deeply. Talking things over with Quint had always allowed him to collect his thoughts. "Gavin always instructed us in a manner where we trusted his decisions, trusted him as a leader, our alpha."

"So, there it is. You're still partial to Gavin and just don't like Cyrus because he's alpha. Not our choice, Brent. It's Lizandra's."

Brent's eyes narrowed. "That's another thing. Did you see the way she looked at Gavin tonight? The heat is still there. She's never looked at Cyrus the way she looks at Gavin."

Quint took his empty glass and brought it back to the mini bar. "Your romantic heart is showing. Our queen has made her choice."

"But is it a permanent one? Yes, I know we need Cyrus to battle the Red Claws. Yes, I know he's powerful and a valuable fighter. I've seen the way he spars." Brent rubbed his jaw. "Felt it, too."

"You're still sore at him because he kicked your ass when you sparred."

"Not sore. I knew I was going to lose, even though I was faster." Strange, until recently, Brent never thought Cyrus had been playing him, learning his moves, studying him as if taking notes for a later time. But, now...he wondered.

"Gavin used to win against you when you practiced with him; you never complained, then."

Brent laughed. "Gavin used to let us win some of the bouts to boost our confidence."

Quint chuckled along with him. "You knew."

"Of course, I knew. Until Cyrus came along, Gavin was always the most powerful among us. And a good friend. He always made it a point to get to know us, hang out with us.

Made sure we knew he always had our back. I've never felt that way with Cyrus."

"Cyrus hasn't been with us nearly half as long. True, he never lets us win any of the fights. But I can understand his reasoning. He doesn't want to instill any false senses of confidence. He gives no quarter, he's relentless, and maybe that's not such a bad thing."

"You think he elicits the sense of loyalty that Gavin does?"

"I didn't say that." Quint shrugged. "They just have different methods of leading. Hey, I like Gavin, too. He's always been our leader, whether he has the title of alpha or not."

Everything Quint was saying made sense, but still, the sense of unease wouldn't subside. "I hope Liz gets back with him."

"You're such a romantic." Quint finished washing and drying his glass. "I love that about you. And, yeah, I'd like to see Liz happy, again. Did you see how she danced and sang with Gavin tonight? It's been too long since I've seen her so filled with...joy. It was nice to see."

Brent was moved by Quint's upbeat attitude; it was infectious and just one of the things he loved about his partner. "Yes, it was. I bet you anything it's just a matter of time before Gavin claims what's his."

"Let them work out their own issues." Quint pulled him out of his chair. "Right now, I can think of another way to get you to relax."

Brent smiled as Quint slid his hand in his and laced their fingers. "I bet you can. Does this plan of yours include getting sweaty?"

Quint winked as he led him back to the bedroom. "It does, indeed."

Brent heard a sensual growl and wasn't sure who emitted it, himself or Quint.

***

Liz couldn't sleep, her mind whirling with scenarios and possible outcomes. She paced back and forth in her private quarters. She was definitely going to meet with Renworth. But not until she had a sit down with her Prime—her inner circle of advisors, who also served as her personal guard. It was imperative that all her consultants were kept updated with what was going on with the Red Claws.

She already knew what Brent and Quint felt; both had made their opinions heard. Logical, precise, and intelligent. She valued their input immensely. Tia had also voiced her concerns and was up for "*whatever my queen advises*".

Maxine was young, but Liz had made her one of her inner circle early on, knowing full well Max had her finger on the pulse of the pack. A clan favorite, many confided in her on issues they might not feel confident in bringing to Liz's attention. She didn't see herself as intimidating, but some in the clan were more submissive than others.

Besides, she liked Max with her multi-colored hair. The youngest member was honest to a fault and never once was her loyalty ever in question.

Liz's brothers, David and Sam, would be instrumental in a war with Renworth. David was muscular and tall. One of the tallest members of the clan and an exceptional fighter. He still hadn't cut his dreads, but he'd had them for so long, Liz couldn't imagine him without them. And, with Sam's police background, she'd consult again with him on updating the electronic surveillance of their borders.

There was one former member of the Prime she missed, but he'd made his home with the vampires of House Valadon: Orion. He was a magnificent Were, and a valuable asset to Black Star Clan. The handsome musician had given concerts in the park to benefit the pack. And she was so damned proud of him.

Drop dead gorgeous, he'd become a rock god, traveling the world, his fame shooting him up above with the stars. A place he richly deserved to be. His voice was one of the best she'd ever heard, but ever since Bastien had become his partner, Orion was more comfortable with the vampires. He'd told her they'd welcomed him with open arms and that was where he belonged.

The last she'd heard, he was touring in South America.

That left Lawe and Gavin. God, they worked well as a team. The best of the best. They implemented tactics and strategies exceedingly well in training exercises. Pride had her back straightening in how proficient they were, how much they were loved and respected by the clan.

But, now, Lawe was busy with his restaurant, so much of the battle readiness would fall on Gavin's shoulders. She had no doubt he was up for the challenge. He'd never failed her, not once in all the years they'd led the clan.

As *Liaison to House Valadon*, a position vacated by Orion, Gavin had learned much about strategies and tactics from the vamp king, as well as his second, Remare. Both vampires had survived numerous conflicts throughout their long centuries and shared their knowledge with Gavin. An accomplished warrior, Remare had even invited Gavin to House Valadon for sparring sessions. Their friendship and alliance had strengthened even more.

The last member of the Prime was also its newest member—Cyrus. Her new alpha was a welcome addition. Cyrus was an industrial engineer, often envisioning ideas for the future of Black Star Clan. And his concepts had paid off lucratively. But, because of his enormous size, he intimidated some of the pack. Was jealousy a factor? Yes, she nodded, it certainly was.

There were other males who had vied for her attention to become her chosen one, but she'd declined all of them.

It also hadn't escaped her notice that loyalties were divided among the clan. Her people easily followed Gavin; they had for years. Some thought Cyrus was too rough, too demanding. Didn't they know she ordered him to be so? She couldn't afford any weakness, any flaws in her people that could be exploited. *So, Cyrus is hard on them, so what?* He made them better, stronger, faster.

They might grumble, now, but they would be thankful later.

A knock on her door broke into her thoughts, and it was as if the devil himself had entered. "I saw your light and knew you were still up. Mind if I come in?" Cyrus waited with brows raised.

"Not at all, come on in and shut the door behind you."

Her alpha was handsome as hell with his wavy blond hair and a physique not easily matched. His muscles rippled when he walked, intimating the animal within. Even the most physically toned males were in awe of him.

She'd watched him when he worked out. Disciplined, focused, and oh so determined to push himself to excel. He was stunning, and when he smiled at her, her stomach did this flip. With his strong jaw, full lips, and piercing green eyes, he was one of the most sensual and desirable Weres she'd ever met.

As he lifted her up in an affectionate bear hug, she recognized the scent of some of the females on him. No big. Weres were inherently affectionate. Touching was a part of who they were. He growled in her ear, "Miss me, gorgeous?"

"Always." She quickly kissed his lips then pulled away. "What has you up so late?" She glanced down at his crotch and arched a brow. "Being entertained thoroughly?"

His laugh reverberated off the walls. "Your women love to dance. As alpha, it's my responsibility to let them know they're...appreciated."

She smirked. "I'll bet."

He released her to flop down on the couch then patted the cushion next to him. She chose her recliner, instead. This way she could see him better when they spoke.

"The Cajun Grill took in a fair amount of revenue tonight. Lawe will bring you the receipts tomorrow, but if we continue like this," Cyrus rubbed his hands together, "Black Star will see a steady and profitable income. Kudos to both Lawe and Gavin. That place is amazing. I loved the food."

"So did I, and the ambience was pretty cool. I love the New Orleans décor inside: the colorful masks, beads, posters of Jazz Festival, and all the other memorabilia from Mardi Gras. I'm proud of them for doing such an outstanding job."

"We should do something special for them." Cyrus stretched out his long legs in front of him. "I'm not sure what, yet, but they definitely deserve something worthy of their efforts. Any ideas?"

With everything else on her mind, she hadn't even considered any kind of reward, but Cyrus was right, both of them merited some sort of commemoration. "I'll give it some thought."

"Good." He leaned forward to put his elbows on his knees. "I got the chance to talk with several of the guys tonight." His tone became serious. "After seeing what happened to Granger, their level of anxiety has significantly increased. I think you might have to address the assembly."

"I'm going to, tomorrow night. What did they tell you?"

"General rumbling. A few of them are spooked. Their fear gets the better of them when they let their imaginations run wild. They spread such rumors about the Red Claws, make them out to be feral monsters."

"Some of them might be." Liz's fingernails beat out a tune along the edge of her recliner. "I've heard they experiment with steroids to increase their muscles."

"Steroids!" Cyrus scoffed. "There's always a price to pay for artificially trying to increase muscle mass. They should know better."

"Some don't care about the long-term consequences, only the short-term benefits."

He rolled his eyes. "Then, they're fools. I've seen the results of steroid abuse. It isn't pretty."

Liz agreed. "What else have you heard?"

"Not surprising, many want to know if we're going to war against Renworth. Some are actually hyped for it. I believe the word 'revenge' was bandied about a bit. What do you think?"

"A war is the last thing anyone should be hyped up about."

Cyrus leaned back and studied her. "That's right; you were a medic in Afghanistan."

She nodded. "And the sights I've seen are enough to hope war is avoidable...even though that might not be the case here."

"Options?"

"That is something I plan to discuss with the Prime tomorrow. Everyone needs to be updated with all pertinent information. I want to hear everyone's thoughts."

After a few moments of silence, he stroked his chin. "You're planning on meeting with him. I mean, Renworth. I know you. You love your people, would do anything to keep them protected. What are you hoping to achieve?"

"Know me so well, do you?"

"Well enough." He arched a brow. "Am I wrong?"

"Not necessarily. But you are right; it is our responsibility to protect our people. I will meet with Renworth. Possibly nothing will be settled, but it's important I do so."

"I knew it. When do you meet with him?"

"Let me talk with the Prime, then I'll decide."

He blew out a breath and then rubbed his neck. "Try to make it before or after I go to Chicago."

Her eyes widened. "Chicago?

Cyrus frowned. "Yeah, the main office sent me an email. They're having problems with one of their operating systems, want me to have a look at it. I'll probably be gone for a day or two, shorter if I discover what's wrong sooner."

"Your timing sucks."

"Hey, work calls." He drummed his fingers on the armrest. "How about this? Why don't I go tomorrow? Meet with the Prime, you already know my thoughts. But don't meet with Renworth without me. I want to be with you when you see him."

"Possible." She considered his words. "You say you'll only be gone a day or two?"

"Shouldn't take more than that, then I'll fly back as soon as I can. I'll keep you updated. Sound good?"

"It will have to be. I'd like you to accompany me, so let me know if you're gonna be gone longer."

He rose as she did. "Will do." His arms circled around her as his voice became sultry. "Want me to stay here tonight?"

Her body was willing, her heart—not so much. "I saw your moves on the dance floor. I think you need your rest."

A throaty purr escaped his mouth. "I think I need more than that." His lips met hers, and then, his tongue was tangling with hers. Cyrus was so inherently sexual, it was difficult to resist him, especially when his erection stirred along her hip. As a Were, her body was instinctual, and she responded to his hunger, her own rising along with his. "It's been too long. Be with me tonight, Lizzie."

No one else ever called her that, she wouldn't allow it, but with him, she did. She was reconsidering satisfying both their needs as he nuzzled her neck, his teeth grazing her earlobe, sending shockwaves throughout her body. She needed a distraction. Something to give her peace for a short while, something to take her mind off everything else, something to make her forget—

Just then, there was another knock on her door.

Gavin entered, and he didn't look happy.

Chapter Six

Cocksucking sonofabitch! Gavin took in the sight before him. Cyrus knew damned well how Gavin felt about Liz. Hell, according to Lawe, everyone in the clan did. That's why, as Cyrus stood behind Lizandra with his arms around her, he smugly smirked up at him. His arrogance, so sure of himself, clear in his eyes. Bastard just had to taunt him by touching what was his. *His!*

Every instinct in his body screamed for him to take the guy down and beat the ever-loving crap out of him. But, as beta, he couldn't do that. Cyrus was alpha, and there was a reason for the hierarchy.

Liz must have sensed the tension in the room because she slipped free of Cyrus' hold. "Is that for me?"

Gavin looked down at the plate with the chocolate cake he was holding. "Yeah, Lawe thought you might like a piece. He didn't think you got a chance to sample his dessert tonight."

"How thoughtful of him. Put it down on the counter, please." Liz walked toward him and laid a hand on his arm. "Tell him thank you for me."

That one simple gesture helped to cool his jets. He looked one last time at Cyrus. "I will."

When he turned to leave, she stopped him. "Stay for a moment. Cyrus was just leaving. He has to be in Chicago tomorrow."

"Now?" Gavin was shocked Cyrus would leave the queen after what had happened tonight. He definitely wouldn't.

Cyrus moved closer to them. "Yes. On business. It can't be avoided, or I'd be here for certain. I've been summoned by the main office. Shouldn't be gone more than a few days." His smile couldn't be any more sarcastic. "I take it you can handle things well enough while I'm away."

"No problem there." Gavin's shoulders relaxed at the thought of Cyrus being away for a few days. If he had his way, it would be for a lot longer. Like forever. "I, assuredly, have enough experience."

Cyrus' smirk returned. "I'm sure you do."

They stared at one another, each taking the other's measure. As sure as he was standing there, Gavin knew the day would come when they would have a throw down. Could he beat Cyrus in a fair fight? Cyrus had more muscle mass, had him in height and weight, but was he as knowledgeable?

Gavin didn't believe Cyrus was one to surrender so easily; neither was he. It would be brutal, probably deadly, but some things were worth fighting for.

It hadn't been the first time they'd locked eyes. It was a contest of wills to see who would break contact first. As it were, neither of them would, until Liz said, "You best be going, Cyrus. The sooner you leave, the sooner you can return."

Cyrus slid his arms around her and pulled her close. He kissed her forehead, and Gavin had to stifle a growl. "Try not to miss me too much while I'm away."

Oh, brother!

She patted Cyrus' hand. "I'll try."

Of course, Cyrus had to bump his shoulder on the way out, but since the guy was leaving, Gavin didn't much care. Once the door was closed, he met Liz's gaze. "Seriously?"

"Don't start." She moved to the cake, removed the clear wrapping and inhaled the chocolaty goodness. "Mmm. Want a piece?"

More than she'd ever know. "Sure."

Liz retrieved a couple of forks and plates from the cabinets and gestured for him to follow her into the kitchen.

He did. "Unfortunate timing for Cyrus to be leaving at this time, don't you think?"

By the breakfast nook, she glided the knife through the cake, placed his slice on a plate, and slid it toward him as he sat on the stool. Then, she took a pitcher of iced tea from the fridge and poured them each a glassful. "Yes, but it's only for a day or two. He'll be back."

"Before you meet with Renworth?"

She tasted the cake, and he watched as the fork slipped between her lips. *Those lips.* "If not, you'll accompany me, along with a few of the Prime."

He broke off a piece of the cake with his fork and raised it to his mouth. His eyes met hers. "Count on it."

"Good; tomorrow night we'll meet in the lounge and discuss strategies and possible options. Cyrus has already informed me of his views."

He knew, as well as she, that any negotiations with Renworth would prove futile. The man was just too aggressive not to declare war on them. "Have you considered asking Valadon to back us? You and he have been friends for years."

She sipped her drink. "Absolutely not. Valadon has his own cold war going on with the Human Order of Light. They tried to assassinate one of his greatest allies in England. Thank God, they failed." She waved her fork in the air. "Besides, if I ask for his assistance, it would be like broadcasting to all the other clans that I can't hold my own territory. It would be a sign of weakness. They would pounce on us the first chance they got."

Maybe yes, maybe no. The vampires of House Valadon were lethal, none more so than Remare, Valadon's brilliant war strategist and second in command. Other clans might think twice about mounting an offensive if they knew they'd have to battle the vamps as well as the clan. "All right, but you mind if I consult with Remare? I want to discuss tactics with him a bit more, see what his views are in defending our territory."

"That would be a wise move. How's he doing, by the way? I know you and he have become good friends since becoming Liaison to House Valadon."

That was true, ever since their trip to Japan, and Orion surrendering his old position, Gavin had become responsible for keeping the lines of communication open. The vamps had been as welcoming with him as they had been with Orion. "As good as to be expected." He shook his head then threw back some of his drink. "I still can't believe Miranda left him the way she did. It's been, what, a year, now?"

Liz nodded her agreement. "More. About a year and a half."

"And you never heard back from her?"

"Not since her last letter assuring me she was all right, learning what it means to be a true *Elemental*, and happy being with her sister, Cassie."

"Nothing more?"

Liz shook her head. "Not a word, not even a whisper."

"She was your best friend."

"I know, but she told me this was something she *had* to do."

Gavin rubbed his jaw. "I guess I just don't get it. I thought she was happy with Remare, that he'd become her family when they got married."

"No." Liz sighed and placed both hands on the edge of the counter. "Miranda has always felt like an outsider. Even here, as much as we welcomed her into the clan, she told me Werehaven was her home away from home, but never her true home."

Gavin liked Miranda. She'd been a good friend to both him and Liz. He was sorry she upped and disappeared the way she had. "I never really thought about it much, but it must have been difficult for her. She didn't have much interest in humans, felt she wasn't one of them; I guess she felt the same way here and with the vampires."

"Yes, that is why I believe she left to be with those of her own kind. All of us seek out those we most identify with, those we call ours. Remember, for many years, Miranda was an orphan, refusing to let anyone get close. For a while, we were the closest thing to a family she had. But there was always some part of her that stayed...detached."

He didn't disagree. It was something he'd also sensed in her. "Man, you should have seen Remare those first few months she was gone. He was livid, nearly took the heads off of those he sparred with during swordsmanship training. Fury raged inside him. Finally, Valadon had to tell him to take some time off before he killed someone. I know he went to London to consult with some of his friends there since that was where the letter was sent from."

"Miranda wrote that she was using a mailing service so that it could not be traced. She said that the coven of *Elementals* she belonged to were fanatic about keeping their location secret, especially when you consider how many of her kind were burned at the stake for supposedly being witches."

He knew the past annals of *Others* well enough. "They won't come out like the vampires and us did?"

She clicked her nails on the table. "No. They are resistive to the idea; given their history, I don't blame them."

"It's a pity. Maybe, then, there would be no need for all this secrecy." He regarded her solemn expression. "Remare must have dogged you for answers; I know he did with me."

She smiled. "He did, indeed, believing I knew more than I was willing to tell him. It took some convincing to make him believe I didn't. And, before you ask, no, I never received any other letters, emails, or texts from her."

He returned her smile. "I know, I just feel bad for the guy." Gavin knew what it was to love a woman so badly it made your insides hurt, as if your heart were being ripped from your chest. The love affair between Remare and Miranda had been one for the books. "Each of them seemed so in love, so devoted to each other. I just don't know how she could have turned her back on him."

Liz stared at him, like she was studying him for any underlining meanings. The unspoken words lie between them. *How could you do it? How could you turn your back on the one you professed to love so much?*

As if reading his mind, she answered him, "In Miranda's case, I suspect there were parts of her Remare could never reach, never really understand. It wasn't his fault. None of us know what it means to be an *Elemental*, not completely, not even Miranda. She had a calling she couldn't refuse."

He shook his head, not understanding the way Miranda had abandoned her spouse. "She could have discussed it with him before she left."

Liz snorted as she placed their plates in the sink. "There's no way he would have let her leave. That's why she left the way she did."

"Maybe he could have gone with her."

"No, the *Elementals* fear vampires. Apparently, there was bad blood between her kind and theirs in the past."

Gavin rubbed the back of his neck. "Well, I hope she returns sometime soon. The guy is going through hell, complete torture, not knowing if she's alive or dead. Or even if she's found someone else. You can't imagine the type of anguish he's going through."

She covered his hand with hers, and he found the gesture warmed his heart. Before Liz and he were lovers, they'd been friends. They'd been able to talk and share the connection that was so strong between them. He missed that; it had been important to him, still was.

"I *do* know the type of anguish you are referring to. I know it well, but as I said before, she did what she *had* to do. That kind of calling, that responsibility to know, cannot be denied."

Gavin sighed. And that was the hell of it all, wasn't it?

***

Cyrus threw his keys on the table and then poured himself half a tumbler of whiskey. Keeping the lights low, he sipped his drink, relishing the slow burn, and gazed out at the city from his Upper West Side apartment window. He was looking forward to going back to Chicago, even if it was only for a day or two. He'd grown up there and knew the people better.

New York was...enchanting, he loved it here, but it wasn't home. The Were clans here certainly had their share of complications. Nothing new there. There'd always been disputes regarding territories throughout many states.

Confrontations and victors, the way of their world.

He downed more of his drink when there was a knock at his door. He glanced at the clock, it was late, and he wasn't expecting anyone. Checking the peephole, he smirked. Sharon. Now, why wasn't he surprised? The way the sexy redhead had danced with him tonight made it clear she found him desirable. He opened the door and said, "A little late for socializing, don't you think?"

Not waiting for an invitation to enter, Sharon strutted past him. "Depends. For those of us who don't have to get up early, not really."

He arched a brow. "And for those of us who do?"

Her smile couldn't be any more suggestive. "Sleep is overrated. I'm sure you'll get by."

He knew damn well why she was there but asked, "So, what brings you here so late?

Sharon gave him the once over, her eyes lingering on his crotch, took the glass from him and downed the rest of his whiskey. She slowly closed her eyes as if savoring the taste and then ran her tongue along her lower lip. "I thought you might want some companionship tonight."

Cyrus retrieved his glass from her, went to the bar to refill it, and poured another. He then handed her the whiskey, and flopped down on his leather recliner.

Ever since it had become apparent that Black Star Clan was going to wind up in a war with the Red Claws, certain females had made their interest in him known. They knew, if it came to war, what the rival clan would do to conquered females, so they'd been slinking up to him, believing he'd be able to protect them.

They weren't interested in him because of who he was, only what he could provide as their alpha.

He glanced up at the clock, again. "You have one hour."

Sharon purred sensuously as she went to his music system and selected a Jeff Buckley song with a heavy percussion, "Forget Her", one of his favorites. Then, she set her glass down, leaned up against his entertainment center and watched him with heavy-lidded eyes. Her musky scent perfumed the air between them.

They both knew where they would end up. Sharon had long, lean legs that would feel real good wrapped around his hips as he drove himself into her. He always preferred females who were confident in their abilities.

He thought of his queen, Lizandra. She was truly one of the most self-assured females he'd ever known. Resolute, intelligent, and grounded in her decision making. She didn't fly off the handle the way some hot heads did. Oh, no, the queen kept her composure under the most dire of circumstances.

It was hard not to respect a woman of her standing.

There was a time when he dreamed of becoming king and sharing the lordship over the clan with her. Unfortunately, the queen didn't share his dreams and made it clear he was her alpha, and nothing more.

Sure, they'd been lovers, on and off, and their nights had been passion-filled, some nights almost brutal in their lust for each other, but always, he knew she was holding back, never really giving herself completely to him.

He scoffed, a smart move on her part.

Cyrus sipped his drink and watched as Sharon swayed to the music, her hands massaging her thighs as she provocatively lifted her skirt higher. He was amused at her attempt at seduction. Truth was, he was still riding high from the excitement of the new restaurant. He was proud to see how his ideas became reality. And, if Sharon wanted to help celebrate with him tonight, he had no complaints.

Would he have preferred another tonight? Maybe. Lizandra was one of the most beautiful and passionate lovers he'd ever known who had the stamina to match his appetite. Few women could keep up with him; that's why he usually preferred two, sometimes three, partners.

Interesting enough, Liz and he had an arrangement. As queen, she had her choice of all the males in the pack, as was her right. But, if he was going to remain alpha, he'd made it clear to her he wasn't going to stay celibate. She had no problem with that as long as both of them treated the other with respect and used discretion when choosing sex partners.

Cyrus was good with that, so as Sharon continued with her striptease, seductively lowering her skirt to the floor and kicking it to the side, he leaned back into his recliner and growled his approval.

He appreciated her well-toned physique and the ample breasts that were barely contained by her black lacy bra. Her matching thong barely covered anything, and he inhaled her womanly fragrance as his cock stirred to life. The heat between them intensified as if someone had turned the thermostat up high.

When she straddled him on the chair, rubbing herself along his erection, a snarl erupted from his mouth, and he took her lips in a bruising kiss. He pulled her closer so that their bodies were pressed tightly together, then he fisted that luxurious mane of red hair that had captivated him. Groaning, she broke from the kiss to strip him of his shirt and toss it aside. Her lips found his jaw and neck, leaving teasing bites along the way. Then, her fingers undid the button and zipper of his jeans and pushed them out of the way to stroke his cock.

God, it felt good to have her hand wrapped around him, and he thrust into her hold, relishing the friction. His pre-cum made for an easy slide that had him growling low in his throat. "On your knees, Sharon. I need your mouth on me, now."

Never one to question his orders, Sharon slipped off his thighs then licked a path from base to tip, her teasing tongue swirling over his slit driving him crazy.

"Suck," he commanded.

When she did, his eyes nearly rolled back. It felt so damned good. He knew, because of his size, it would be impossible for her to swallow him whole, even though she was making every effort. But, before he would allow himself the release his body craved so badly, he pulled her off him and stood.

While she gazed up at him, panting her arousal, he let his pants and boxers fall to the floor and stepped out of them.

Then, he bent and lifted her up in his arms. "Let's continue this in my bedroom."

Her laughing eyes glinted as she purred, "Let's."

Fuck, there was no way he was going to make the early flight he'd booked on the way home. Not with the exertions he had planned. Oh well, he'd catch the next flight. Tonight, he needed to unwind, and Sharon was providing a most enjoyable alternative to a cold, lonely bed.

Chapter Seven

The Were King prowled through the great hall of Renworth Castle to where the cage fights were going on. The arousing aroma of blood, sweat, and riveting excitement permeated the air, as did the sweltering heat of many bodies present tonight. And, if he wasn't wrong, he smirked, the sweet scent of sex also perfumed the vast room.

He paused, for a moment, to inhale the vibrancy, the exhilaration his people experienced while watching physical prowess in action. It was as if he could absorb the intense anticipation emanating from his people, making him feel more powerful.

There were those who thought the competitions too brutal, too bloody, but they weren't Weres. Humans could never comprehend what it meant to be Were. It was in their animal nature to compete, to fight, to push their limits, and strive for supremacy.

It was the only way to bask in the glory of triumph.

As more of his people became aware of his presence, they raucously applauded and cheered; pride surging through him, he waved his approval and gestured for them to continue watching the sport before them. Their shouts became a thunderous symphony of celebration. It was music to his ears. No others could ever enjoy the thrill of living as well as they did.

To be truly alive meant to challenge yourself as if you flirted with death. No fear, no hesitation in the dance of darkness. *I fucking love it.*

Renworth climbed the steps up to his throne, situated high up on the elevated dais. Once seated, he scrutinized his people. Their energy levels ignited the air around them. His approbation swelled, knowing their aggression motivated them to excel, to conquer and prove dominance.

Of course, the drugs supplied by Ehrlich Pharmaceuticals only enhanced their performance, even if they were still illegal. He'd met the CEO, Stuart Blackmore, at a cocktail party and discovered the two had much in common. He was looking forward to seeing him, again; they had much to discuss.

Another bellowing shout went up as Curtis, one of his best enforcers, landed a punishing blow to Aaron, who seemed dazed for a moment then rejoined the combat. All his people were caught up in the rush of the fight, relishing the volatility between the opponents.

Almost all.

Scanning his realm, his eyes landed on the one who did not seem to share their enthusiasm. The one who kept himself reserved with his arms crossed over his chest and a reticent countenance. Victor.

When their eyes met, Renworth gestured for his second to join him on the dais. Another might be concerned with his second's seeming remoteness. But he liked that Victor didn't share his lust for bloodshed. Gren would never challenge him for the throne; he didn't have the stomach for it. In a way, Victor balanced him, kept him grounded, and considering his depth of interests, that was a commendable feat.

As Gren ascended the stairs, Renworth pointed to the chair closest to him. "You don't seem as entertained by our games as everyone else. Are you becoming too jaded?"

Victor leaned closer to him. "Difficult to become jaded when so much is going on. But you are right; the bloodletting doesn't excite me as it once did."

"Oh, and what does?"

His second seemed to think about it then replied, "Stability." At his king's raised brow, he added, "Prosperity for the future."

Renworth snorted. "On that, we agree."

A particularly vicious blow to Curtis had blood spewing on those too close to the cage. "We do."

The pack master eyed his pensive friend. "Spit it out, Victor. What's on your mind?"

"If we go to war, there will be losses on both sides. I thought it would be in our best interests to reevaluate options."

The king growled as he shifted in his seat. "We explored those alternatives. The commissioner ruled in favor of the Black Stars, repeatedly. The bitch queen turned down my offer of uniting the clans, so tell me, Victor, what options do we have left?"

Gren stroked his chin. "If our goal is to tap into the potential wealth of Central Park, your sports pavilion may have more appeal to the queen...if you offer to share profits with her."

Renworth scoffed at the idea. "She would never agree to such terms."

"Lizandra is an intelligent woman. She knows, if it comes to war between our clans, she will lose. If we make our offer generous, say...an even split of the revenue, she may reconsider."

The king considered his second's suggestion. The sports pavilion was a major aspiration of his, something that consumed his reveries. Inclement weather forced people indoors. So, he had designed a facility that would house a basketball court, tennis and racquetball courts, and various other recreation rooms.

As a media mogul, he had many interactive games to offer, as well as a museum wing that would house the history of sports. His archives possessed a ton of videos and never-before-seen memorabilia. Oh, what income such a complex would generate.

"Percentages?"

Victor shook his head. "The queen would never contemplate anything less than fifty percent. I'm sure, if we made the offer, her advisors would recommend she ask for more. We, however, would not settle for less."

The crowd again roared, this time, even louder than before. The king watched as Curtis threw his hands in the air after defeating his opponent and saluted him. The blood that ran down the side of Curtis' face was almost as dark as his skin. Renworth nodded his approval and smiled.

Now, the females in the clan would compete. Carita and Dori were up next. Each was reasonably built and deadly in a fight. There were those who thought they couldn't fight as well as the males. But he knew better. He'd overseen their training himself, rooting out the weakest and giving them the boot.

The women of Red Claw Clan were dangerous, cunning, maybe even more so than some of the men. They were strong enough to throw hits that did serious damage. And lithe on their feet. He liked how they danced around their opponents then struck with incredible speed and alacrity.

He thought of Lizandra and how toned her body was. She was the strongest female in her pack. Dori had fought her once, studied her moves, style, and how quickly she rebounded. After being discovered as an enemy agent and ousted from Werehaven, Dori had been able to report to him on what she had learned while at the Black Star sanctuary. And, it had been quite a lot.

But not as much as his present agent. His grin returned. Like the females, he enjoyed playing with his prey before he pounced. "All right, then. Make the arrangements. We'll see if the queen bites. If not...prepare yourself for a more aggressive turn of events."

As if satisfied with his reply, Victor bowed his head in deference. "Will do."

As the two female combatants fought in the cage, he admired their form and their bloodthirsty natures. Each was dressed scantily in leather that just barely covered their softer parts. A low, lusty growl emitted from his mouth. The female body was a fucking work of art, a delicious meal to be savored. Perhaps he would reward the victor with a night in his bed. "Send the winner of the match to my rooms, when they're finished."

When he rose, he spotted an amorous couple in the corner with the female straddled over the lap of the male. The way their hips were moving made it clear they weren't waiting for the matches to end to enjoy a good hard fuck. "Who's that with Xander?"

Victor followed his line of sight. "Alana."

"Are they mated?"

"Ah, I believe so."

"Pity, she knows how to move her hips really well." Renworth continued his descent. He usually didn't bother with mated members of the clan. Of course, there were exceptions. He remembered the time Sloan had failed him by giving him a positive proposal on a project at work. When the venture had plummeted, he'd ordered Sloan's mate to his bed. She hadn't complained one bit. It was considered an honor among the females to be invited to his bedroom. But making Sloan watch as he vigorously fucked her may have been too severe a punishment.

Then again, Sloan had never brought him another failed project.

***

The next night, at Werehaven, Lizandra ascended the stairs to her VIP lounge, aka The Throne Room, where many vital decisions concerning the clan were made. From here, she could gaze out the large, tinted window at the massive dance floor and twin bars on either side where most of her people congregated. But tonight, her Prime Nine awaited. Well, with Cyrus still in Chicago, it was her Prime Eight. *Doesn't have the same ring to it as Prime Nine. Maybe the Elite Eight? Nah.*

"I see everyone's here." She sat in her favorite recliner and faced her inner circle. Tia sat on her left, and Gavin to her right. She smirked at Gavin's choice. It had once been a foregone conclusion that was his place. The seat suited him, even though it now belonged to Cyrus. "Let's get started. Where are we?"

Quint, the clan's lawyer, spoke first. "We received an interesting invitation from Alexa Cantrell, Edgar Renworth's lawyer. The Red Claw King wants to meet at a mutually agreed upon location. He suggests you bring two—no more, no less—of your advisors and he will do the same."

David, her brother, snorted. "As if he would only have two of his people with him."

"He's not to be trusted." Lawe leaned forward. "You know he'll surely have more of his men nearby."

"Of course, he will. And, so would I," Liz exclaimed.

Ever coolheaded, Gavin asked, "Did he mention the reason for the meeting?"

Quint exhaled. "Something about generating goodwill between the clans."

Brent shook his head, disgust etched in his face. "He says this as he prepares for war against us."

Max, the youngest member of the group, spoke up. Neither excited, nor distraught, her face seemed more contemplative. "Is that a definite? I know many in the clan think it will happen, but is it a foregone conclusion?"

Liz rhythmically tapped her nails on the armrest. She didn't want to alarm any of her Prime, but she believed in full disclosure. These were her people, her most trusted advisors. "All reports indicate it is certainly a possibility." She stared at Brent. "Unless, he's grown a heart in the last few days and decided to spare the lives of his clan. Somehow, I hardly think that's feasible."

"We have a few spies in his court. All indicators point to him readying his forces. If it does come to war, I believe it will be imminent."

At Brent's declaration, some of the members seemed uncomfortable and shifted position in their chairs.

"Come, now, we've been expecting this for some time. It should not come as a surprise to any of us." Liz looked Gavin's way. Her rock, as always. How she admired his composure, his confidence. Even without touching, she could feel his support streaming her way. "I understand our troops are in optimum condition."

"All of us are in the best shape possible. We've always conditioned ourselves for any acts of aggression, by the Red Claws or any of the neighboring clans in nearby states." Gavin's voice didn't waver one iota. "If they do attack, we're ready for them."

Liz imagined Gavin as an ancient warrior of a far-off land, wearing a kilt, with a sword in his hand. She half-expected him to make a fist and hold it over his chest in a gesture of deference to her.

Tia's voice held vitriol. "No one's ever attacked us, except for the Red Claws."

"He's had his eye on our territory for some time" Lawe gazed her way. "He's determined to have it. One way or another."

Liz smirked. "Well, we certainly won't make it easy for him, will we?"

"Hell, no!" Variations of similar responses reverberated loudly around them.

God, Liz loved her people, they were so passionate, so proudful, each one willing to risk their lives for her. No one could ask for a better group of friends and advisors.

"I think we should meet with him."

At Sam's remark, everyone faced her youngest brother as he rubbed his palms together.

"We should see what he has to say. Be in a better position to gauge his intent. Listen, I agree with everyone here. War, at this time, seems unavoidable, but maybe he'll let something slip that could serve us."

The room stayed quiet as everyone contemplated Sam's remarks. Finally, Liz spoke up. "I planned on seeing him, anyway."

"Surely, you haven't agreed to his proposal of marriage?" Horror was written all over Tia's face.

"Not in a million years. But his request does stir deeper consideration, does it not? Renworth could easily attack us at any time he wishes. Why ask for a meeting? What's he looking for? What does he hope to gain?"

Brent frowned. "His way of appeasing the Commissioner of Clans when they ask him why he made war on us. This way, he can say he at least tried to negotiate a peace treaty."

"A peace treaty?" Lawe looked shocked. "That's the last thing on his mind."

"Perhaps," Liz agreed. "Could be he's trying to gauge us as much as we are him." She slyly peered up at Brent. "Rumor has it Renworth has insinuated a spy...among us."

"In the Prime?" Tia asked, her voice heightened. "No fucking way!"

Liz admired her people for their outrage at the thought of one of their own betraying them; she'd never had cause for suspicion, trusted every one of them with her life. When they finally settled down, she said. "A few members of the general assembly have informed me that Renworth offered them considerable bribes if they relayed information to his confederates."

Gavin narrowed his eyes and leaned forward. "Who?"

"Renworth has specifically targeted packmates who are under harsh financial stress, either with medical bills for family or escalating college costs, or those in severe credit card debt. He, apparently, had our people scrutinized for monetary deficiencies." Liz leaned back in her chair. "Ruthless, wouldn't you say?"

Lawe crossed his arms over his chest. "Conniving bastard."

"I would expect nothing less." Liz's nails dug into the leather. "Quint?"

"Yes?"

"Set up the meeting." She met Gavin's eyes. "Where would you suggest?"

"My first gut response would be the park. Just in case this meeting is nothing more than a lure to get us to leave our territory vulnerable without its most fierce warriors."

Quint negated that idea. "No way would he agree. He specified a neutral place. I'd suggest a restaurant in Mid-town."

Liz considered all the places she'd frequented. *Mid-town, hmm.* And then, a thought occurred. "I think we should meet at a park, but not this one. Bryant Park, adjacent to the New York Public Library. Forty-second and Fifth. We can have our people scattered throughout, as I'm sure Renworth will do the same. The space is wide-open enough to spot any surprises he may decide to hit us with. Besides, it's a human territory, he would have to have some pretty big brass ones to inflict harm on the humans who frequent the park."

Sam shrugged. "Unless, he considers humans collateral damage."

"No, I don't think so. Even Renworth wouldn't be so brazen. He would lose the allies in the human world. Quint, set it up for tomorrow. At noon. This way he has little chance for planning anything nefarious."

"Will do."

She met Gavin's gaze. "We'll see what the Red Claw King has in mind. Should be interesting."

Chapter Eight

Later that night, Liz found herself tickling the ivories of her grand piano at Songhaven, Werehaven's tiered amphitheater, a place that offered solace as she composed songs while the others found succor at the bar and on the dance floor. She played around with a tune that had been spinning around in the back of her mind, then paused to write down the lyrics and notes.

She smiled when Gavin's face came to mind. She'd titled the song, "My Rock". Most people, when they heard it, would probably think she was writing about her clan. They'd be half-right. But the heart of the song belonged to Gavin.

The music flowing freely through her, she stepped down on the pedal to emphasize the emotion she was conveying. It was as if the song took on a life of its own with her being merely the tool that elicited the magic. She started humming the melody until she was happy with it and then let the notes fly from her mouth.

With the acoustics in this room, and the music echoing off the walls, anyone could hear the ache, the want, in her voice as she continued crooning desires that had gone too long unanswered.

Unlike Orion, she'd never aspired to become a professional singer. She'd been taught music by her grandparents and sang for her family, friends, and the grace of God. That was enough for her. Always had been, always would be.

"My Rock"

Forever and always on my mind

Always the one to help me unwind
Your gentle touch soothes my aching soul
Basking in the shadows of my goal

Your faith in me is unwavering
To the peace I find myself craving
Forever my lonely heart, my cure
You are the one reason I endure

Denial is such an ugly beast
When dining on an empty feast
I long for our moments of light
To keep us warm in the dark of night

Liz yawned. Another time, she'd finish it, but tonight, she just wanted to focus on the music. Feel it as it coursed through her into the keys, surrounding her with its enchantments, giving her hope. Music was a soothing balm, a curative, to everything that had her wound up. She raised her shoulders and rubbed her neck, hoping to loosen the knot of tension there.

"Why'd you stop? I was loving the song."

She didn't have to turn around to know who had entered. His scent was a dead giveaway. She'd know it anywhere. Only Gavin smelled of pine after a hard rain. She loved the intoxicating effect it had on her. Closing her eyes, she breathed him deep into her lungs. So soothing, so masculine, it made her body shimmer.

She looked over her shoulder to see him walking toward her with that crooked smile she adored plastered on his face. So wrapped up in the music, she'd hardly heard him enter and wondered how long he'd been there watching her. "It's not finished, yet." She flexed her neck muscles by rotating her head.

"A little stiff there?" He approached her and used his fingers to massage her neck and shoulders.

All Weres enjoyed touching and being touched, so the familiarity was not only welcomed, but deeply appreciated. Her animal stirred, yearning to be with him. She almost groaned. "A little."

"I think more than a little. Everyone's under some level of stress." He leaned lower to whisper in her ear. His breath along her skin doing nothing to quell the butterflies taking flight in her belly. "It's okay to admit you're not Wonder Woman."

She laughed. "I never said I was."

He continued to rub his thumbs in a circular motion along the tight muscles of her neck and shoulders until they relaxed; it felt like heaven. "No, you only act like you are. Even WW must have her moments where she didn't want to be a superhero and just be...a woman."

Liz rolled her eyes as she turned to face him. "Never wanted to be a superhero, it's tough enough being queen." *Some days, you feel like a pawn. Other days, you're a queen. And damn, it sure feels good to be the queen.*

He gave her arm one last rub then leaned up against the piano. "I know. That's why you have us. To bear what you cannot. You're not alone, Liz. You have me. You always did."

They stared at each other for a moment before she moved closer and whispered, "Good to hear, but fairly certain I already knew that." Pulling back, she said, "I noticed you didn't mention you were at ValCorp during the meeting. What did your pal, Remare, have to say?"

Gavin checked the tiers for any sign of movement. He needn't have bothered. Either one of them would have caught the scent if any of the others were nearby. "Not here. Y'know, I could work those kinks out of your back a lot better on my table in the infirmary."

I bet you could. And then some. It was the "then some" that had her worried. She tapped her fingers on the piano and considered his desire for privacy for whatever he needed to tell her. "I've got a better idea."

"Oh?"

"A couple of beers, my quarters, an old movie, and whatever I can find in the fridge. I think I may have some leftover blueberry pie."

"With real whipped cream?"

She arched a brow as if to say *you doubt my culinary skills?* "Of course."

"Mmm, my favorite."

"I know. Mine, too." She rose and lifted the lid to the bench and placed her notebook and pen inside.

As they walked down the hall, he grinned. "Promise me no chick-flicks tonight."

She certainly wasn't up for anything too heavy or sentimental. She returned his smile. "I promise nothing, but I'm sort of in the mood for something fast-paced, action, fight scenes, hero stuff."

"Sounds promising."

"Yeah, we haven't seen *The Mummy* in a long time. Heroes and sheroes. Guaranteed not to fall asleep watching. That work for you?"

"Pretty much. As long as it's the Brendan Fraser version and not the remake."

She gave him an exaggerated look of being appalled he would ever suggest such a thing. "Hell, yeah, even the villain was a hottie in the film."

He paused outside her rooms and narrowed his eyes. "I knew you'd say that."

She unlocked the door and flipped on the lights. "He was. So was Oded Fehr in his black robes. Mhmm. Y'know that actor always reminded me of Remare. Anyway, I'm eager to hear how your day went."

"Damned interesting, to say the least."

Liz retrieved the pie and beers from the fridge, then cut two slices while Gavin set up the TV. "Wanna get the beers?"

He nodded as she placed one of the plates on the coffee table and took her usual seat on the recliner. Once situated, he hit the remote to start the movie and then tasted the dessert. His moan of approval sounded more like a purr. "This is the best pie ever."

"Glad you like it." She, too, enjoyed the sweet, delectable blueberries, but her response wasn't nearly as loud as his. "So, give me details."

He lifted his index finger. "One moment, I'm still savoring." When she stared his way, he finished swallowing. "It's a good thing I caught Remare today. He's leaving for Europe soon. Not only are the European vamps fending off attacks by the HOL and propaganda by its leader, Stuart Blackmore—who excels at inciting fear and hatred toward the vampires, they're having major differences of opinion in their ruling court concerning their new chancellor. All kinds of shenanigans going on there."

"So I've been told. Lately, it seems like the whole world has gone crazy. What did Remare tell you?"

"Pretty much what we expected. He thinks if Renworth attacks, it will certainly be at night, when no humans are in the park. Remare suggested more guards at all the entrances and exits since that is the probable point of entry. We've already done that. Also, to expect his people to attack in waves. The Red Claw King will send his 'pawns' in first and hold back his seasoned warriors until he's ready for the major fighting to begin. He'll try to surround us, but we have the upper hand as it is our territory and know it better than anyone."

She rubbed her chin. High Lord Valadon's second, Remare, was a thousand-year-old vampire who had served in many wars. You didn't get to live that long unless you knew what the hell you were doing. And Valadon didn't get to be High Lord without surrounding himself by the best people possible. "I see. What else did he say?"

Gavin swallowed another bite of his pie and leaned back in the cushions. "Renworth won't launch an offensive from just one direction. He'll pounce from different locations. He won't care that he'll have to sacrifice some of his men. He'll do it, anyway. Remare believes that Renworth has had our territory and people under surveillance for some time."

"I would expect nothing less from Renworth." She considered doing the same for Riverside Park, scrutinize his comings and goings. The thought even occurred that maybe she should plan an offensive, teach the motherfucker not to vex her. But she has no desire for Renworth's territory or to fight him on his own turf. *I'm not that suicidal.*

Gavin seemed perplexed. "You really think Renworth had one of his people infiltrate us? I mean The Prime?"

Liz began playing out a tune with her fingers on the armrest. "Something hasn't felt right in some time. We already know he's offered bribes to several of our people. He may not actually have to try to seduce one of our own inner circle, but rather someone who is close to us, stealthy, one who socializes well with our people. Someone we'd never expect. A person who keeps a low profile, says all the right things, but harbors duplicity. Money may not be the motivating factor. Renworth owns several cable channels and news stations, perhaps career advancement opportunities would appeal." Her gaze met his. "It could be anyone."

Gavin shook his head. "Both of us have known our people for so many years. I've watched them as we trained, as we socialized, I can't fathom any one of our people betraying us so blatantly."

She didn't disagree. "I tried to come up with ideas of who I might have pissed off, angered, or offended so badly they would turn on us." She placed her empty plate on the table. Liz leaned back, then her eyes met his and lingered there for a moment. "The only person I could think of was...you."

He glared at her, wiped his mouth on the napkin, and tossed his plate on top of hers. "You pissed me off royally, humiliated me in front of the clan. And, *still,* I would *never* betray you or the pack. Not. Fucking. Ever."

"I know." She leaned forward to squeeze his hand reassuringly and felt a zing buzz through her, their connection a palpable thing. "That makes it all the more painful that, if there is a spy in our ranks, it's someone we trust, have faith in, laughed with, and partied with as a brother or a sister."

"So, you do believe it?"

"I think it is something we need to be vigilant about. My mind is outraged that it could be true, wants to deny it, but...my gut tells me the possibility is very real."

"I trust your gut." His ire was clearly stoked by the way he kept tightening his fists. "It just sucks and infuriates me. After everything you've done for the clan—offering medical care, housing, emergency funds, scholarships—how someone could even consider siding with Renworth is fucking unbelievable."

"I don't want to believe it either, but we must consider that Renworth has stacked the deck in his favor and has been doing so for some time."

Gavin took a long swallow of his beer and set the bottle down. After a moment, he reached for her hand, again. "Are you ready for tomorrow?"

"As ready as can be. I don't believe Renworth will do anything reprehensible, not with so many humans around. This is a scouting mission on his part. He wants to check us out, see if he could spot any weakness, sniff out any fear. Try to manipulate and intimidate me. I've met men like him all my life. He thinks I'm an easy mark. Easily conquered. He doesn't know me. I do so hate to disappoint him." Her smirk turned evil. "But I will."

Gavin's body betrayed him, his scent stronger, more potent, as it lingered in the air, caressing her as easily as if it were his lips. He was clearly aroused by her confidence, and she, in turn, by his desire. He liked the beast that lurked beneath her skin, her spirit, her sass.

He'd told her long ago that was what had first attracted him to her. Some men preferred the damsel in distress, some blonde, blue-eyed feminine piece of fluff. That wasn't her, though she'd had friends that aptly fit the description. Come to think of it, their teeth were just as sharp as those with harder edges. And could be just as dangerous. More so, since you weren't expecting it.

Knowing Gavin was turned on by her comments had her heart skipping a beat. Was there ever a time when her body didn't respond to him? Those whiskey-colored eyes of his that lured her in, held her captive in their depths as he shared a part of himself with her. She'd been attracted to him from the moment she laid eyes on him. The fact that he had the physique of a god was a plus, a really good plus.

Their bodies so close together, she could feel the air around them heating as the electricity between them arced and pulsed. She wanted to believe their chemistry was just a physical thing, that would be the easy way out, but it was so much more than that. She respected him and his opinions, liked the way he got along with everyone in the clan.

True, he was strong, but he was also kind. His compassion and empathy called out to her. What they shared was so powerful, their connection bound them together in ways no one else ever had.

"Oh, Liz." As if reading her mind, he reached for her, their foreheads touching as their breaths became ragged.

His exhalations whispered over her skin, sending a thrill through her. Her mind melted as instinct stirred. Part of her wanted him to stay and was reminded of a song she'd always liked: Rihanna's "Stay", the lyrics of unrelenting longing floated around inside her, stroking her where she wanted him touching her. The singer's ache so apparent in her voice, the incessant need to feel connected to someone so undeniable.

Why was it so hard for her to vocalize all that she was feeling? They'd been lovers for years; she knew what he was like in bed, knew his generosity, his moves. Images started surfacing in her mind of the evenings they'd been together. Maybe, a night of good, hard fucking was just what they needed—a release from all the sexual tension that held them tightly in its grip.

He kissed her, and her world started spinning out of control. The man had a lethal mouth that made her insides turn to mush. And she knew she was having the same effect on him as she passionately returned his kiss. Too long, too damned long, they'd been apart, their bodies demanding time together, the connection each of them shared with the other sorely missed.

But she couldn't do this. Not tonight. If it was just a fuck, a release from pent-up sexual need, she could see it through to its blissful end. But Gavin wasn't a piece of meat to be toyed with. His feelings for her were genuine. She'd broken his heart once; she wasn't going to do it, again. She tore her lips away. Her heart was beating so loud, she was sure he could hear it. She panted. "You can steal the breath from someone."

His crooked smile had her stomach flipping. "Glad to see you remembered."

He reached for her, again, but she braced her hands against his chest. "No. It's not right. Not now."

His hands stroked her arms. "When will it be right?"

She stared into those fathomless, mesmerizing orbs of his. She could drown in those depths if she let herself go. "I don't know."

Gavin's animal wanted to howl in frustration, break free from its cage. He knew, beyond a fucking doubt, she wanted him. Her arousal was as strong as his and permeated the air around them. Why would she put the brakes on, now? Only one possibility surfaced, and the thought infuriated him. "Are you waiting on Cyrus?"

"No." She was struggling to get her breathing under control, and that pleased him. "He texted me earlier. He said he'd try but wasn't sure he'd be back in time for the meet with Renworth. Apparently, the problems in his main office were more complicated than he first believed."

His shoulders relaxed a little, his anger retreating along with his inner animal. "Who are you planning on taking with you tomorrow?"

"You and Quint. In a way, it's a good thing Cyrus is still in Chicago. Renworth knows our key people and will be expecting him to be accompanying me... Let him think Cyrus is watching over the territory."

"Who will you put in charge while we're away?"

"Brent. His organizational skills are great, and he's respected by everyone in the clan."

"Good choice. His strength has been steadily increasing over the years." Gavin's eyes flicked to the TV screen, and his lips quirked. "Gotta have some sympathy for the villain. He loved his woman so much, he was willing to risk everything to be with her. Even death."

She held onto his biceps then pulled away. "It didn't work out so well for either of them in the end."

No, it didn't. He rose to leave then remembered something and fished out the flashdrive in his pocket and handed it to her. "Oh, a present from Remare. He downloaded everything they had on Renworth. Stuff not easily accessed. Evidently, Renworth and Valadon had been business competitors in the past, and the High Lord had ordered a thorough background check on him and kept his files updated. I skimmed most of it. Renworth has some interesting political connections. Brent might find his financials interesting."

She accepted the flashdrive. "I'll look it over first then let him peruse it."

At the door, Gavin turned back toward her. "Remare offered us use of his arsenal, any weapons we might desire. He assured me they had an abundance readily available."

Liz smiled as she flipped the flashdrive up and down in her hand. "Renworth has bought many friends. But I think we have the better allies. Tell Remare thank you, but confrontations between clans warrant no weapons, and tradition dictates we fight with claws and fangs only."

"No disagreement there." Though, he'd be a fool to believe Renworth would fight fairly. The Were King surely had some nasty surprises in store for them. Gavin smirked. He wasn't the only one. "Get some sleep, Liz. Tomorrow's a big day."

Chapter Nine

The sun was shining brightly when Lizandra, Gavin, and Quint strolled into Bryant Park where people who worked in the area had congregated for their midday meal or perused the vendors located along the edge of the park. Some had gathered by the fountain to take selfies or munch on the pretzels they'd bought at the concession stand. Tourists loved to hang out here after visiting the New York Public Library and exploring all the artwork housed inside.

Lizandra liked that the park was packed—less chance for an undesirable outcome. And she knew, without a doubt, Renworth had his people strategically placed throughout.

For that matter, so did she.

Her hair done up and make-up perfected, Liz had chosen the Vera Wang gray suit she reserved for important business meetings she usually had with the Commissioner of Clans or the Council of Others. As the leader of Black Star, she occasionally served as one of the magistrates when court issues arose concerning *Others*.

With her Prada bag, Jimmy Choo shoes, and Dior sunglasses, she looked the epitome of a successful corporate executive and carried herself with confidence. She may not have the wealth Renworth possessed, but she was still a queen.

And today, she felt as regal as she ever did. Her responsibility for her clan was foremost on her mind. Today would be vital in determining their fate, and yet, a strange calm had settled over her. Perhaps part of the reason was the man standing to her right.

Gavin looked stunning in his dark blue suit—Armani, if she wasn't mistaken. And it did little to hide his muscular physique. He'd donned aviator sunshades, but the planes and angles of his handsome face were still apparent.

Anyone who thought to tangle with him would think twice if they got a gander at his stern visage. He was as concerned about the meeting as she was and just as intensely protective of their clan.

If Gavin had a fierceness to his disposition, Quint relayed a more relaxed tone with his tan Saint Laurent suit and approachable demeanor. The rest of her people were casually located nearby. She spotted Max playing Frisbee with Granger, who had healed up completely with no noticeable scars. Tiago and Dorn, two of her best fighters, were buying stuff at the merchant stalls.

She chose one of the tables nearest the fountain, sat, and removed her sunglasses. She scouted the area until her eyes lit on Renworth entering the park from the southern entrance.

The Red Claw King was dressed in a dark suit, cut perfectly to emphasize his broad shoulders, and was flanked by his lawyer, Alexa Cantrell, who was dressed in a similar power suit as her. Also impeccably dressed and on his right was his second, Victor Gren, who seemed to have an uneasy air about him, like he was anxious about the meeting. *Now, why would that be?*

As if knowing exactly where they were located, the Red Claws approached, and Liz wondered if they were wearing ear buds to communicate with all the people they said wouldn't be there.

"Lizandra, it's good to see you, again. And you, Gavin McCray, a pleasure as always." Renworth shook his hand, and Gavin replied, "Likewise, I'm sure."

Quint extended his hand. "A good day for negotiations. Quentin Rodgers, I'm the Black Star lawyer."

Renworth shook Quint's hand and then introduced Victor and Alexa. Once all social niceties were complete, each party stepped back so that she and Renworth could talk.

"You look stunning today, Lizandra. Would it be brazen of me to expect you've reconsidered my offer of uniting the clans through marriage?" The king smiled sardonically, as if he already knew her answer.

Fat chance. She smiled cordially and waved her hand nonchalantly. "I've already had two husbands, Edgar, don't need a third." She thought she saw the corner of Gavin's mouth tip slightly upward.

"I've had three wives myself. You learn something new with each experience."

Yeah, like to stop doing it.

Renworth leaned close enough she could smell his Tom Ford cologne. "It can be quite stimulating with the right partner."

She gave him the once over. Had she not known of his penchant for violence, she would have almost considered him handsome. Now in his mid-forties, the slight gray near his temples enhanced his attraction, but too many years trying to rule the business world and too many self-indulgences had taken a toll on him and caused a few lines near his eyes.

His face had a savage beauty to it, good breeding evident in his bone structure. Renworth kept himself in excellent shape. *Ego. Disciplined.* He stood about six-foot-tall with a frame most would consider stocky if they didn't know how well-defined his muscles were.

From what she learned over the years, Edgar Renworth was not a man to deny himself any of the world's pleasures. Men like him were too used to getting everything they wanted and not being denied a single blasted thing. No matter who got hurt in the process.

The info Remare had gifted her had provided details of Renworth's daily routine, as well as his business life. She wondered if the vampires had spies themselves in Renworth's court they would never admit to having. *Probably.*

"Please sit." She gestured with a wave of her hand. "The noon sun can get hot."

"And, yet, neither one of us is sweating."

As he sat beside her, she got a better view of the man whose most striking feature were his deeply-set, dark eyes that were now studying her. No fear, no hesitation lived there. Only cold, precise calculation.

"I don't think either one of us sweats easily." She decided to cut to the chase. "Your people have been antagonizing mine, on our own territory, as I'm sure you've been informed." She returned his stare, refusing to blink. "Is there a reason for such behavior?"

"Ah, youth. At that age, testosterone runs high. Men need to release the energy that builds up," he answered unapologetically.

"And your cage games don't offer a suitable method of...release?"

He leaned back, his eyes narrowed, assessing, as if wondering how she knew what went on in his castle. His voice took on a more formidable tone. "For some, they do. Others require more...stimulation."

Liz relaxed back into her seat. Renworth kept his feral nature just below the surface. She could almost hear his wolf snarling, wanting to break free. Most Weres knew how to control the beast that lurked beneath. After all, they were civilized, and their human forms were dominant.

At least that was true for most Weres.

Of course, there were exceptions where the wolf ruled supreme, and the human part was less in control, less dominant. She wondered if that was true in Renworth's case, and if through the years, he had polished his veneer to such a luster that most couldn't see his true nature.

But she did. She maintained the equanimity in her voice as she spoke. "There's a reason you want control over my territory. It has nothing to do with uniting our clans or any desire for marriage. What is it?"

"Who's to say our united clans wouldn't be a good venture? Can you imagine how strong, how exquisite we could become? How powerful. I suspect, with our combined clans, there would be very little we could not achieve."

"We have each accomplished much in our separate clans. Much to be proud of. What more could you possibly desire?"

His eyes scanned over the terrain. "The future, Lizandra. No matter how much we've attained in the past, it is never certain it will be enough for a progressive and prosperous future. Your current alpha has built some admirable money-making endeavors. But his scope is somewhat limited. I could build far more superior projects that would significantly enhance our financial portfolios."

"You have my attention. Such as?"

He signaled for Cantrell to come forward. She handed him a binder then stepped back to stand beside Gren. He pushed the leather toward Liz. "Have a look."

It wasn't lost on her that, during their discussion, Alexa had been smiling, giving Gavin the once over, and Liz wondered if the woman was quietly imagining some X-rated fantasies. Liz opened the binder and scrutinized the contents. After a moment, she asked, "You want to build this pavilion in the park?" *My fucking park!* "Do you really think the city officials would allow such a structure built?"

"Why not? They, too, would benefit from it...financially."

Because the founding fathers designed the park as a place to recreate, to relax, not to compete in indoor games in this monstrosity. "Why not just build it on your own territory? You have plenty of space."

"We both know Central Park has the advantage of location. Riverside Park has some awesome vistas, but more people frequent New York's premier park. Therefore, more revenue is to be gleaned from the project being constructed there."

She stroked her bottom lip, as if she were considering his proposal. There was no doubt in her mind Renworth would do whatever it took to have his pavilion built. He practically salivated when he discussed it, his fangs almost protruded from his jaws, as if he could already taste it.

He had no intention of taking no for an answer. Before they had even sat down to discuss options, before he'd even sent the invitation, he'd already had his mind made up.

Today had nothing to do with negotiations. It was all about posturing, getting a bead on an adversary, sizing up the enemy. This would not end pretty.

She exhaled slowly, choosing her next words carefully. "And, if I refuse?"

"You've prevailed admirably in the courts." He leaned forward, the beast shining brightly in his eyes. "How much longer do you think you will endure?"

Ah, there's his wolf. She'd been wondering when he'd make his threats known, no matter how cunningly covered up by pretty words. Out of the corner of her eye, she saw Gavin almost take a step forward then lean back. Her hand rose in a soothing gesture. *Steady, my love. I've got this.*

Now, it was her turn to lean forward, her claws itching to break free, her voice, authoritative. "We are both people used to playing by our own rules. We rule our territory as we see fit, make decisions that are in the best interest of our people. All our people. Would you so callously lead your people in a war where we *both* would suffer substantial losses?"

He didn't flinch at all. "In a fucking heartbeat."

No fucking shit.

He wore his confidence like it was an accessory specifically designed for him. "Especially when I know I'll triumph. You can't win a war with me, Liz, and you know it. You don't have the numbers."

His arrogance chafed, but she refused to back down. "Don't be so sure. People who defend their territory fight with all they have. What do your people fight for? Greed?"

He barely contained his growl, and she knew, if humans weren't populating the area, he'd lunge for her to tear out her throat. "You're playing with fire."

She held his stare as her tone turned icy. "A man's reach shouldn't exceed his grasp. Better men than you have fallen for failing to acknowledge their limits. And even you, Edgar, have limits."

He stood, his patience clearly exasperated. "We shall see. Keep the prospectus." When he tried to invade her personal space, Gavin stepped closer and shook his head once, negating any forward movement by the Were King, who eyed him, then her. "Think long and hard before you make your decision. You stand to lose far more than me." He signaled for his people to accompany him and then left the way they came.

Liz let out a breath she hadn't realized she'd been holding.

Gavin asked, "You okay?"

"Yes." She was sure he and Quint had heard every word and handed the leather binder to Quint, who remarked, "There are others leaving the park in the same direction as Renworth. Evidently, he'd had close to a dozen of his clan placed among the humans." Her lawyer faced her. "What's your take?"

She donned her sunglasses. "We have much to discuss. Let's do it back at Werehaven."

***

"So, what do you think?" Gren asked as they drove in the limo to The Algonquin Room for lunch.

Renworth smirked. "You heard everything, still think the Black Star Queen will acquiesce to our request?"

"Give her time to go over the proposal with her advisors. Many in her pack are young. She's not going to risk a war that could potentially get them killed."

The king considered his second's words. "You didn't see her eyes. Maintaining control of her clan over the years has given her some depth of character, an inner strength that's almost admirable. Central Park has been in her family for generations. She won't share that land with anyone who isn't a Black Star member."

Cantrell said, "She should have taken you up on your marriage proposal. It would have saved a great deal of work and effort on our part."

Renworth massaged her knee. "Ah, Alexa, bloodthirsty as always. I like the way your mind works. Give me your take away."

Cantrell shook her head. "She's not going to back down. The Were Queen is defensive and possessive of her people and her territory. If she has to go to war with you to protect them, she will. Stupid as it is since you gave her a viable option. Pride will be her undoing."

"Gren?"

His second shrugged. "Maybe yes, maybe no. As I said," he reached for the Lagavulin in the limo's paneled bar and poured them each a glass, "give her time to confer with her Prime. I'm sure we'll be hearing from her either way sometime soon."

"No doubt." Renworth threw back the scotch. "What do you think of her, as a woman?"

Gren held his stare. "Intelligent, not easily ruffled. She'll carefully consider all options, look at it from all angles, before she makes her decision. It's her Prime I'm concerned with. Some will advise her to take the deal, others... I'm not so sure about."

"I agree, but what do you think of her as a female?"

Gren glanced Alexa's way. "I think, if pushed against a wall, she'll come back at you with everything she has. Her claws nearly erupted from her fingers when you made your point clear. She's not a woman easily intimidated. She'll fight for what she considers hers."

"Cantrell?"

"She'll have a meeting with her advisors and listen intently to what each and every member of the group has to say, but when all is said and done, I get the feeling she'll do exactly as she wants."

The king sipped his drink. "And what is that?"

Cantrell swallowed leisurely then faced him. "Plan for war."

He nodded his agreement. "What did you think of her beta, Gavin McCray? I noticed you eyeing him during the meeting."

She grinned and smacked her lips. "De-licious. If I could seduce him, I wonder what he might whisper to me. Rumor has it, it's never sat well with McCray that she demoted him to beta after he was alpha for so many years. I bet there's some underlying resentment there. Might be worth looking into."

Renworth laughed. "See to it, then."

Gren swallowed the rest of his drink. "I wonder why she didn't bring her alpha. Or perhaps she wanted him guarding her territory while she was away."

"The same reason I didn't bring Curtis. She knew there would be no hostilities today; she trusts me as much as I do her." He downed the last of his whiskey in a single gulp. "Don't worry about her alpha." A wide grin appeared across his face. "Leave him to me."

Chapter Ten

Wanting privacy, the Were Queen invited the Prime to the sound-proofed conference room located farthest from Werehaven's main area. Everyone was seated around the long mahogany table when she entered with Gavin by her side. She took her place at the head of the table as Gavin shut the door behind them. This was a conversation she wanted kept under strict silence.

If necessary, through a flick of a switch, she could hear her techies next door in the communications room and peer out the large glass windows to see where her people—Mila, Jaxx, and Kael—kept watch over her territory through camera feeds on a multitude of screens.

"I trust everyone has been updated by Quint. I'm going to have copies made for everyone present of criteria all of you should have. Gavin was able to procure vital information about Renworth not easily accessed. I suggest everyone study the data thoroughly." In gratitude, she nodded his way, and the others followed suit, acknowledging the man they knew to be worthy of respect.

"So, it's certain, then?" Max asked the first question. "Renworth is willing to go to war?"

Liz maintained her composure, hoping to assuage the tension in the room. "It appears so. Unless, of course, I agree to marry him, which will never happen." She eyed her financial advisor, who seemed contemplative as he rubbed his jaw. "You have an opinion, Brent?"

"I've read through the prospectus. As Renworth indicated, the sports pavilion has the potential to generate a ton of income, especially since he states he would fund the construction. He knows we don't have the finances he has, so he's offering an auspicious bribe, but a bribe, nonetheless. Of all the machinations I'd imagined him purporting, I never thought he would venture something this bold."

"It certainly is substantial." Her brother, David, tossed the leatherette on the table.

Obviously, the Prime had discussed the situation before her arrival. Her brothers would never challenge her decisions in front of the others; her mother had taught them right, even if they did, occasionally, have disagreements. "Come now, brother, state your mind. Do you think this is something we should acquiesce to?"

"I didn't say that." David crossed his arms over his expansive chest, making his muscles appear more defined. "You'd think, with all the wealth he has, he wouldn't covet more, I mean to go to war over."

"Some men are never satisfied with what they have." Tia spoke up. "They always want more."

Liz smirked, wondering if Tia wasn't just referring to their adversary. "Renworth said he was planning for the future."

"I bet he is. And has been for a very long while." Sam, a member of the NYPD, looked out over the communication room he'd helped design. It was similar to what she suspected they had on the police force. Through his connections, they'd been able to acquire state-of-the-art equipment.

"No doubt about that." Liz swiveled in her chair, regarded her closest friends, and wondered how many of them wanted to take the deal. "Does anyone here think allowing Renworth to build his pavilion on our grounds a viable option?"

They stayed silent, with a few of them averting her gaze. She now knew who were leery of going to war. "Please, speak up, now, or forever hold your..."

She was surprised when it was Brent who voiced his concern. "I think we have to accept the likelihood that, if you were to acquiesce to the Were King on this matter, you'd be opening the door to more audacious ventures. There's no telling what Renworth would instigate. If he is, in fact, planning for the future. My gut tells me this pavilion of his is only a starting point. I dread to think what else he may be considering."

Liz noted the looks of surprise on some of her people. She'd already considered what Brent was voicing as a distinct possibility. "I agree. Once Renworth got his foot in the door, he would only want more propitious endeavors."

"He would destroy the natural beauty of the park to line his pockets. Our territory wouldn't be ours, anymore." Gavin kept his voice even as he eyed all the others at the table. "Renworth would defile the geography and its environment without any care of the consequences. Can you imagine how much contamination would be generated by his proposals, how much harm he would do to the landscape? It would be a nightmare we could never undo."

She appreciated Gavin's support and agreed with him. She turned to the one who had remained quiet throughout the meeting. "Lawe?"

"Everything Gavin and the others say is true. We let Renworth in, and he'll destroy the park, turn it into an amusement park, like fucking Disney World. How long before he petitions that humans use the park after dark? This park belongs to *us* at night, so we Weres have some place to roam, stretch our animals' limbs, hunt in our natural habitat, run along its trails."

Having a pretty good idea where he was going with his insights, she gestured for Lawe to continue.

"It belongs to the humans during the day—the separation is needed to maintain the peace. If they saw our more feral natures, they would learn to fear us, as some do the vampires. Not good. I'm with Brent; we'd be opening the door to much more than we'd bargained for. Let Renworth build his sports complex someplace else."

Liz appreciated that everyone seemed to be contemplating the risks of such a proposal.

"Yeah, like New Jersey," Max huffed. Which had everyone snorting their agreements.

She was surprised that Lawe had been so wordy in his response. He usually kept his remarks more succinct. "Anyone else have an opinion they think needs further discussion?"

When nobody else spoke up, she said, "All right, then, there's no telling when Renworth will attack. In all honesty, I believe it won't be imminently. I suspect he will wait until after the Lunar Run when the moon isn't so full and bright. Which gives us less than a week. I suggest we do all we can to prepare."

Everyone in the room seemed to come alive at her last announcement.

"Gavin, instruct your men to dig trenches with traps near the entrances to the park. Make sure they're deep enough so that they can't jump out and are not on the trails the humans use. David, I want you to erect snares with nets, using the ropes and pulleys we have in storage. This way, if any of Renworth's people make it over our walls, they'll have a surprise or two waiting for them."

Sam added, "I think we should use the scented macadam near the entrances, as well. Make sure the fragrant plants are close to our walls; their aromas will cling to whoever touches them. Since the Red Claws are using scent blockers, we'll smell them before they even get close."

"We'll be using scent modifiers, as well. ValCorp perfected the formula years ago. Somehow, Renworth either got his hands on it or had his own R & D people come up with something similar. As with everything else in this meeting, that information is confidential. For now, keep it to yourselves. All right," her nails scratched along the surface of the table, "any other ideas to deal with our belligerent neighbors?"

"Besides the stepped-up patrols," Gavin offered, "I think we should have more sentries situated high up in the trees. I know we already have the cameras around the perimeter, but just in case Renworth spots them or somehow has them disarmed, we'll still know if he encroaches on our territory."

"Good idea. Make sure they're supplied with the proper communication equipment." Liz eyed the monitors in the other room. "I'll want them in constant contact."

"Will do."

"Okay, everyone out. If anyone else has any other suggestions, text me. Lawe, Gavin, a moment, please. The rest of you go about your business. I'll address the assembly in due time and apprise them of the situation. I doubt this will come as a surprise to anyone."

After everyone else had left and Brent closed the door behind him, she faced her two commanders. "I already have an overview of our people's status, but I want fitness reports on the people you've been working with. I need to be kept current on who our strongest people are and those who have weaknesses. Not a judgment against someone's lack of ability, but something I need to know precisely for strategic planning."

Gavin nodded. "We've already done that and completed the assessments. Lawe and I have kept close scrutiny of our fighters, so we know who is best prepared for battle." He breathed out with an apparent sense of pride. "You'll find only a few who have temporary afflictions that make them unsuitable for war.

"We've got this, Lizandra." Lawe reached for her hand. "We've been training for years in case something like this arose. Have faith, sistah."

She patted his hand. "Always." When Lawe and Gavin rose, she stopped one from leaving. "Gavin, stay for a minute."

She thought Lawe was saluting her as he left but then realized it might have been Gavin he winked at as he left. When her beta faced her, she said, "I need you and Lawe to accelerate the training exercises, increase night maneuvers."

He nodded. "I can do that."

"I...hesitate to ask you. You've given so much of your time," she placed her hand over his and met his striking eyes, the longing present in those depths, "are you sure you're not hindering your chiropractor practice?"

"No, not at all. There's always an uptick in the winter months, injuries from people lifting more than they should. Besides, I always take vacation time in the summer." He winked at her. "Benefits of being your own boss."

The chemistry that had always been there between them simmered, warming her, making her want things she shouldn't. "I cannot tell you how much I've appreciated everything you've done for the clan. I'm not perfect, I've made mistakes, but always, I've tried to do what was in the best interest of the pack."

His voice conveyed not only his approval, but his affection for her. "No one doubts that, Liz. We know what you're going through. It isn't pleasant for anyone. But this is our home, our territory, and we'll defend it to the best of our abilities."

She bowed her head, wanting—no, *needing*—his opinion. "Do you think I'm making the right decision?"

He lifted her chin, his touch sending tendrils of heat spiraling through her. "I do. Everyone does. Don't start second-guessing yourself. You're making the right decision."

Thank you. "I know. That's what scares me." As if realizing how alone they were for the first time, and afraid she might act on her more basic desires, she said, "Walk with me back to my rooms."

"My pleasure."

After securing the lock to the conference room and nodding at the techies, she smiled as they walked down the hall together. *Just like old times.* Gavin always had the ability to make her feel stronger, more confident. Few men possessed that trait. She almost reached for his hand, their fingers nearly touching, but then, she refrained. "We may never be the same after this."

"We might be stronger, more united. War has a way of making people realize what's most precious to them."

Ain't that the truth?

His voice sounded self-assured. "We're gonna kick ass and who knows? We might even emerge wiser, better for the experience."

"We might, indeed." She unlocked the door to her rooms and would have flicked the switch if the lights weren't already on. His scent hit her almost immediately. Sitting leisurely in the corner with his legs outstretched, one ankle over the other, and his arm hanging over the back of the couch, was her alpha.

Cyrus stood, his impressive size always commanding the attention of others. "Liz, Gavin. I had hoped you could have postponed your meeting with Renworth until after I got back."

"I decided it was in our best interest not to give him any time to plan something nefarious." She moved farther into the room. "When did you get back?"

"Just now. I ran into some members of the Prime out in the hall." He gestured with his chin as he adjusted the waistband of his pants. "They updated me with what's been going on." He stood with both hands on his hips. "I've read all your emails and texts. I think we should talk."

"Yes, of course." Before the testosterone in the room spiked, she turned to Gavin, stroked his bicep, and hoped her eyes conveyed more than what she was saying. "Thank you for your support today; as always, I appreciate everything you do."

He stood frozen, rigid, as he eyed Cyrus. He didn't say a word, but she could spot the tic below his left eye easily enough and almost heard him grinding his molars. "As my queen wishes." Gavin then took her hand and kissed her knuckles. It wasn't something he usually did, but she supposed it was his way of making sure Cyrus knew he had her affection.

When the door closed behind him, she grabbed a couple of bottles of water from the fridge and turned to Cyrus. "Quint fill you in on Renworth's proposal?"

"Yes, and I've read through it." He let out a low whistle. "Guy doesn't dream small, does he?"

She handed him one of the bottles then gestured for him to sit. "No, he doesn't."

He exhaled then ran a hand through his blond locks as he leaned back into the cushions. "I wanted to be the one who accompanied you to the meeting." Frustration and regret laced his voice. "I apologize for not getting here sooner. Please believe me, I did all I could to hasten my departure, but some things necessitated me staying longer than planned."

"I know."

He swallowed a few gulps of water, then lowered the bottle to the table, and rubbed his palms together. "Are you disappointed with me?"

"No." She sank down in her recliner, set her bottle down, and grasped his hand. His usually sparkling green eyes seemed muted, more yellow. *Must be the jet lag.* "It's not lost on me the amount of demands I'm making on my people. In the days to come, I suspect those burdens will double." She stroked his jaw. "With some more than others."

"We live to serve." He covered her hand with his then leaned in and kissed her, but when he tried to deepen the kiss, she pulled back. He sighed his disappointment. "What is it, Liz? Are you apprehensive about Renworth?"

"He means to make war on us. At the meeting earlier today, I saw it clearly enough in his eyes. He intends to take our territory, or try his damnedest." She reached for the water. "Gavin and Lawe are going to increase the training exercises and night maneuvers, as I've instructed they do." She swallowed a few sips. "If he wants a war, we'll goddamn give him one."

"That. We. Will. I'm beginning to think this might actually be a good thing."

When she gave him a look, he clarified, "It's the not knowing one way or the other that keeps people tense, on edge. Knowing for certain energizes people, brings out the best in them. We'll pull together, stronger, united. Give that sonofabitch something to think twice about before deciding to make war against us, ever again. I say bring it on, show him who we are."

Liz didn't disagree with him. "No matter how bloody things get?"

"Has there ever been a war where blood hasn't been shed? Look, I know we may lose people, but I'm gonna do my best to keep the damage to a minimum." He jutted his chin at the door. "I'm sure your other commanders feel the same."

Through all of the complications associated with defending her territory, the one thing that stayed constant was the love of her people. "They do. It's what gives me hope that we may emerge victorious."

"We will." After a while, he said, "How's Gavin doing?"

"He's prepping the teams to the best of his ability, as is Lawe."

Cyrus scoffed. "That's not what I mean, and you know it." He rested his elbows on his knees. "I'm not blind, Liz. I can see you still have feelings for him. I get it. It couldn't have been easy for him getting demoted to beta and losing you in the process."

She rubbed her forehead. "It's been over for some time, now, Cyrus."

"Has it? I don't think so." He glanced downward and lowered his voice. "I would never make demands of you. I know you have feelings for me. And that it's not just gratitude for my presence or fighting ability. And...you still have feelings for him." He offered her one of his sexiest smirks. "No one ever said you had to choose. Why should you? You're queen, so...have both of us."

She wasn't sure she heard him right and shook her head. "What are you saying?"

"I'm saying you don't have to choose. I would be just as happy with him in the bed with us as I would be with you alone. And, if I'm not wrong, he would jump at the opportunity to be with us, or you, even if I was included."

"A three-way?" *Is he nuts?* "You're suggesting a three-way?"

His smile increased. "Why not? We've both had others in bed with us. Neither one of us is completely vanilla."

Liz shook her head, surprised at what she was hearing. Never once, had she imagined a scenario where both, Cyrus and Gavin, would be in bed with her. "Not discounting that, but I doubt Gavin is the sharing kind."

His eyes glinted. "Don't be so sure. It all depends on what's being offered. I'm not saying forever, but I'd like to give it a try. See if it works. If it doesn't, if one party gets too possessive, we don't do it, again. No harm, no foul."

Try as she might, she just couldn't imagine it. Gavin and she had once let another in their bed. God, that was so long ago and under different circumstances. They'd come so much further since then.

"Look, the guy still has feelings for you. It's painfully obvious. Talk it over with him. Let him decide."

She gave him an exasperated look. "I'll consider it. Now, leave. I'm tired and I want to get some sleep."

"Okay." He leaned his body over and sucked her bottom lip between his then kissed her forehead. "Promise me you'll talk to him."

She pressed her palms to his chest. "I said I'll think about it."

"You do that. Meanwhile, I'll be fantasizing about it. Just think how you'd be killing two birds with one," he glanced down at her crotch and gave a wicked grin, "heat."

She snorted. "Go, before you get me all hot."

He laughed then brushed his lips over hers before he made for the door. "Okay, I'll see you tomorrow. We'll discuss strategies and tactics. Good night, my beauty."

"Good night, Cyrus."

Chapter Eleven

Gavin made his way to Lawe's new restaurant. He needed some fresh air and was feeling too wired to sleep. Just seeing Cyrus in Lizandra's quarters irked him to no end. Yeah, the guy had a body like a Greek god, so what? Gavin wasn't that insecure about his own physique not to acknowledge that annoying fact.

What he and Liz had once shared was so much more than just physical attraction. *It was real.* And it grated that Liz wouldn't succumb to him. He knew she cared about him, he could see it plainly in her eyes, smell it in her scent, but she put clan first, and that meant Cyrus was her chosen one. *Fuck!*

As he sidled up to the bar, Lawe threw the towel over his shoulder and laid his elbows down in front of him, his dark eyes assessing. "Let me guess, Cyrus is with Lizandra. I saw him earlier entering her rooms. Only one thing makes you get that look you're sporting, bro."

He was in no mood for the ribbing when he parked his butt on the stool, even if it was his best friend jabbing at him. "Just pour me a scotch and leave my love life out of this. And make it a double."

"Easy enough," Lawe grabbed the bottle of Remy Martin, Gavin's favorite, poured a generous portion, then slid it toward him, "if you actually had a love life."

"Har, har." Gavin downed the liquor, relishing its smooth burn, lamenting the fact that it was the only warmth he was getting this evening. "How's the place doing tonight?"

"Good. We're pulling in a decent income." Lawe looked over his personal kingdom, the pride etched in his face as he shook his head. "I can't believe how great this place turned out to be. Y'know, when I saw the sketches, the paneling, and the tables and chairs, I never fully envisioned it looking this grand, but hot damn, this surpassed all my expectations."

Gavin was happy for his friend. It was a great thing to realize your dreams, and Lawe had been wanting a place of his own for so long. "You deserve it, pal. I'm proud of the way it turned out, too."

Sharon, one of The Cajun Grill's waitresses, stopped by. "Okay, the condiments are filled and all supplies refreshed, ready for tomorrow. I'm gonna clock out." Her gaze shifted to Gavin as she undid her black apron. "Unless you need me for anything else."

"No, you go on, honey. I'll close up here later. Thanks for the help." Lawe winked her way, the way he did all the females in the clan.

"You guys must be so proud of yourselves." She patted Gavin's arm. "When it was under construction, I kept trying to imagine what it would look like, but now, it's even better than all the drawings." She smiled back at Lawe. "I still think the décor with the plants and Mardi Gras stuff is what polished it off."

Lawe wiped down the bar and glanced up at her. "I don't disagree."

"Okay, I'm off." She slung her backpack over her shoulder. "See you guys tomorrow."

"Later, babe." Lawe watched as she strutted out the door. "Mhmm. Now, that is one fine-looking redhead. Don't know about you, Gavin. I think you're losing your touch. You could have had her. She was glancing down at your crotch, or didn't you notice?"

Gavin nearly sputtered his drink. "She was not."

"Yes, she was, but you didn't notice because," he circled his hand in the air, "your head is somewhere else."

"With what's happening lately, do you blame me?"

"Hey, man, no matter what is going on, there's always time for the ladies. Gotta keep the home girls satisfied." Grinning, he leaned lower and whispered conspiratorially, "They get a little lonely on these hot summer nights."

Yeah, I know all about loneliness. Gavin downed the rest of his drink. "Make it another."

"Sure thing." He reached back for the bottle of scotch. "You gonna tell me what happened down below?" Lawe gestured to the entrance to Werehaven.

"Nothing happened. Not a damn thing."

Lawe refilled his drink then poured himself a short one. "Well, my friend, nothing is gonna happen if you don't make *some*thing happen."

Gavin lifted his glass halfway to his mouth then lowered it back to the bar. "I just might have, if Cyrus hadn't shown up. Man, there is just something about that guy that...bugs the ever-loving shit out of me." People would say male pride, jealousy, whatever. But it was more than that; he just couldn't put his finger on it.

"No shit. The thing is, I don't think Lizandra is all that crazy about him." When he looked up, Lawe continued, "I mean, I know we need him. He's an excellent fighter, fearless, in fact. But other than what he can do for the clan, I don't believe she's all that hot for him."

Gavin sipped his drink. "And you know this, how?"

"Oh, right, you're Mister Oblivious when it comes to women. Females have a way of telegraphing their desires without having to say a single word."

"You don't say. I think I'm quite aware of the way women work."

Lawe grinned, again, this time, showing off a couple of his gold teeth. "So, I'm supposing you see the way they arch their spines, lean in a little closer so we males get a whiff of their scent that drives us fucking crazy. The extra special care they take in their appearance. Or the way they jut out their fine breasts, just ripe for the plucking, like Sharon did a minute ago."

"She didn't jut. You're delusional. She's just naturally endowed."

Lawe boomed out a laugh. "I'd say so. Look, all I'm saying is that Liz acts a certain way when you're around, and she don't act that way with Cyrus."

Gavin swirled his drink. It was true; he'd caught her looking at him when she didn't think he was aware. He was certain there'd been longing in her gaze. And he knew her well enough to notice the little things Lawe thought he was blind to. "Women aren't the only ones who send signals out. I've all but rubbed myself against her. She knows how I feel."

"Maybe you should remind her how good you two were together. If you want," Lawe stroked his thumbnail against his hairline as if thinking, "I can distract Cyrus, tell him I have a problem he needs looking into. Pull him away for a while so you and Liz can have some alone time."

Gavin mulled over the prospect. But what could he say to her that he hadn't already said? He'd made his feelings known to her on more than one occasion. He downed more of the scotch. "Not sure that will work."

Lawe shrugged. "Maybe yes, maybe no. Don't know 'til you try."

He knew what his friend was telling him was true, but how much more torture did he want to subject himself to? How much of a masochist was he? "I've already humbled myself to her, plenty of times. Not sure I want to keep going down dead ends."

Lawe rolled his eyes. "Man, I see you two and just wonder when one of you is going to come to your senses. Look, she needs him now, with all the aggression the Red Claws are throwing our way. But this war that's looming on the horizon, it ain't gonna last forever. Maybe you should remind her of that."

Before he could respond, the phone behind the bar rang, and Lawe went to answer it. Gavin scrubbed his face with both hands, his friend's comments swirling in his head, then he downed the last of his scotch and was about to call it a night when Lawe approached with a big ole smile on his face. "You're not going to believe this, but a certain lady wants your attention, and twenty bucks says you'll never guess who."

Gavin's eyes narrowed. "Liz?"

"You're not that lucky, *mi amigo*. Try, again."

Gavin couldn't imagine who else would be calling him. It couldn't be any of the females in the clan. Then, a thought occurred. "It's not Miranda, is it?"

He scoffed. "Magic Mira disappeared with the wind. Get this, it's Alexa Cantrell, Renworth's lawyer. She's at the bar in the Plaza Hotel's Oak Room. Said she met you at the meeting today and wants to know if you'll meet her for a drink."

Stunned, Gavin didn't believe Lawe for a minute. "You're shitting me."

"No, sir." Lawe shook his head. "Not about this. Now, why would Renworth's premier attorney be calling you?"

Gavin tried to shake off the effects of the alcohol. "I have no clue. We didn't even speak at the meeting."

"Well, you must have made some kind of impression. She told me to give you her number and for you to call her back if you're interested." Lawe passed a bar napkin his way. "She said what she had to say to you was private and to come alone. Think it's worth investigating?"

"Come alone. Yeah, right, like I'm gonna fall for that. I get there then get jumped by some of her goons. No thanks."

"Want me to go with you?"

"No way. I'm not going there."

They stayed silent a minute. Then, Lawe said, "Y'know, the Plaza Hotel is a human establishment. Humans all around. It would be very risky to pull something there."

Yeah, it would. He pondered calling her back and telling her he was wise to her shit, but what if what she had to say was important? Would he be missing out on an opportunity? Hmm. Only one way to find out.

Once outside, he hesitated punching in her number, knew half of what she had to say was probably BS, but he was curious. He hit send.

A woman's sultry voice answered. "Well, hello there. I wasn't sure you'd return my call."

"Now, why would Renworth's number one attorney be calling me this late in the evening?"

"Just finished up with a client and happen to be in your neck of the woods. Not everyone at Riverside is gung-ho about starting a war, Gavin. Some of us have even argued against it."

"I'm listening, Alexa. You have my undivided attention."

"Not over the phone. Why don't you meet me at The Oak Room for a friendly drink?"

Not in this lifetime. "I wasn't born yesterday. Not a chance, sweetheart."

Her feminine laughter echoed over the phone. "A man who's cautious. I like that, but I assure you, nothing nefarious is going on here. Just a casual drink between members of different clans. What do you have to lose?"

My neck. "What is so important that you need to discuss with me? If it pertains to clan business, why aren't you calling Lizandra or Cyrus? They run the pack."

"Somehow, I don't think Queen Liz would be all that receptive to me after today's meeting. Edgar can get...a bit temperamental when he wants something he can't have."

"So, why call me?"

"You fascinated me. Obviously, Renworth said things that were upsetting, but you restrained yourself, even though your need to protect your queen was more than apparent. I like men who know when to show reserve."

"If you like restraint so much, then you know why I must refuse your offer. Not sure my queen would like me socializing with an enemy."

"Are we enemies, Gavin? How are either of our clans ever going to get along if we don't first get to know one another? I understand your hesitancy, but the Plaza is loaded with people. Neither of our clans are foolish enough to do anything that would bring bad press our way. I can guarantee your safety."

Gavin contemplated what she was saying. She had a point; there was no way they were ever going to be on good terms. One of the clans had to make the first move in that direction. And the Plaza was neutral territory. "Guarantee it, how, Ms. Cantrell?"

She purred. "I give you my word, no harm shall come to you here, tonight. I am alone, I promise you that. I just thought it would be a good idea for us to get to know one another a little better, maybe foster goodwill between the clans. Was I so wrong?"

"Then, why request I come alone?"

"I'm not familiar with everyone in Black Star Clan. I prefer to keep this meeting secret. Even Renworth doesn't know I contacted you. I'd prefer to keep it that way. He has an aggressive nature, doesn't always take the proper amount of time to think things through, consider viable options. That's one of his fallacies."

Gavin remained silent, thinking over her words. What if he did show up? Was there the potential to learn something that might be beneficial later on?

"Just one drink, Gavin. Promise, you'll be safe, but if you want, then, by all means, bring as many of your men as you want."

Cantrell was certainly eager to meet with him. How big a fool was he that he was even entertaining the possibility of seeing her? He could scout out the area before his arrival. Have one of the guys canvass the room first. "One drink, huh?"

"That's all. Who knows? We might even have mutual ground to cover."

He waited a moment, not wanting to sound too eager for this meet and greet. "All right, Ms. Cantrell, but if I get one whiff of any underhanded business, I'm history, got it?"

"It's just a drink, Gavin, just a drink."

"Half hour."

"Looking forward to it."

Gavin didn't answer her, instead pressed end. What the hell was he thinking? This was probably a bad idea. More than likely, he was making a mistake. He turned to see Lawe leaning up against the façade of his restaurant. "You heard?"

"Most of it. You're not going there without backup."

"I know." He considered Lawe's size and musculature. No way he'd blend into the background. "Now, who can we get to do recon?"

Just then, one of the blond twins, Daniel, approached. "I cleaned up the kitchen. Everything's put away where it belongs." Noting the way they were sizing him up, he glanced from Lawe to Gavin with an inquisitive look. "What's up?"

If anyone looked innocuous, it was Dan—medium height, slender build, and, although handsome, he didn't give off that intimidating vibe other members of the clan possessed. "Well, Danny, how would you like to do a little scouting mission?"

He didn't hesitate. "Sure thing." He sniffed his arm. "I think I still smell like seafood, though."

Gavin nearly laughed as he palmed Dan's shoulder. "You'll be fine. Now, this is what I want you to do."

Chapter Twelve

After Danny had scouted out the Oak Room and reported he couldn't detect any other Were enforcers, neither by scent nor bearing, Gavin decided he was reasonably secure. And, if he wasn't, Lawe would be close by if the situation warranted it.

There was always the chance a Red Claw or two had average builds and were stealthily located nearby, but if that was the case, Gavin was more than able to deal with them. The fact that the Red Claws were now using scent-blockers vexed him. It made things more complicated, but not impossible.

When Gavin entered the Oak Room, he scanned the area, noting the murals on the walls and the chandeliers. Only a few humans were drinking and too busy socializing to notice him. He quickly spotted Alexa by the bar. *Damn!* She'd changed from the business suit she'd worn earlier to something more casual. Much more casual, considering the cleavage she was now sporting. She'd donned a stunning deep-green dress that clung to her voluptuous curves.

He'd never been attracted to women who kept themselves so thin they resembled anorexics. He much preferred women with curves, who looked healthy and wouldn't break if you hugged them too hard.

When Alexa glanced around and met his eyes, her smile—reminiscent of a shark—widened. Perfect white teeth in a face that was a few shades darker than Lizandra, and just as beautiful. He remembered her impressive height and the way she moved from earlier in the day. Some women had a natural grace to the way they held themselves, their movements resembling that of a dancer: effortlessly fluid, elegant, and well-choreographed. Female predator. *Now, why do I always find the dangerous ones so damned appealing?*

"As requested, Ms. Cantrell." He slipped onto the barstool beside her.

"Oh, please, call me Alexa." She played with the gold links in her necklace, drawing attention to the valley between her breasts. Her gaze slid seductively over him then up to meet his.

Dangerous ground. What was it Lawe told him before about the signals women sent out when they wanted...companionship? Strange, he didn't remember Cantrell being this attractive and sultry during their earlier meeting. Obviously, she worked out, her body toned to tempt and had his cock taking notice. *Down, boy. Wrong time, wrong place, and definitely wrong woman.*

The bartender, a robust man in his fifties dressed in a gray vest and bow tie, lay down a coaster in front of him. "What would you like this evening?"

Oh, so many things. After the two doubles he had back at The Cajun Grill, he thought he'd lighten up a bit on the alcohol. "Scotch and soda, on the rocks."

When he took out his credit card, Alexa placed her hand over his. "No, I invited you out tonight; let me get it. I'm already running a tab."

Gavin wasn't used to women buying him drinks, but tonight, he capitulated. "All right, but remember, I'm here for just one."

Her smile widened as her eyes glinted with amusement. "So am I."

The bartender brought his drink then stepped away to serve his other customers.

Gavin sipped his drink. "Come here a lot, do you?"

She laughed at his obvious uneasiness. "Not really. On occasion, I meet out-of-town clients who stay here on business. I figured it was close enough to your park for you to feel comfortable. Home turf and all that." She took a sip of her gin and tonic.

After a moment passed, he said, "All right, I'll bite. Why did you summon me here?"

"It was hardly a summons, more of a request." She swiveled in her seat. "Don't you think it's unnecessary for all the hostility between us? Surely, we have some mutual ground."

"Your pack master has made it clear he wants our territory. I'd say that's very good grounds for hostility."

"Maybe." She sipped her drink, and a droplet slid down her chin. He watched as it traveled down the column of her neck and down between her breasts before she casually wiped it away. "Edgar has made certain overtures that could make a truce between our clans. I knew Lizandra would never accept his marriage proposal. I'd have been shocked if she agreed so easily. Still, I think it shows Renworth was willing to consider options."

Gavin faced the mirror behind the bar, scanning the movements behind him. "Options, like wanting to build his complex on our land?"

"He said he'd be willing to share the profits the pavilion would bring in. He's even prepared to meet all the costs of construction. If nothing else, it shows good form." She sighed. "Not everything has to end in violence."

"Speaking of violence, people from your clan have been molesting my packmates for months. What's with that?"

"You're right. It's unfortunate, but I think we both can agree that each of our clans has members who are more truculent than others."

"Unfortunate?" His temper spiked. "Tell that to the youth that got mauled by one of your pack."

"What?" Her face and body language betrayed no duplicity, only surprise.

"Surely, you're aware of the increased attacks Renworth has waged against the Black Stars. He seems to favor the young."

She seemed to consider his words. "I advise Renworth on the legal implications of his investments. He doesn't update me on his, or the clan's, day-to-day activities."

"Maybe you should ask him, then. It seems, when he doesn't get the answer he's been hoping for, he sends one of his enforcers to tangle with us."

She turned from him and stirred her drink. "I'd like to say I'm surprised, but I know Renworth and certain members of the clan who relish belligerent behavior. All I can tell you is not everyone at Riverside shares their hostile nature. Not everyone wants to see this end in war."

"Then, what do you propose to stop it?"

She tapped her nails on the bar, similar to the way Liz did when deep in thought. "I know enough about Liz to guess she'll do whatever she believes is right for the clan. I also believe it would be wise if she gave careful consideration to Renworth's offer."

He didn't disagree. He knew Liz very well and the way her mind worked. "And if she's not careful?"

Her dark eyes caught his and didn't waver. "You and I both know the answer to that."

"Do you really see this ending any other way?"

Alexa smoothed her finger along her bottom lip. "I will be saddened and regretful if it comes to that. My purpose in inviting you here tonight was to consider ways of avoiding war between our peoples. If, in fact, war is inevitable, there will be losses on both sides." She licked her lips. "There are some members of the Red Claws who occupy a special place in my heart. I don't want them hurt or injured in any way. I'm sure there are those you are close to and feel the same about."

"True enough, but the decision doesn't lie in either of our hands."

"No, it doesn't. I think my hope was that we could advise our leaders to lean in a direction that is non-violent."

"Would your king listen to such a request?"

"Would your queen follow likewise?"

While she'd been talking, he'd watched the way she crossed her legs with her dress riding casually up her thighs. *Accidental? Doubtful.* Her skin was smooth enough that she didn't bother wearing stockings. He'd known she was on a fishing expedition from the minute he set foot in the place.

But, then again, so was he. Her goal tonight: Find out what direction the Black Star Queen was leaning. His goal: To get a bead on who she was, see if she'd let anything slip, give a hint as to how the animosity between the clans would play out.

Before he knew he was going to say it, the words fell from his mouth. "This isn't going to end pretty for either one of us."

She sighed as her lids fluttered closed. "My greatest fear."

"If that's so, why don't you advise Renworth against making war on us? He's been the aggressor in all our confrontations."

She tilted her head in his direction. "I already have. If you knew Renworth at all, you would know he's a man set in his ways." She looked him straight in the eye. "He will do whatever it takes to get what he wants. He's not a man to let obstacles stand in his way. He's been downright ruthless during business negotiations—almost terrifying in his bullishness. In the end, he will take whatever measures he needs to become victorious. That has always been his way...and always will be." She downed the rest of her drink.

So noted. He knew he should leave, now. There was nothing else to be gleaned from this meeting. Both of them had said what they intended. But something compelled him to stay. Even if her feminine scent hadn't been saturating the air around them and her heavy-lidded eyes hadn't conveyed her desire, he would've known she wanted him.

It had been a real long time since he'd allowed himself to be attracted to a woman who wasn't Liz. He'd never thought to consider anyone else. He ground his molars together. Liz and Cyrus were probably in the throes of passion, their bodies slick with sweat. But, tonight, Gavin wouldn't torture himself, wouldn't allow his jealousy to run wild. Instead, he stood and considered what type of woman Alexa Cantrell was.

As if reading his mind, she leaned forward, her breath whispering over his jaw. "From your investigation of me, you know I live in New Jersey. But, tonight, I booked a room here to avoid the drive."

"Of course, you did."

A slight rise in the corner of her mouth. "Would you like to come up for a nightcap?"

He had no delusions of what would happen once he got there. Visions of their intertwined bodies danced in his mind. He wondered if her skin would feel as warm and smooth as it appeared, if she liked it hard and rough or slow and sensual. Maybe a combination of the two. Run those sharp nails down his back, drawing rivulets of blood—wounds that quickly healed. With her muscle tone, she could ride him long and steady until he popped.

His dick throbbed, wanting, needing a release from all his pent-up emotions. Would it hurt to spend one night in the bed of a woman who obviously desired him? A woman who wouldn't keep him at arm's length, but stroke him where his itch needed scratching?

He bet she'd be warm and wet before he even entered her. Their bodies coated with a fine layer of perspiration, over-heated from their exertions, they'd fall to the mattress in blissful satisfaction.

He blinked and shook his head, as if someone hit him with a bolt of reality, then leaned forward to whisper in her ear. "It would have been even better than what you're now imagining."

She kept her voice low and husky. "I'm not the only one imagining it."

True that. But, before he let his dick make a move he was certain he'd regret, he said, "I hope when we meet next, it's under far better circumstances. Goodnight, Alexa. Thanks for the drink." Then, he turned and walked away, telling his shaft to calm the fuck down.

His hearing was acute enough to hear her whisper, "Anytime."

Once outside, he weaved through the traffic to meet with Lawe who was standing with one foot leaning against the gate to the park. "If you didn't come out in the next ten minutes, I was gonna go in there. How'd it go?"

Gavin glanced back at the hotel. "There is no doubt in my mind, that dark times are coming, my brother. Renworth is going to throw everything he has at us."

Lawe unlocked the gate then fastened it once they were inside. "She told you that?"

"Pretty much. Listen, I need to burn off some energy. You wanna race with me back to Werehaven?"

Lawe grinned. "Excess DSB, huh?"

Fuck! Deadly Sperm Buildup. Yeah, I'd say so. "Keep my dick out of this."

He laughed. "I always do. Okay, you're on. I'm still gonna beat your ass."

"Think so?"

"Shit, yeah. So, wolf form or human?"

"Human. The full moon is only days away. We'll race in our wolf skin, then. Ready?"

"I was born ready."

Gavin returned his grin as they crouched down. "I knew you were going to say that."

"One, two…"

And they were off, neither one of them waiting for three. They never did.

Gavin loved to run, to stretch his muscles and challenge himself to see how much he could increase his velocity. Side by side, hearts pounding, they jumped over rock formations, sped around the pond, down the trails, past the carousel, and really let out their speed as they closed the distance to the entrance to their home base.

If they'd been in wolf form, both would be howling their complete exultation of the moment. By the wide grin on Lawe's face, he knew his friend felt the same.

Once they neared their compound, they both collapsed on the lawn and laughed until they couldn't laugh anymore. Sweat dripping from both their faces, Gavin wasn't even sure why he was laughing so hard, but a sense of unrelenting euphoria streamed over him.

The exhilaration of the race, the fresh scent of the outdoors, being with his best pal. It all made him feel alive, feel energized. He rolled to his side. "Man, I needed that."

"Hell, yeah." Lawe panted. "We were never meant to be confined in cubicles," he pointed to the skyscrapers in the distance, "in those office buildings. The open terrain, the fresh air. This is us; this is where we belong."

"Absolutely. Thanks."

Lawe rolled to all fours and then sat up. "For what?"

"Coming with me tonight. Being there when I need someone."

They fist bumped. "Yeah, well, no one else would put up with your broody ass."

"I'm not broody."

"Yeah, right." Lawe stood, dusted himself off, offered Gavin a hand up, and then led the way to Werehaven.

Gavin followed closely behind. "I'm not."

Lawe turned, gave him a look that said, "Keep telling yourself that, buddy."

***

Alexa flicked on the lights to her hotel room and didn't have to turn around to know who was standing in the corner in his usual pose with his arms crossed over his chest. She tossed her purse on the table. "Don't you think it might have been awkward if I'd brought McCray up here?"

"Nice try, Alexa. He was never going to join you."

She smiled. "Didn't hurt to try. Mmm." She flexed her shoulders. "He is one delicious male. I wouldn't have minded taking a bite out of him one bit."

"Besides noting his culinary appeal, did you find out anything else, something that may be of import?"

She shrugged, still feeling a little lightheaded from being with Gavin in the bar. "Nothing we didn't already know. He's loyal to his queen, not easily tempted."

"You're losing your touch, Alexa."

"Not really." She kicked off her shoes and regarded Victor as he watched her. Now that her body was vibrating with need, she considered seducing Renworth's second, but he'd never showed any interest in her or, for that matter, any of the females at Riverside.

Neither did he display interest in any of the males. How dull and incredibly boring not to experience passion. She supposed the only desire he had was to serve their fearless leader. And maybe that was a good thing. He balanced Edgar, a man who knew no limits to his fervors.

"Oh?"

"Nothing easy is worth having. Besides, it was only one meeting. Before he trusts me, he'll need more than just one get-together. It takes time to develop faith in someone, earn their confidence."

"Renworth know of your grand plans?"

Feeling hot and too confined in her dress, she shimmied out of it and tossed it on the chair, then, wearing only her bra and thong, lay down on the bed. "Edgar is going to plunge us into war; he'll make a bloody mess of everything."

"Yes, he will." His eyes traveled leisurely over her body. Maybe she'd been wrong about his predilections. "And you thought you could avert that by…?"

"Negotiation. The Black Stars don't want war either." She remembered how irate Gavin had been about the younger members of his clan being annoyed by the Red Claws, and how resolute he was about defending his territory. "But it's their turf; they'll defend it to the bitter end."

"No argument there." He moved closer. "What did you have to give up in order to 'earn' his trust?"

She almost purred as she hugged the pillow beneath her. "Nothing vital. I told him not every Red Claw wants war, that there are those who would prefer a peaceful outcome."

Victor seemed to be studying her. Finally, he said, "You're not falling for the guy, are you? Because, if you are, that would be very unwise."

She laughed as she rolled to her back, her hands sliding over her breasts and ribs. "How big a fool do you think I am?" She thought back to the way McCray's breaths had increased when she fingered the droplet of water between her breasts. "We flirted, that's all."

"The thing about playing with fire, Alexa, is that ultimately someone winds up getting burned."

She nearly rolled her eyes. "I'm well aware."

"Are you? Good, so I won't have to remind you, again. We're on the eve of war. There are those in the pack who might not understand the games you play and misconstrue the reason for the meeting with McCray. Use discretion." And, with that, he opened the door and left.

She sighed at his comments then smiled as she remembered the way Gavin had eyed her. He'd been envisioning them together just as much as she'd been. She was sure of it. A moan escaped her mouth. Damn, he'd make a fine lover. With his maturity and experience, he'd know how to keep his partner begging for more, his movements measured, and oh so fine. Undoubtedly, Gavin was a man who could go all night and never tire.

Unconsciously, her hand slipped down over her abs and went lower. She knew he would touch her exactly the way she liked. She bit her lip and groaned loudly.

They could've had a lot of fun together; it was just too damned bad that he was a Black Star.

Chapter Thirteen

Unable to sleep, Liz trekked through the tree-lined path up to Summit Rock, a place where she could gaze out over her territory. Central Park was truly a wonder. She couldn't imagine any other park as grand as this one with the lakes, zoo, carousel, and her favorite, Bethesda Fountain, a place she'd often hung out with her best friend, Miranda.

God, Liz missed her, missed having someone to talk to who really knew her and didn't treat her like a queen as so many of the others did. Wherever Magic Mira was, Liz hoped she was happy, unlike herself.

A cool breeze swept over her, making her skin tingle. She sniffed the air, laden with a familiar scent, then crept to the edge of the precipice and peered down below. Granger and Max were going at it. Apparently, he'd fully recovered, and no ill effects were bothering him. She smiled. Young love, so pure and beautiful. Still in their early twenties, neither of them knew the complications that came with age.

Hell, she was only in her mid-thirties, but lately, she felt a lot older. She backed away far enough to give them their privacy, looked out at the hills, and supposed several couples were mating, needing the intimacy, as war loomed on the horizon.

If she could spare them that, she would. But the price Renworth would exact from them would be too high. As Gavin said, some things were worth fighting for, and the right to rule their land as she saw fit was definitely worth it.

She sat on the boulder and circled her knees with her arms, then closed her eyes and breathed in the night air. Sounds drifted upward, music that sounded familiar;

someone was playing Orion's latest hit single, "Starfire", a song his lover had written for him.

Liz hummed along as Orion crooned out a haunting melody about finding someone who set your world on fire, brought you so much love they became the light of your life, your reason for living—your starfire.

> *The night never shown so brightly*
> *The night never knew of beauty*
> *Until the gods flung your essence*
> *So high above the earth's torrents*
> *Higher and higher, my starfire*
>
> *We soar together, you and I*
> *Where no one can reach as we fly*
> *Above the forgotten world below*
> *To a place they will never know*
> *Ever higher, my starfire*
>
> *With the speed of fire, you enthrall*
> *With your heart on fire, you call*
> *The night is yours to take at will*
> *You overwhelm me as you thrill*
> *With the heat of your starfire*
>
> *Your eyes are on fire with love*
> *So pure, so rare, as like a dove*
> *You warm me on the coldest night*
> *Be my love, be my only light*
> *My starfire, my starfire.*

The lyrics touched her, warming her from the inside, as she wished Orion and Bas a long and happy relationship. Each deserved the obvious joy they'd found in one another. She bowed her head. Why couldn't she make her relationships last? Was she unworthy of the love that others found? No. She'd chosen her path.

As queen, she had to make sacrifices; that came with the territory. She exhaled slowly. No one could have it all; no matter how hard they tried. Not even a monarch.

"Hey there." One of the twins, Danny, came to sit by her, thoroughly rousing her from her reveries. "Why are you out here alone? Shouldn't one of your guards be with you?"

She gestured to their surroundings. "The night is just so lovely. Peaceful." She sighed as she stared off into the distance. "Sometimes, you just need a break from it all." Liz understood his concern for her safety, but she felt reasonably secure. "What are you doing out here? It's pretty late."

"Oh, I just came back from a scouting mission Gavin and Lawe had me on."

"Ah, checking the perimeters."

"Umm, no. Gavin wanted to have drinks with some woman, so he had me case out the bar at the Plaza."

What the hell did he just say? Liz felt her heart nearly explode out of her chest as her body buzzed with heightened awareness. "What woman?"

Dan scratched his head. "I didn't ask. But pretty sure she was one of the Red Claws."

Flames danced in front of her eyes, but she kept her voice steady. "Is that so?" *And they didn't inform me?* "What else did they tell you?"

He shrugged. "Just to check out the place, make sure there were no other Weres in the vicinity."

Liz was proud of herself for holding back her growl from erupting. "Are they still there?"

"I don't know. After I reported in, they said they didn't need me anymore, so I left." He tilted his head to the side. "Is everything okay?"

"Yes, everything's fine, but you should get inside. It's late, and you shouldn't be out here by yourself."

"Look who's talking." He winked. "Want me to escort you back?"

"No, you go on. I want to stay out here a moment longer." *And try not to kill anyone!*

"Okay." He scampered back down the hill.

When he was gone, Liz breathed deep. She needed a few minutes to calm down. Her blood coursed through her veins with startling speed. Drinks? *Who the fuck is Gavin meeting with? A fucking Red Claw?* Her nails became claws, and fur started to flare up along her arms.

Restraint, she needed to contain the animal within threatening to break loose and hunt down her beta. *Deep breaths, deep breaths.*

How dare he pursue another? Her snout felt like it was protruding, and she reined it in before it burst forth. She never lost control like this; what the hell was wrong with her? She'd been the one to cut Gavin loose. He had every right to date another.

Fuck no! She was on her feet and staring in the direction of the Plaza. Was he still with the woman? Would they be up in one of the rooms now, lying together between the silky sheets, their bodies glistening with sweat? Liz had spent New Year's Eve there once and knew just how smooth those sheets were.

Visions of Gavin and some faceless woman danced in front of her eyes. *Oh, hell, no!* She tried to clear her head, but the images persisted. Arms and legs intertwined. Soft growls and pants echoing in her mind made her ears hurt.

She was down the hill faster than she'd known it was possible.

Once inside the compound, she paced outside Gavin's door, knowing he was inside because his scent was still lingering in the hall. She deliberated on whether or not she should confront him. No matter how many times she'd counted to ten, her ire would not abate. Finally, she decided to open the door and have a conversation with the guy.

Closing the door quietly behind her, she scanned his living space and found it empty. Then, she heard the shower running. She crept silently and pushed the bathroom door open. The room was filled with steam. Was he washing off another woman's perfume? *Grrrr!*

She banked the raging beast within and inhaled. No female scents greeted her. Perhaps she was too late, and any female fragrance was now down the drain.

As the steam cleared, she could make out his form. He was faced away from her, and she watched as the water sluiced down the rippling muscles of his back and the curve of his ass. An ass she'd sunk her teeth into many times in the past. He was perfect, fucking beautiful.

Her beast demanded she join him. To open the shower door and wrap her arms around him, press her body to his, absorb his warmth. He'd welcome her, hold her, and kiss her senseless until she couldn't think, anymore. She wanted that; she wanted it badly. To mark him as hers so no other female would ever touch him. So, everyone would know he belonged to her and no one else.

And, because she wanted it to the very depths of her being, that was the reason she made for the bedroom door and quietly left his quarters.

Liz would not allow herself to make decisions when her emotions were this heightened. She knew better, had been taught clan came first, and there was a war to plan for. She was Queen and would act like one.

She'd be a woman another day.

After drying off and tossing the towel back into the bathroom, Gavin slipped between the cool, crisp sheets and sighed in contentment. He felt more relaxed than he'd had in months. He was sure it had something to do with the exciting fervor of racing with Lawe.

It felt so damned good to fly through the park with the carefree abandonment of youth, to just have fun and laugh at nothing in particular, other than the joy of being alive.

And his best pal always made him smile. But that wasn't the only thing on his mind. Something else was making his lips curve and his cock twitch—something, or someone, in a green dress.

Damn, you'd think taking care of himself twice under the hot spray would have done the trick. Yeah, not so much. Sure, he knew Cantrell was the enemy, knew beyond a doubt she was playing some sort of game. But she'd wanted him. He'd seen it in her eyes and the way she held her body. That much was clear, and it stroked something besides his ego.

Other females in the clan had made their interest in him known. Lawe wasn't wrong in pointing that out, especially when it came to Sharon. But the thing was, he'd known most of the women for years, knew what their lives were about, their lovers; they were like sisters to him.

Pretty hard for him to think of them as anything else. And most were familiar with his history with Lizandra; some respected that and kept their distance.

But Alexa didn't care about his past, and that pleased him. He ran his hand leisurely over his semi. She would have done her best to rock his boat, and that had him moaning. He imagined all the ways she would have gotten him off: slowly stimulating at first, and then hard and fast. The erotic images coursed through his mind, each scenario more carnal than the last, more arousing. His lust ramped up to a ten. There was no doubt in his mind it would have been wicked hot.

But some things were just never meant to be.

He rolled to his side, and a memory of long ago came to him. It was fall, the leaves were turning vibrant colors, and an invigorating aroma scented the air. Late that night, not quite the full moon, but almost, Liz and he had decided to go for a run and get away from the clan for an hour or two. The queen and her alpha. They loped through the woods, worry-free, their howls music in the night, both of them thrilled for the chance of alone time.

When they were far enough away from Werehaven, they abandoned the trails and lay down in the soft grass near one of the rock formations. Since it had rained the night before, the air had never smelled fresher, cleaner. It was a perfect autumn night. The sounds of the city were far off echoes that barely registered. Neither cold nor hot, they lay naked side by side. Content to look at each other, to enjoy their shared moment.

There were no threats from rival clans, no exigent matters to deal with, no injuries to administer to. It was just them enjoying time together. He remembered the way she laughed at some stupid joke he'd told, how melodic her voice had sounded. They'd been a couple then, the love they shared obvious in the way they held each other, stared into one another's eyes.

God, he'd thought they would stay that way forever. Each of them so hot for the other, they couldn't keep their hands off one another.

They'd made love that night, all that night, fiercely and sensuously, no fear of discovery, so obsessed with giving and taking pleasure. They'd whispered so many things, of promises and hopes. The future had been so crystal clear in his mind. Was it a dream? Or had it been real? It had felt real to him. He loved her, and he was sure she felt the same.

So, what had gone wrong? They'd been together for so long, years, in fact. He thought he knew her and what she wanted. Except...

Oh, yes, now, he remembered. In a foolish moment of sentimentality, he'd asked Liz to marry him. He'd forgotten she'd been married twice before and sworn off marriage. He remembered the devastating look she'd had in her eye: shock, disappointment. But what had hurt the most was the gradual distancing that happened soon after. He'd tried to talk to her, get her to open up to him, but she kept putting him off until it became clear the paths they were on were separate and irreconcilable.

Why couldn't he have kept his mouth shut? They could have continued on as they always were. But he wasn't satisfied that she might choose to be with another male, as was the right of the queen. That was something he could not accept. He'd wanted more, a commitment, and that was something she'd never give.

Gavin rolled over and punched his pillow until he found a comfortable position. He had to believe she would come around. She just needed time to be on her own. What was it they all said? "Distance makes the heart grow fonder"? But they never told you how much distance or how long it would take.

He needed a plan. A way to prove to her no one could ever take his place; prove he was the best fucking thing that ever happened to her. He would win her back.

Or die trying.

Chapter Fourteen

Edgar Renworth knew it was late. He never went to bed earlier than midnight; his body only required a few hours' sleep. There'd be plenty of time to sleep when he was in his coffin. But this particular night, his brain would not turn off. There was always so much to do, so much to plan for.

At his desk, he examined the blueprints and read outs his people had prepared for him. Topographical and geological reports on Central Park with special interest given to depths of rock formations. His photographer had done a good job in capturing striking images of the park.

During the past few days, he'd had his experts do land surveys on the park's terrain, scouting out the best possible regions to build with an eye out for easy accessibility. He would see his sports pavilion built, if it was the last thing he did. But, first, he needed all pertinent data concerning the park, and that took time. As requested, his assistants had researched information going back nearly a century.

Aside from excelling in economics while in college, he'd taken a keen interest in history, particularly in historical architecture. He loved scrutinizing the images of the underground subway systems, the artwork of the mosaics that decorated the stations. Back then, artisans had taken the time to do quality work, took pride in their accomplishments.

Although structurally sound, some of the newly renovated transportation stations left little to admire aesthetically.

There were several train lines on the West Side, but only the one on the East Side—the Lexington Line. He studied the tunnels and the reasons why some had to be abandoned and remain unfinished.

Unknown to many New Yorkers, there were three underground rivers that flowed deep beneath the surface of Manhattan. Important information to have if you were planning new construction. The land had to be able support the mass of the building to avoid any type of cave-in.

He rose and walked to his anteroom where he had the model of Central Park, built to scale, on a large conference table. He'd marked where the best three locations of his pet project would be most beneficial. He still hadn't made his final decision, as yet, since each location had its particular advantages. He would give it some more thought then make his choice.

It was a magnificent park that would only be made greater with his new addition. Why couldn't the queen understand that? *Foolish, foolish woman. You give no thought to the future and what this project could mean for your people, as well as mine.* No worries. In time, it would be built.

He moved to the next model, a mock-up of his sports pavilion. The designers were keen on every detail. He loved seeing the miniature and imagining what the real thing would look like when completed.

"Admiring your new brain child?" Victor entered, wearing his robe and slippers.

"It is worthy of admiration and so much more."

"I'm sure it will be." Victor studied the layout. "Impressive, to say the least. I can imagine the crowds it will attract."

"And the money it will bring in. A very worthy investment."

After perusing the pavilion, Victor moved toward the panoramic of Central Park. "Have the geologists finished with their assessments?"

"Not yet, but soon. They are still analyzing soil samples with their depth gauges."

Victor pointed to the red X's near the edge of the park. "What are these marks over here?"

"Subway exits. The majority of people will use mass transportation to enter the park. Do you have any idea, over time, how many subway stations had construction started, only to be abandoned because of deficiencies in the land mass?"

Victor scratched his head. "No, but I have a feeling you're going to tell me."

Renworth scoffed. "Several, poor planning by the founding fathers of the city. In some cases, it wasn't until they started excavating that they realized the ground was unsuitable and had to alter the course of the subway system. Can you imagine how much more efficient the subways would have been if they could have traveled in straight lines, without having to curve in certain areas."

"Speed trains. Like they have in Japan."

"Good analogy. In the not-too-distant future, the engineers are going to have to rebuild the entire underground system. The one they have now is antiquated and deteriorating, rapidly, since the storm caused the salt water to enter the subway lines and erode the tracks."

"Not a bill I'd want to have to pay."

Renworth laughed. "No one would. The cost of travel would surge to meet the demands of construction. No one wants to tackle such a profound undertaking."

"Good God, you're not thinking of investing in such a project."

"Relax, Gren, I have other more important ideas in development." He gestured to the model of the pavilion. "One major venture at a time."

"Agreed. You should get some sleep, unless you need me for anything else."

"No. You go on. The others all have their assignments?"

Victor was near the door when he turned. "Yes, I'll advise you when I hear from each of them and finalize their reports."

"Good." He returned Gren's nod and watched as he closed the door behind him.

Edgar supposed he should have shared some of his other endeavors with his second. But there were those choice undertakings he preferred to keep close to the vest. *Plans and preparations.* It felt powerful to have knowledge others did not. No matter, in time, everyone would know of his schemes and be in awe of his cunning and calculation. For some, it would come as quite a shock, for others, a stunning victory.

***

The next day, Gavin watched over his troops as they practiced their martial arts outdoors, close to their home base. Lawe was doing the same with his men. Gavin wasn't happy with the exercises in aikido, feeling the moves were more for self-defense and not aggressive enough for fighting, so he ordered the other commanders to run practices with a combination of tae kwon do and jujitsu. He wanted more challenging regimens with judo that used an opponent's strength and weight against them, as seemed the case with Brent.

For a man of average muscle mass, Brent was surprisingly adept at judo, his moves lightning quick and just as deadly. Highly impressive for a taciturn man who sat at a desk and crunched numbers for a living. When their eyes met, the financial advisor closed his fist over his heart then saluted him. Gavin returned the gesture.

Brent's sign of respect reminded Gavin of the techniques he learned while serving first as Lord Valadon's bodyguard, and then with Miranda and Remare while in Japan. Now, that had been a learning experience.

Previously, he'd studied karate, muay thai, and other forms of combat, had earned his black belts, but the warriors he'd met in Lord Huay's court in Sapporo were some of the best fighters in the world. He felt fortunate to have been able to not only observe, but participate in their workouts. True, their programs were tough, nearly brutal; humans probably wouldn't survive the vigor, but for vamps and Weres, the results were incredible.

Working out with Remare and his Torian guards, twice a week, for the last year and a half was another awe-inspiring experience. He'd always believed Weres were faster, stronger than vampires. And that was true, depending on the age of the vamp. But the Torians were several hundred years old, and Remare was over a thousand.

Lord Valadon's second was an expert fighter who taught Gavin it wasn't enough to excel in just one type of martial arts, but that a warrior needed to be adroit in all areas. The master swordsman had centuries of experience, not only in sword fighting, but also in every known form of physical conditioning.

Remare had introduced him to a form of combat that was considered the most dangerous in all the world: krav maga, the Israeli form of fighting. It had taken Gavin months to perfect the techniques. Gavin remembered how mesmerized the other Torians had been by their leader.

The only one who came remotely close to Remare's level of expertise was Orion's partner, Bastien. The speed both combatants displayed when sparring was unbelievable. Orion divulged he'd once witnessed Remare fencing with the High Lord himself, and that their moves were so incredibly fast he'd had a hard time tracking them.

Gavin had been told Lord Valadon was older by a couple of centuries and stronger than Remare, but his second was faster. Remare had advised him, when confronting an enemy who was stronger, speed was crucial in defeating that opponent.

Lawe, his navy T-shirt covered in sweat, came over to offer Gavin a water bottle, which he gladly accepted and gulped down a few mouthfuls. "Not too shabby an army, if I say so myself. These guys are pumped for what's coming; they're giving it their all."

Twisting the cap back on, Gavin asked, "Any complaints?"

"Not so far. I can tell when I've pushed them beyond what they *thought* they could handle, but no further. They know me; I'll never ask from them anything I wouldn't do myself."

On that, they both agreed. Each knew their people, their strengths and their weaknesses and knew when they needed a break. "Gotta say, they're looking good. I'm pleased with several of the younger ones; they've exceeded my expectations. Brent's looking really good."

Lawe nodded. "He's got stamina, bested a few of my guys with moves I haven't seen him use before. Stays cool, too, hardly breaks a sweat."

"That is impressive." Gavin knew Lawe's men; they were tough fighters.

Lawe grinned. "The ladies are the ones who've impressed the hell out of me. Whoever said they were the weaker sex had no fuckin' clue whatsoever. These women fight like their protecting their young; they show no hesitation, no mercy."

Gavin had reviewed the tapes and respected the female warriors. Even Max. What she lacked in size, standing at only five-foot two, she made up for in spirit and flexibility. She had acrobatic moves, similar to gymnasts, the others didn't, and that would benefit her when the time came.

Cyrus approached, holding an ice pack over his eye. "McCray, you gotta talk to Liz; she listens to you. I've never seen her workout like this. She's got Tia and Sharon sidelined in the training room with sore ribs. She's kickboxing like she's out for blood."

Gavin and Lawe smiled knowingly. Both said, "She's in a mood."

Gavin pointed to Cyrus' black eye. "She do that to you?"

"All I asked was if she was PMSing, and before I knew she was going to do it, she clocked me. Nearly knocked me off my feet, and in front of everyone."

Gavin bit his lip, trying to stifle a chuckle. "Bad move, Alpha."

"Oh, man," Lawe laughed as he clasped Cyrus' shoulder, "you don't go around asking females that. They get a little perturbed when you say shit like that."

Cyrus gave him an exasperated look. "No kidding."

"Okay, I'll go below and have a word with her." Gavin used the towel he'd wrapped around his neck to wipe his face. "She's probably just getting herself pumped."

"Tell her to save it for when it's needed," Cyrus groused as Lawe led him to where the soldiers were. Gavin nearly snickered when he heard Lawe trying to give the guy advice on what *not* to say to women.

Once in the training room, he spotted Liz near the long punching bags. She'd already split the seam but was still going strong with single-minded focus. Dressed in a black sports bra and yoga pants, rivulets of perspiration were running down her neck and chest. Like him, she had a third-degree black belt in kickboxing.

He admired her level of concentration. Not only was she throwing powerful kicks, she was using a combination of hook, scissor, and butterfly kicks in rapid succession. He stood transfixed. She was beautiful, her form flawless and her footwork nearly perfect. Great balance. Simply amazing.

Tia sidled up to him. "She's been going at it for hours. Barely taking time out for breaks. She nearly took Sharon's head off with a flying roundhouse, but Sharon moved away at the last second."

He spotted Sharon breathing heavily on the sidelines, her body bent over and coated in sweat as she watched their queen decimate the punching bag.

"Why don't you take Sharon and go up top, get some fresh air? You two look like you could use a break. I'll talk with Liz."

"Uh huh." Tia's eyes nearly bugged out. "Just so you know, your name came up, once or twice, accompanied by some choice words you never hear in church, when she was punching the hell out of the bag."

"Is that so?" he muttered, more to himself. "Go, now." He signaled for Sharon to follow, who seemed relieved for the chance to leave. He watched as the women, holding their sides, slowly climbed the stairs. Alone with his queen, he approached carefully, so as not to distract her.

"How are the men doing outside?" Liz gave one last reverse kick and then spun in his direction. Her incendiary stare would have flayed a lesser man. Gavin wasn't lesser, and he'd be damned if he let another make him feel that way.

"They're meeting and exceeding their personal best. Lawe commented his men have been training hard, surpassing all our expectations."

"Good. Then, what are you doing down here?" Her voice grated like broken glass. "Shouldn't you be up top, too?"

Okaaay, she really was in a mood. "I saw the black eye you gave Cyrus." He shrugged. "Just wanted to make sure everything was all right down here."

"Obviously, it is," she continued kicking the bag with amazing force, "so you can turn around and join your pals outside."

"I will. After you tell me what's got you so wired."

She spun in his direction, her rage just barely banked. "We're on the brink of war, and you ask me that?"

He stood his ground and crossed his arms over his chest. "Tia tells me you almost injured Sharon. What's that about?"

"Fucking Sharon." A high kick, using the heel of her foot for maximum impact. "She was getting sloppy. I thought I'd give her a little reminder to keep her head up."

"By nearly taking it off?"

A low growl escaped her lips. "I don't answer to you."

"No, you don't, but maybe you should answer to someone." He couldn't remember the last time he'd seen her so infuriated. She was spoiling for a fight, but why?

She narrowed her eyes. "And I suppose you think that person should be you?"

He was getting tired of her mocking tone and spied the punching gloves. "Fine. You need to work out whatever's got you aggravated, let's work out." He tossed her a pair of the gloves then slipped his hands into his own.

"I'm not in a mood to show mercy today." She pulled them on. "So, don't expect any."

"No one asked for any. Come on, Liz," he bounced on his feet, "show me what you got. Do your worst."

The corners of her mouth tilted upward. "I will."

He wasn't concerned. Years ago, they had trained with the same instructors. He knew her moves, her speed, and the techniques she used. They'd sparred before, and even though she could pack a wallop in her hits, he'd taken worse before. "Bring it on." He returned her smirk then used the one word he knew irritated the hell out of her. "Queenie."

A snarl reverberated around the room. She bounced on the balls of her feet, her movements fluid and quick. She started with a few short jabs then switched to uppercuts.

He parried every one of her blows with no intention to cause her any harm. She increased her speed, keeping her punches at eye level. And so it went until he nearly took a hit, but deflected her right hook, one of her most lethal blows. "Keep your elbows tucked."

"I *am* keeping my fucking elbows tucked."

"No, you're not. Combine your punches."

Huffing, she did just that, shuffling away when she thought he'd retaliate. Both sped up their moves, evading the other. He always pulled his punches with her; never attacked with full force. She must have realized what he was doing and got impatient with him because she decided to throw a spinning kick his way he wasn't prepared for and went flying to the ground. He rubbed his jaw as he gave her a look. "Mind telling me what the hell that was for?"

Releasing the gloves, she grabbed her water bottle and swallowed a few sips. "Mind telling me what the fuck you were doing at the Plaza last night?"

Oooh, so that's what this is about. "Lawe tell you about the meeting with Cantrell?"

Her eyes blazed. "You meet with an enemy Red Claw and don't inform me about it?"

Her temper was beginning to incite his own. "It was nothing. I would have mentioned it at the next meeting. Why don't you just admit what's really bugging the hell out of you?"

She put the water bottle down. Her voice deceptively calm. "I just did."

"No." He lifted himself and threw off the gloves. "You're still using evasive maneuvers."

She stood with her hand on her hip. "What are you talking about?"

Bending at the knees, he raised his hands and gestured for her to land her blows on his palms. "You know what I'm talking about. You don't need me to spell it out."

"Enlighten me." She threw a few punches into his palms that stung like hell, but he wouldn't flinch.

He threw a lopsided grin her way. "Admit it, you were jealous. That's why you've been in this mood all day."

Her eyes flared at him. "I don't have time to be jealous of anyone."

"Sure, you don't."

"What's that supposed to mean?" When she pulled back, rotating her hips clockwise—a prelude to her next move—he knew what to expect.

He quickly sidestepped her punch and grabbed her arm, then slid his foot around her ankle so that both of them toppled to the mats. Keeping his weight just slightly above hers, he pushed her legs wider so he fit snugly between them. His body ramped with lust, he crushed his lips to hers as his arms surrounded her and he pinned her down. He halfway expected her to fight him and sighed blissfully when her arms circled his neck.

"I'll tell you." Then, he kissed her, again, deeper, their tongues tangling, and this time, he brushed his length against her core, eliciting a groan. Music to his fucking ears.

"I'm listening," she panted as she rolled them to their sides.

"You need to be fucked—thoroughly, skillfully, and soon." He didn't wait for her to respond before he deepened their kiss as each of them fought for dominance. But he was not going to let her take the top position, not now.

When she broke from the kiss and pressed her palms to his chest, she looked up at him and said, "That may be, but what makes you think I'd come to you for satisfaction?"

Still pissed off at me, huh? He was not going to let her barb get to him. He knew better. "Because no one else can give you what I can, obviously." He rubbed himself against her, watching as her eyes nearly rolled back.

"You think you know me so well?"

"I know I do. I also know you've been depriving yourself of any joy because of this goddamned war that's looming, but you know what?"

Her eyes were heavy lidded with ardor. "What?"

"Fuck that, and fuck me, instead."

Chapter Fifteen

Liz was thinking that exact thing as her body vibrated with need. When Gavin had first started rubbing himself against her core, she'd felt sensations waking that had laid dormant for far too long. She wanted him, her traitorous body wanted him, every fiber of her being was screaming for her to reverse their positions so she could ride him until his body erupted in soaring pleasure.

All the emotions she'd been so careful to bank, had carefully ignored, came blazing to the surface demanding satisfaction. But, before she'd give in, there was one little matter to be taken care of. "Before this goes any further, tell me what happened with Cantrell. And don't leave anything out."

"Fuck." He sounded deflated as he lay his forehead against hers. "Sure you don't want to wait until later to hear?"

"I'm sure, *Reddy*." She used the nickname she knew he hated. She supposed most redheads did, even though his hair was an enticing mixture of reds and browns. Payback for what he called her before.

He rolled them to their sides. "Don't fucking call me that."

"I won't if you don't use 'Queenie' when talking to me."

"Deal." He braced himself on one elbow. "Cantrell called me, not the other way around. Just so you know. Lawe took the call while we were in the restaurant. I didn't even want to go at first, but then, I thought I might be able to elicit some key piece of information for my," he kissed her knuckles, "queen."

Her brow rose. "And did you elicit...anything?"

"Not what you're thinking, though I'm sure she wouldn't have turned me down if I did make a move. Anyway, we talked about Renworth and the upcoming war. I think she was trying to get a bead on whether or not you were seriously considering Renworth's offer."

"Gavin, you're handsome as hell, but you had to know she was there for information, not your Adonis body."

He chuckled. "Would it have bothered you if I had taken her upstairs and let her have her wicked way with me?"

Liz lifted one finger to his face and stroked his jawline with her sharpest nail. "Yes. It would have."

He held her hand in place. "Didn't happen. I know a player when I see one. That woman has shark teeth."

Liz leaned forward. "Any other key pieces of information you happened to glean from sharklady?"

He smirked as his eyes darkened. "Maybe. She did tell me not all Red Claws are as keen on this war as Renworth is. That surprised me. Up until then, I thought all the Red Claws were united in single purpose."

"It's not surprising. Not everyone in our clan favors war either. In any large group, there are always dissenters."

He released her hand; his eyes seemed to be assessing her. "You've already made up your mind, haven't you?"

She nodded. "What Brent and the others said is true. We let Renworth build his complex on our land, it will certainly open the door to other things we're not prepared for or desire. No ruler wants war, but in this situation, we don't have much of a choice."

"I agree. In time, he'd appropriate more and more land. From what else Cantrell said, Renworth won't back down; he's too used to getting what he wants."

"Of course, he is. We've both read the files on him; he's relentless in his pursuits." She grasped his hand. "Because of his greed, his need for a structure to stroke his ego—a monument to proclaim how wonderful he is—he's going to plunge us into war. Innocent lives will be lost because of him."

He conveyed his admiration of her through the way he held her gaze, stroked her fingers, by always being there for her when she was at her best and her worst. She couldn't remember a time when she hadn't had his complete support, and that warmed her heart even more.

She slid one leg over his and assumed the top position. Bracing her hands on his chest, she looked down into those whiskey-colored eyes she loved so much and smiled. "You've been a very naughty boy, Mr. McCray. I should punish you for upsetting your queen."

He returned her smile. "Punish away...Queenie."

Before she could grouse, he pulled her down for a soul-searing kiss she felt all the way to her toes. Groans echoed around them as their bodies communicated in the most primal of ways. Lust surged within as he broke through the last of her barriers. For so long, she'd tried to keep him at bay, making Cyrus her alpha and lover. But his appeal had diminished soon after. Always, there was someone else invading her dreams, her memories, his essence keeping her warm on the coldest of nights.

Gavin reversed their positions, his body fitting snugly against hers, and all she could think was that he was finally home. A warrior returning from the wars, reacquainting himself with what was his. And it felt so good, so right, she would not fight him for dominance. For once, she didn't have to be in control; she could let someone else be strong as she surrendered to the hunger that haunted her.

He trailed kisses down her neck and chest, each kiss more arousing than the last. Bliss, that's what being together was, complete and utter bliss, but when she moved at an awkward angle, a zinger of pain shot through her right shoulder, causing her to groan mournfully.

He lifted his head. "What's wrong?"

She rubbed the afflicted area. "I think I might have overdone it today."

"No kidding. If that punching bag were Red Claws, I'd say you effectively killed at least a half dozen. Turn over; let me look at it."

When she complied with his request, he ran his fingers over the sore muscles, causing her to wince. "Shit, that's tender."

"I bet. Your back is a mass of tightened nerves. Wouldn't be surprised if you pulled something. Take your top off. I'll work the muscles."

"Spoken as only a chiropractor can."

"Guilty as charged." He got up and retrieved a couple of towels and a small bottle from the supply closet. After rolling one towel into a pillow, he spread the other beside her. "Lay on this."

She did, grateful for the pillow to lay her head on.

"This oil is not only good for conditioning leather; it will help soothe your muscles."

"Oh God, I'm going to smell like leather."

"Not a bad scent to have. Everyone will think you're a dominatrix and whipped my butt."

She laughed at that then moaned sensually as he worked those talented fingers into her shoulder. "Mmm. That feels like heaven."

"Consider it an appetizer, my lady. If you're a good queen, you'll get to feast tonight."

God, she missed the easy banter between them, the way they always flirted with one another, the way his voice got all sexy, promising wicked delights in the dark. And that was it, the title of the song she'd been composing about him that had been banging around in her head. "Wicked Delights". As his hands worked their magic, lyrics danced in front of her, of the way he made her feel, gave her hope for an inspiring future.

Feeling sublime, she didn't need painkillers to float this high from reality; all she really needed was him by her side, offering a connection so strong, so powerful, she could never completely ruin it, even though she had tried.

It stung to realize how cruel she'd been to him, doing everything she could to create distance between them, to make him turn from her. Had the situation been reversed, she wasn't sure how she'd react. Certainly not with as much grace as he had. "I'm sorry, Gavin."

"What for?" he asked as he continued to massage away the ache in her back.

"Being a total bitch." She twisted around and looked up at him when he stopped. "Not just for today, for always. I thought it was for the best. Cyrus... The clan needed him."

"And what do you need, my queen?"

She wrapped her palm around his neck. "My name is Lizandra, and what I need is...you."

His lips met hers, and it felt like paradise. It always had. He broke from the kiss, his breaths ragged. "You already have me, Liz; you always have."

She reached up to pull him closer, their bodies pressed oh so tightly together. She was about to drag him down over her when movement to the side caught her attention.

"Jesus. You two have incredible timing." Brent stayed by the entrance, his face flushed. "You both need to see something."

"What is it?" She nearly growled at the interruption.

"Forgive the intrusion. We caught a spy in our midst, a Red Claw filming our training exercises. The same prick who fought Granger. We put him in the interrogation room."

***

After quickly showering and throwing on fresh clothes, Liz met Gavin out in the hallway. His hair was still wet from his shower and combed back. She'd chosen the purple leather tunic and pants with the violet sash that indicated royalty. She rarely wore the outfit, except when meeting with the heads of other clans, but tonight, she felt like emphasizing her status as queen.

When she entered the observation room that faced the interrogation room, she assumed her seat in the chair on the raised platform. Members of her nine were seated just below her.

Through the one-way mirror, they could see the spy, but he could not see them. Brent handed her the Red Claw's ID. "His name is Robin Carnack, lives on West 45th near 10th. Works for Renworth's construction company."

Cyrus nodded to her. "We wanted to wait before questioning him, let him sweat a little."

"Good. Has anyone spoken to him as yet?"

David said, "When I apprehended him, the little shit insisted he was only taking pictures of the park, but when we viewed the pictures, he'd managed to video our training sessions."

Her other brother, Sam, said, "He tried to run, fought us like he was fighting for his life. All the good it did him. We handcuffed him to the chair. He's going nowhere."

Liz nodded. "Knowing Renworth's reaction to him getting caught is what's got him anxious."

Cyrus asked, "Want me start the interrogation?"

She studied him for a moment. "No, I don't want him knowing your strength. Guys, give me a moment. Cyrus, Gavin, stay. Everyone else outside."

No one needed to be told twice; they filed out with Max closing the door behind her.

"I'll question him," Gavin offered. "I've done it before. Remember, not too long ago, we had some goons in who hurt one of our own."

Cyrus looked inquisitive, but Liz had no time to explain what had happened before he'd joined the Black Stars. She could never forget the members of the Human Order of Light who had viciously murdered one of her Weres. She'd returned the favor in kind, much to the gratitude of the vamp king who considered the HOL some of his worst enemies. "Never forget," she muttered. "But, no, not you. I want you here with me analyzing his reactions."

"Who, then?" Cyrus asked.

"What about Lawe?" Gavin suggested. "If anyone could elicit the truth, it would be him."

Lawe was certainly intimidating by his size alone. Even though he could convey a menacing, threatening façade, underneath, he was more warmhearted than he let on. "No, he'd have to live with what goes down tonight, and I suspect things are going to get ugly real soon."

"Surely, you're not thinking of interrogating him yourself?"

She glanced up at Cyrus. "It wouldn't be a first. I assure you, I'm more than capable. But no. I want someone levelheaded, someone who's detached, keeps his emotions controlled, stays cool under pressure. Unreadable. Someone who can pace himself, ask the right questions, mindfuck Renworth's spy into revealing more than he thinks he's divulging."

Gavin sighed. "Only one person seems to fit your criteria. You think he has the cajones to administer pain when necessary? Because I can tell you, now," he pointed at the window, "that guy in there won't break easily."

"That's why I want someone who's patient, deliberate, and focused. Call Brent inside."

Gavin opened the door and gestured for him to enter. Brent looked around inquisitively. "What did you decide?"

"You up to interrogating our guest tonight?" she asked.

At first, he seemed surprised by her question. "You want me to question him?"

"And torture, if need be. Of everyone here, you keep your emotions in check. Hell, half the time, I can't figure out what you're thinking." She gestured to the window. "I want that mutt in there to get anxious; I want him to know fear. Can you do that?"

Brent exhaled slowly and ran a hand through his hair. "I could. I'm going to need a few supplies." His gaze shifted to her. "On one condition, if you see fit to indulge me. I don't want the others to watch. I find it unbecoming for women, such as Tia and Max, to observe. You can have David and Sam in there with me, but only to stand by the door. Tell the others to wait outside. Let me handle this the way I best see fit."

She was impressed as fuck that Brent's voice never once quivered at what she requested of him. She knew she was asking a lot, but she'd seen the way he trained with Master Quen when he came to visit New York City and gave classes in the park. Under the most grueling instructions, he'd segued from tai chi to some serious mental and physical conditioning. Even when the more muscular people in her clan collapsed from the vigor, Brent was last man standing. A fact only a few knew, since they'd been faced away. "I grant your request."

When Brent stepped outside, presumably to talk to Quint, Gavin asked that Sam and David stay, and for the others to take a break. After much grumbling, he told them he'd let them know what they found out, if anything. Reluctantly, they left.

Cyrus bent down to her. "Are you sure you know what you're doing?"

"Yes, quite sure." Her nails scraped along the armrest. "Come sit on my left, tell me what you observe in the prisoner."

After getting situated, he said, "If Brent gets tired in there, I'll take over for him."

She smirked knowingly. "He won't."

Chapter Sixteen

Dan was laughing as he disembarked from the evening Circle Line cruise, which docked at the West 42ⁿᵈ Street pier, that he'd taken with Lisa Martinez. God, he loved her smile. Ever since he'd moved to New York City, he'd wanted to go on one of those boat rides he'd seen advertised everywhere, the one that circled the entire island of Manhattan. Sure, it was a touristy thing to do, but still so much fun.

Breathing in the cool, fresh air off the Hudson River was so invigorating. And being with Lisa made him feel like a million dollars. He hoped she felt the same way about him.

"That had to be one of the most exciting outings I've had in a long time. Thank you, Danny, for taking me."

"No problem. I thoroughly enjoyed it, too." He pointed to the tavern at the corner. "Hey, wanna get a drink at that bar?"

"Okay."

They walked arm in arm as they crossed 12ᵗʰ Avenue, careful of the cabs scurrying away with other tourists who had debarked with them. It was a lovely night out, being on the boat, seeing so many of Manhattan's sites; they'd even been able to see a few stars in the night sky.

But it was Lisa who'd held most of his attention. He'd met her at a club in Mid-town a few months ago and had been seeing her ever since. With her dark brown hair and golden-brown eyes, Lisa enchanted him with her carefree laughter. He'd never met anyone like her.

Once they were seated at a booth, they ordered beers and gazed out the window, then at each other. "How's your brother doing?" She smiled up at him. "You used to talk about him all the time."

He thought about his twin, Drew, and his girlfriend, Sasha. As brothers, they were close, but being twins—there was a bond most people didn't understand. How could they? Half the time, he wasn't even sure he knew. "Drew's doing great. We were discussing going back to California for the holidays but haven't made any definite plans, yet. You?"

"That's months away. I haven't even thought about it. You know me; I like to be spontaneous. I don't always make plans."

"I know." He grinned. It was just one of the things he liked about her. Like when they'd decided to go to the Brooklyn Aquarium despite the downpour. She'd liked the stingrays best, but he thought the shark tank was awesome. It had been a great day, even with the rain. When the waiter brought their drinks, Dan thanked him and then watched as Lisa sipped her beer.

"Still not going to introduce me to him, huh?"

He relaxed back into the booth. Drew and he always talked about everything: sports, careers, girls. But this? Sheesh, it was complicated. "Not an easy call to make. Not sure how he's going to respond."

"You've been saying that for months, now. They're going to find out sooner or later, y'know."

He shrugged. He'd prefer later, like, *much* later. "I guess."

She put down her beer. "You're not ashamed of me, are you?"

"Oh, Lisa, far from it. It's just that," he scratched his head, "they might not understand."

"What do you think's gonna happen? That I'm gonna bite one of them?"

"Of course not." He fingered the side of his bottle. "It's just that..."

Her lids closed over those beautiful brown eyes he loved so much. "Go on, just say it."

Dan didn't want to admit that their differences would not go over well if his friends found out who he was dating. They'd never expect who he'd been seeing. His queen might even kill him.

She grasped his hand and held it snugly in hers. "It's because of my clan, isn't it?"

"Lisa, our clans are on the brink of war; tensions are running high. Surely, it must be the same in your pack."

"And I told you, not all Red Claws are aggressive. There are several of us who don't want to make war on the Black Stars, don't want anything to do with it."

Dan asked the one question that had been bothering him for some time. "But, if your pack master calls for it, will you fight against us?"

"I don't even want to think about it. I'm not exactly primed for fighting." She lifted her arm and attempted to make a muscle.

He nearly chuckled at how slender she was. She definitely didn't have the physique of the warrior females in his clan.

"Don't you dare laugh. I work out all the time, but my body just doesn't develop the way others do."

"You need to eat more protein-enriched foods."

"I do." She looked exasperated, but in a humorous way. "It doesn't help."

In a way he was glad, he liked her petite frame. Some men liked the athletic type, but he preferred his women soft. "Maybe, in time, it will." He finished his beer. "Wanna head home? It's a clear night, and your place isn't far; we can walk it."

"I am a little tired. I think it's all the fresh air. I had a great time tonight." She drank the rest of her beer and set the glass down. "Okay."

After dropping a few bills on the table, they walked out into the cool, brisk air. He still felt happy, even if the conversation had turned serious. As they strolled up the avenue, he probably should have been concerned about how close they were to Riverside Park—Red Claw territory, but this area, around the piers, was heavily human populated so he wasn't concerned over much.

He should have been.

They were about halfway to her apartment when a niggling feeling started creeping up his spine. Usually, he was good at detecting when someone was following him. The first month he'd been in New York, he'd gotten mugged not even a block after emerging from the subway. Ever since then, he'd been vigilant about his surroundings, but tonight, he was preoccupied.

A gruff voice sounded behind them. "Hey, Lisa, how come you weren't at the meeting tonight?"

They turned to see three young men approaching, each one of them muscularly built. One of guys had red teardrop tattoos under his right eye. Fuck! Not only were they Red Claws, they were enforcers.

Lisa showed no fear in staring the guys down. "I wasn't aware there was a meeting."

"Well, maybe if you had checked your messages, you would've known."

She jutted out her hip and put her hand on it, looking bored. "Anything of import?"

Teardrop guy was eying Dan suspiciously. "Yes, Renworth wants all of us assembled."

"Whatever for, this time?"

"Report in and find out. Who's your boyfriend?"

Before Dan could say anything, Lisa said, "A friend from work. Tell Renworth I'll be at the next one."

Teardrop guy sniffed the air and pinned Dan with a stare. "A rogue?"

Lone wolves were rare in the city, so a rogue wolf without a pack was unlikely, especially when Weres believed in safety in numbers, most belonging to a clan. Before he could pull his words back, he uttered, "Not quite."

Teardrop smirked like he'd sighted prey and couldn't wait to take a bite. Dan could fight, maybe, two of them, but three? This was not going to go well.

"Well, Sunshine," the Red Claw drew closer, "there's someone we'd like you to meet."

He'd been called that before, because of his blond hair, so it didn't bother him. But there was no doubt in Dan's mind, whoever they had in mind wasn't anyone he was interested in becoming acquainted with.

When Teardrop grabbed his arm, he tried to shrug him off, but one of the other guys pinned his other arm behind him and whispered, "Don't make a fuss; it will only go bad for you."

When the other Were pulled Lisa away, Dan shouted, "Don't you touch her!"

"Don't worry, Sunshine, we would never hurt one of our own. But you..."

They were quickly ushered into a waiting car and sped away into traffic. As soon as they entered Riverside Park, Dan knew where they were going. They were now deep in Red Claw territory. Once inside Renworth's castle, Dan was led upstairs and shoved into a chair in some sort of antechamber. His insides still hurt from the punches he'd taken when he tried to fight them.

He'd told Lisa with his eyes to remain silent; he'd handle this. More than likely, they'd ransom him to Lizandra. Man, his queen was going to be so pissed off at him.

He heard a deep voice grouse, "Bring him in."

Teardrop hauled him up by his shirt and dragged him inside a magnificent room overlooking the Hudson River. He didn't have time to admire his surroundings when a voice echoed from the chair faced away from him, "So, you're one of Queen Lizandra's. Now, what would a Black Star be doing with a Red Claw? Spying for your queen?"

Dan thought he'd be brought to one of Renworth's lieutenants; he never suspected he'd come face to face with the Red Claw King, himself. *Holy shit!* He knew better than to say anything provocative, even though the devil in him wanted to. But, if they were going to rough him up, he wanted to make one thing clear. "Lisa's loyal to you. She never once said anything against you or the clan, and I never asked for anything. We were just dating, that's all."

"I'll deal with Martinez later."

His fear for what might happen to his girlfriend erupted, and the guys had to tighten their hold on him. "Don't you hurt her."

"You're in no position to make any sort of demands." Renworth smirked. "This one's got some fight in him." He seemed to be thinking about something then said, "Put him in the cage. With Curtis. Maybe that'll loosen his tongue a bit."

Dan swallowed hard as Victor Gren entered the room. "Is this the one?"

Teardrop nodded.

Gren gave him the once over, snickered, then advised, "You put him in with Curtis, he won't last two minutes. Not exactly entertaining."

Renworth swiveled his chair. "You may be right. Now, who should we choose to entertain our guest?" After a moment he said, "I've got it. Put him in with Bali."

Bali? Dan didn't have time to wonder who this person was before he was led away.

***

"I've got to hand it to you. You were right about him," Cyrus whispered in Liz's ear as they watched Brent continue with his interrogation of Robin.

Time had passed slowly since Brent had begun grilling the spy. Liz said, "It's been what, two, three hours since he started, and Brent still hasn't broken a sweat."

"He's methodical," Gavin said from where he stood with his arms crossed, "asking the same questions, over and over, just rephrasing them each time. So systematical, so amazingly patient. Brent tripped him up a couple of times."

Indeed. It was similar to what her brother, Sam, said law enforcement agencies did to elicit answers. But nowhere in Brent's resume indicated he'd ever served. *Interesting.* "I know. If I put anyone else in there, they would have become frustrated with Robin's lack of info and reverted to violence."

"I would have beaten the truth out of him." Cyrus stood, cracked his knuckles, and stretched his legs. "It would have saved us some time."

"Maybe." Liz signaled for them to remain quiet as she listened to Brent. She wondered, not for the first time, if in fact, Brent had some vampire blood in him because the way he used his voice was compelling, like that of the vamps, mesmerizing. He didn't shout; he didn't terrorize the prisoner. He didn't have to; he left that to Liz's brothers, David and Sam, who'd backhanded Robin hard enough when he'd given a sarcastic retort that he'd spit blood.

But it was Brent who held her attention. He never blinked, not once, as far as she could tell, just maintained his stare. It was eerie, unnatural. He'd gotten the basics from Robin, like who ordered him to spy, who he reported to, how long he'd been spying, but the one question she wanted resolved most still remained unanswered: How many agents did the Red Claw King have in her court? If, in fact, there were spies. That stuck in her craw more than anything. "Renworth trains his men well."

Cyrus barked, "He's just a stubborn sonofabitch."

"It's fear that motivates him." Gavin uncrossed his arms. "He fears what Renworth will do to him if he gives anything pertinent away."

Liz quickly leaned forward. "Wait, what was that he murmured?"

"Say that, again, Robin; I didn't hear you." Brent moved closer to the man handcuffed to the chair.

"Your queen is going down," he said between gritted teeth as David increased the charge to the electrodes attached to Robin's forehead and appendages. He hissed in agony then, enraged, faced the mirror, as if he knew she was watching. "He's going to destroy you, and you'll never see it coming."

"Tell me what you meant by that, and he'll lessen the pain. You don't have to suffer, Robin." Brent tapped his prisoner's forehead. "Is your loyalty to your king so important, you'd let him fry your circuitry?"

"Go to hell," Robin wheezed as blood began to drip from his nose.

"He will only increase the pain until you suffer an aneurism and your head explodes from the pressure. Is your king worth the sacrifice of your life?" Brent's voice never wavered. "Would he do the same for you?"

Liz found the calm that Brent maintained throughout the session admirable. Who had composure like that?

Before she could listen further, Quint knocked then entered the room. "I've got an important message from the Red Claw King. He says it's urgent he speak with you."

Cyrus scoffed. "Probably figured out his spy didn't report in."

When Liz gestured for him to come closer, he gave her his phone. She took it, annoyed at the interruption. "What is it, Renworth?"

"I think we should negotiate a trade, Lizandra. I hear you took one of my men prisoner. I'd like him back."

"Now, why would I do that? He's been such interesting company."

"Because, Liz, I have one of yours here. Would you like to say hello?"

On the screen was Danny, the twin who'd sat with her on Summit Rock. His face looked like it had been worked over, one eye was swollen shut, and his shirt was covered in blood.

She rasped, "You bastard."

Renworth laughed. "So I've been told. Many times. Meet me in front of the Museum of Natural History. One hour. I don't think your man will last much longer. Ta."

Chapter Seventeen

Liz, still dressed in her leather uniform and royal sash, exited the park, accompanied by her lawyer, Quint, and her alpha, Cyrus. Bringing up the rear were Sam and David, who held Robin between them. Other members of her Prime were stealthily hidden among the trees, careful not to set off the traps that had been deftly camouflaged. Since the museum was considered human territory, she didn't expect violence would occur, but with Renworth, you never knew.

It was dark out, but she easily spotted Renworth's limo twenty yards away. He'd gotten there before her and casually stepped out of his vehicle with Gren and another of his flunkies. The door to the car behind his opened, and two goons emerged. She kept her voice authoritative. "Where's Daniel?"

"First, you give us Robin."

"Like hell." *How big of a fool does he think I am?* "Is he with you?"

Renworth gestured for his men to retrieve Danny, who slowly stepped out of the car. His shirt was in tatters and covered in blood, a few streaks stained his pants. He looked exhausted, as if he'd crumble to the ground if the man holding him up let go.

"Step closer," she ordered her brothers, who held Robin firmly in their grips, in case he decided to make a run for it. When they were thirty feet apart from Renworth, she said, "That's close enough. Give us Danny."

The guy holding Danny said, "Walk."

Her packmate shuffled toward her, dragging one leg behind. Her brothers released Robin, who strolled gingerly toward his clan. She didn't hear what Robin whispered when he passed Danny, but saw clearly enough when he bumped shoulders, causing Danny to stumble. He quickly caught himself, and Cyrus was there in a heartbeat to help him cross the street. His low growl of warning was loud enough for all to hear.

Renworth seemed to be scrutinizing her alpha, taking his measure. A look passed over the king's face, but was quickly gone before she could decipher it. "This could have easily been avoided. You should tell your pack not to trespass on our territory."

"And would you do the same?" Liz's voice was strong as it echoed around them.

"The next time we meet, it won't be under such peaceful terms." Renworth held the door for Robin to enter.

"No, I don't believe it will be." She glared mercilessly. "I suspect this is the last time we'll ever set eyes on one another."

"Most likely." Renworth saluted her then got in his car, and she watched as they drove off.

Danny moaned as he clutched his stomach. "I don't feel so good."

Before he passed out, Cyrus scooped him up in his arms.

Liz scanned the area one last time. "Let's get him back to the infirmary."

Once there, Cyrus lay Danny on the exam table. Gavin was already there, with Drew, Max, and Sasha. "Everyone out," Liz ordered. "Let Gavin treat him."

"You okay, bro?" Drew took his brother's hand and squeezed.

"Kinda numb, right now."

Liz said, "He's probably in shock. Go, now; you'll talk to him later."

"I'll be right outside." Drew laid Danny's hand on the table.

Cyrus said, "I'll check the perimeters, make sure Renworth doesn't have any other surprises for us."

Liz nodded, closed the door after the others left, then faced Gavin as he cut off what remained of Danny's blood-stained shirt and discarded it. "Jesus. His stomach looks shredded." His chest was covered in gashes. Some looked like they had begun to heal while others were still oozing. The smell of Were blood saturated the air.

Gavin undid Dan's belt then unbuttoned his jeans and used the palm of his hand to test his internal organs. "Thank God, no other wounds."

"Hey, stop looking at my tattoo; that's for my girlfriend only."

Liz was glad Danny was joking, but she was sure the blood loss contributed to his lack of coherence. He almost appeared inebriated.

Gavin assured him, "I wasn't looking."

"But you should have seen the other guy," Danny wheezed. "I think he was a guy. I'm not sure really. He/she smelled like both."

"You've lost a lot of blood." Liz grabbed one of the blankets and covered his lower half to keep him warm. "You're not thinking straight."

"No, I am." He seemed confused. "I mean, she looked like a girl, but something was off about her. I'm telling you she/he/it had both scents."

"That can't be right. You were probably smelling others in the vicinity."

"No, I got a good whiff of her when she slashed at me."

Startled, Liz glanced up and tilted her head. "Hermaphrodite?"

Gavin shrugged. "Could be, but they are exceedingly rare." He used a betadine solution to clean Danny's wounds.

"Danny, you're going to need a lot of stitches. Do you want me to give you something for the pain?"

"No. I don't really feel anything anymore." He coughed, his breathing labored. "But, before, it was hell."

"Who did this to you?" Liz asked.

Another cough as he tried to focus. "Bali. I'm pretty sure that's what they called her when they put me in the fighting ring. I never saw anyone move like her." He winced, as if it hurt to shift on the table. "Bali moved like a snake, very fast, struck with incredible speed. At first, she played with me, only scratches, then worked herself up. I defended myself as best I could, but she was just too fast."

"They put you in the cage?" Liz was outraged. "You rest, now." She stroked the side of his face, one of the few places that wasn't covered in blood. "I'm going to kill that sonofabitch."

"Save your anger for later. For now, I need you to assist." Gavin pointed to the table with the medical supplies. "Get out more sutures. He's gonna need a shitload."

As she helped with the sutures, she asked before Dan conked out, "What were you doing in Red Claw territory?"

Danny wheezed, again, as if he were growing weary. "I wasn't in their territory. I was walking my girlfriend home." His stomach rose slightly with the cadence of his speech. "That's when the Red Claws accosted us."

"Your girlfriend?" Liz stopped for a moment to meet his glassy eyes.

"Yeah, please don't be mad. She's not like the others, I swear; Lisa's good." His eyelids fluttered closed. "She has no interest in fighting."

Liz was confused and moved closer to Dan. "Why would I be mad, Danny? You did nothing wrong."

Danny reached up for her hand as he slowly opened his eyes. "Promise me nothing bad will happen to her. Please."

She met Gavin's gaze for a moment before he resumed stitching his patient. "Is Lisa a Were?" Danny didn't immediately answer. And Liz felt her heart lurch. "Danny, is Lisa a Red Claw?"

Silence for a moment, then. "I'm sorry. I didn't know when we first started dating." His voice slowed. "I didn't find out until we'd been dating for several weeks. Don't be angry at me, okay?"

As Liz looked over the shredded mess of his torso, she was torn between offering him solace and wanting to kill something. "I'm not angry at you, Danny. But you must have suspected she was leading you on, possibly an agent for Renworth?"

"No." He surprised her with the force of his answer. "No way. She told me there are others who think like she does. They want no part of the war."

"Of course not." When she glanced up at Gavin, he shook his head, as if to say stop with the questioning already. "One last thing, Danny. What's your girlfriend's last name?"

"Lisa, Lisa Martinez. She's so beautiful." His lids lowered. "You'd like her. And funny." He seemed to slip into unconsciousness.

"Good, he's asleep."

"Not surprising. He's lost a lot of blood." Gavin used the forceps to remove a piece of metal from Danny's ribcage. "Look familiar?"

She'd seen them before, had one imbedded in her side by a traitor who was really a Red Claw. "Sure does, you never quite forget the sting."

She watched as Gavin went methodically about stitching up Danny's wounds. God, he had so many. She examined the cuts on his arms; these were shallow and not nearly as deep as the ones on his stomach. "He's so young."

"That works in his favor. Why don't you do the sutures on your side, and I'll do the ones closest to me."

"Like old times." She worked alongside him for as long as it took to finish, then covered Danny's wounds with a dressing. "He looks so angelic."

Gavin disposed of the soaked gauze and placed his instruments in the sterilizer. After washing his hands, he stood beside her. "He's so pale. I guess most blonds are."

Liz studied Dan's unmoving form. He was so still. It wasn't until a moment passed before real dread settled in. "How come his chest's not rising and falling with his breaths?"

Gavin sniffed the air, the panic etched in his face as he immediately reached for Dan's wrist. "He's ice cold. Something's wrong. Danny! Danny, can you hear me?" he shouted as he valiantly tried to rouse him.

Liz didn't have to inhale the air to know death when she saw it. "He's gone."

"Impossible. We closed all his wounds." Trepidation flashed in his eyes as he met hers. "Didn't we?"

Dismayed, she looked below the table to see the red pool. "He bled out."

"From where?" Gavin gently lifted Dan to check his back. "No gashes." Laying him down, he tore the blanket off him and ripped open Dan's pants. The horror of the truth stared back at them. "They cut his femoral artery. Not a major laceration, just enough for him to bleed out."

Gavin's fists tightened, and the veins in his neck bulged as he threw his head back and growled menacingly. He looked like he wanted to kill someone. "This was done deliberately. Renworth's cruelty. He let us believe we could save him, when..."

"He knew Dan wouldn't make it."

"Oh, God." Horrified, Gavin stumbled back from her. "I didn't think to check." A howl of pain roared from him. "I should have checked. My God, what have I done?"

"This isn't your fault." Her heart was laden with sorrow for Danny and for him. "I thought the streaks on his pants were from his chest wounds." She held Gavin in her arms as he grieved the loss. And he held onto her as though she was his lifeline. And she supposed she was. "We did what we thought was best."

"But…" His voice shook with bitter agony.

Empathizing, she palmed his cheek and shook her head. "No buts. The Red Claws are responsible."

He covered her palm with his and closed his eyes in quiet despair.

She whispered, "My heart aches for him. He was such a kind soul, a good man. We'll have to tell the others."

His breath was ragged. "What will we tell them?"

"Dan died of blood loss, and no matter how quickly we stitched him up, it wasn't fast enough. That's the truth."

Gavin shook his head. "I have to tell his brother. How am I going to face him, now?"

"I will inform him. That's my job."

He breathed deep. "Dan's death will haunt me until the day I die."

"The same for me. This is a burden we will both share. Nothing else will ease the pain of loss."

He pulled away from her and nodded.

"I'm going to get Drew. Do you want a few minutes first?"

He tilted his head back and then slowly exhaled, "No."

Liz went to Dan's body and lovingly covered his chest with the blanket. "Goodnight, sweet prince." She kissed his hand. "We'll meet, again, another day."

She waited until Gavin slumped into his chair before opening the door. She was met by three doleful faces. This was going to wrench her gut more than she realized. Before she could stop them, the tears fell down her face.

"No!" Drew shouted as he rushed past her, with Max and Sasha slowly approaching.

"He bled out before we could finish stitching him up. He died on the table."

Sobs erupted as both women embraced, seeking comfort in each other. Liz didn't think her heart could break any more as she enveloped both women in her arms.

A howl, impassioned and soulful, rent the air as Drew pulled back the blanket. Gavin quickly wrapped his arms around Drew, offering what comfort he could. Liz and Gavin's gaze met in a bittersweet moment of shared solidarity. Soon, the whole clan would know one of their own had fallen.

A few moments later, the girls left with Drew, vowing not to leave him alone. Liz spotted her brothers coming down the hall. After informing them of Danny's death, David went to offer Drew his condolences.

She pulled Sam far away so no one could overhear them. "Do you still have friends outside the police force who owe you favors?"

Sam moved a strand of hair away from her cheek. "You know it. What do you need done, sis?"

She was resolute in her answer. "Will he eliminate someone if you ask him?"

Sam clicked his teeth. "For a price."

"You wrote down Robin's address from the ID you found in his wallet?"

Sam nodded. "Oh, yes."

Steeling her resolve, Liz's vision turned dark, and her voice held that thin edge that cut deeply. "Tell your friend to make it look like an accident. I'll pay whatever price he asks for. Go, now."

Chapter Eighteen

Feeling wired from the night's events, Liz paced in her rooms. Renworth knew, the fucker knew Danny was lethally injured, probably instructed Bali to cut him shallow where it would do the most harm. *Bastard!* As much as Liz regretted war, the beast that lived within her soul, desired it, craved the vengeance she would visit on her enemy. "Blood will have blood."

A knock at her door broke into her reveries. "Come in."

Cyrus entered. "I patrolled the area then checked all the camera feeds at the entrances and exits. No movement near any of them. We're good. No one else is getting killed on my watch."

No, she didn't suppose Renworth would orchestrate an attack tonight. Too busy gloating over his recent triumph. He'd want to wait, so would she. Liz turned to Cyrus. "Thank you."

"It's late. Do you want to get some sleep?"

"No. Not yet." She continued pacing.

Cyrus came up behind her and massaged her shoulders. It felt good. She hadn't even been aware of how much tension her body was holding. "You know, there are other ways to induce sleep." He turned her in his arms and whispered, "Do you remember how good it used to be between us?"

"The last thing I have on my mind is sex, Cyrus. We lost someone tonight. Danny. He was only twenty-four years old."

"I know, Liz. Everyone in the clan knows. We all feel terrible about it. Fuck, I carried him in my arms this evening; I brought him to the infirmary. He felt so light, so weak. I had no idea he would die tonight."

"No one did." She broke from his hold. "Gavin is very upset about it. We tried to stem the bleeding, but he had too many wounds. We couldn't get them all closed fast enough."

"I ran into his brother, Drew, and gave him my condolences." Cyrus ran a hand through his long hair. "I'm not sure he heard a word I said, though. The guy looked like he was in shock."

"I'm sure he is. Twins have a special bond. At least he's got Sasha to offer him comfort. And Granger and Max are his friends. I'm glad he's not alone tonight."

"You don't have to be either. You should go to him."

"I've already expressed my sympathies. I think I'm the last face he wants to see, now."

"No, I didn't mean Drew. I meant Gavin. The two of you have been through hell. And I know he's the one you think about. The one you want." He offered her a half smile. "The *only* one."

Liz didn't want this conversation tonight; she was too tired and too emotional. "You think you know me so well?"

"Kinda obvious. I know you have feelings for me. We're united in our need to protect the clan, the love we share for our people. But I'm not the one your eyes track whenever Gavin and I are in the same room together. Your body reacts in ways I don't even think you're aware of. You want him. So, be with him."

"You don't mind?"

"Hell, yeah, I mind, but I don't play second fiddle to anyone. Make him your lover, but keep me as alpha, allow me *some* dignity."

She thought he would've given her a stronger argument. Cyrus desired her. He'd been a vigorous lover when they'd been together. His appetite was voracious. "What made you change your mind? The last time we spoke you wanted a threesome."

He shrugged then laughed. "Every man needs his fantasies." The corner of his mouth quirked up, making him almost appear boyish, despite his imposing size. "But I know reality when it slaps me in the face. You're never going to come to my bed, and if you did, it would be maybe out of loyalty, maybe out of gratitude. Doesn't matter. Doesn't change the fact that you want Gavin. I'm man enough to accept that."

She stood in amazement. There was more to her Viking warrior than she'd expected. "I doubt he wants me after the way I treated him. I pushed him aside; it seems like long ago, now."

"Oh, he still wants you, Liz. Anyone with a pair of eyes can see that. Sure, I'm disappointed. I had hoped... Well, that doesn't matter now. Go to him. He must be feeling really crappy tonight."

"Yeah, he is."

Cyrus got up and made for the door. "I'll still fight my heart out for you. You know that, right?"

"Sure. And, Cyrus?" When he turned back to her, she said, "Thanks."

***

Gavin stared at the walls of his room in Werehaven and felt too closed in. Grabbing his keys, he wasn't sure where he was going, but he was not staying here. No matter how many times he'd washed his hands, he could still smell the putrid scent of blood. He was halfway to the door, when someone knocked and entered.

"I heard what happened. You okay?" Lawe stepped inside and shut the door behind him.

Gavin shook his head. "I don't think I'll ever be okay."

"Hey, man," Lawe gave him a bear hug, "it wasn't your fault. There wasn't anything more you could do for the guy."

Yes, there was, like save his life, check his body for more wounds. He backed away from Lawe's embrace and rubbed the nape of his neck, barely able to look his best friend in the eye. "I gotta get out of here. I need some fresh air."

Lawe was regarding him, as if he was trying to read his mind. "Want some company?"

"I think I need a drink and then some alone time. I'm not gonna be good to be around for a while."

Lawe squeezed his shoulder. "You know, if you need to talk, I'm good at listening."

Gavin nodded. "I know, but not tonight."

"Walk with me to the restaurant." Lawe opened the door. "I might have what you need."

Gavin did, but when they got there, the place was locked down for the night.

"I've got the keys." Lawe unlocked the door and went straight to the bar. He opened up a cabinet and returned with an unopened bottle of Remy Martin whiskey.

"You're crazy. You know how much that stuff goes for?"

"Sure do. I was saving it for a special occasion but figured you need it now." Lawe pulled him in for another hug. "Don't beat yourself up too much, huh. Some things are just out of our control." He handed Gavin the bottle. "Just save it for when you get to where you're going."

"Thanks." Gavin was grateful for their friendship, but right now... "I'm gonna head on out. Go down to my apartment. I haven't been there in days." He looked over the park. "I need to get away from here."

"Want me to drive?"

"Not this time. Thanks for the bottle." They fist bumped. "I'll be in touch."

He had just stepped out of the restaurant when he heard, "You take care, now."

"I'll do my best," he murmured to the night.

Once in his car, he hopped on the West Side Highway that would take him down to his place in the West Village. He rolled down the window, letting in the breezes that flowed off the river. He breathed deep and thought about turning on the radio but, wanting some peace and quiet, negated the idea.

After he drove for a while, his mind began to clear, and instead of sorrow engulfing him, a quiet rage surged through him. Taking the next exit, he pulled over to the side and reached for his phone.

"Well, hello there. I didn't think I'd hear from you again so soon."

Gavin noted the seductive tone Cantrell used in her last two words. "That makes two of us. So, tell me, are the Red Claws celebrating tonight?"

She stuttered, "I, uh...I don't know what you're talking about."

"I just bet you don't." His sarcasm took on a hard edge. "Renworth and his guys get a real kick out of watching one of my men get mauled tonight?"

"Gavin, I'm in New Jersey. Tell me what happened."

"Oh, you gonna tell me you know nothing about the Red Claws abducting one of my people. Forcing him to fight in the cage with someone named Bali?"

She hissed into the phone. "My God."

His rage only increased as he spoke. "Gonna deny you know nothing about how she cut up Danny? How Renworth traded him for his little spy he had photographing Black Stars in Central Park?"

"Is he okay?"

"Your spy is just fine. We don't torture people to the point of death, Alexa. Wish I could say the same for your clan. Danny had so many gashes, he bled out. Fuck, he was only twenty-four years old." His voice reached a crescendo. "Think about that, will you? He was just a kid walking his date home when your guys jumped him. He did nothing that warranted him getting killed."

"I...I'm so sorry."

"Yeah, me, too. Renworth's little joke didn't intimidate us, Alexa. He comes after us, we'll show him the same kind of mercy he showed Danny. Next time you see Renworth, tell him to fuck off for me." He hung up before he said anything more. He didn't believe for a minute that Renworth's number one lawyer knew nothing about the trade. She was probably the one who advised him to do it.

He got back on the highway and drove home. As soon as got there, he was going to pour himself a tumbler full of liquor, then go up to the roof and howl his outrage. He'd probably wake his neighbors, but tonight, he just didn't give a damn.

Gavin drove down his street and was able to find a parking spot relatively close. He took the steps two at a time and unlocked his door. Once it was closed behind him, he laid his head back against it. "Well, today was one giant shitstorm." He closed his eyes. "God, please don't let tomorrow get any worse."

He marched into the kitchen, flicked on the lights, and went to the fridge to get some ice, then poured himself a tumbler full. He needed to get good and drunk tonight. The only way he would get any sleep without the nightmares of blood and death haunting him. Sitting at the kitchen table, he rubbed his head then took a long swallow. "Thank you, Lawe." Booze this expensive had a smooth burn as it slid down his throat.

Gavin wasn't sure how long he remained sitting and drinking when he heard the front door open. "What the fuck?" He was on his feet in an instant, his instincts prepared for whoever just invaded his place. Who even knew he was here? He was all but ready for a fight when her scent hit him, and he sat and relaxed back into his seat. He inwardly smirked. "How'd you get in? I distinctly remember locking the door."

Liz dangled her key. "Miranda gave me one, a long time ago, when she used to live here." She had switched out of her leathers into black jeans and a silky top.

"Figures. Lawe tell you where I was?"

"Yeah, reluctantly, so don't bust a cap on him. He's a good man."

Gavin poured another tumbler full. "Yes, he is. Want a drink?"

She sat across from him and whistled when she read the label. "Remy Martin. Someone spared no expense."

"Lawe gave it to me. Said I looked like I needed it."

Liz rose, checked his fridge and retrieved a beer. "I'll stick with a Sammy Adams."

"Sorry, no Coronas."

She shrugged. He knew that was her favorite beer. "No big." After twisting the cap off and downing a mouthful, she said, "Let's go inside the living room. More comfortable there."

Liz was hoping he'd sit beside her, but he chose the couch across from her. After placing his glass down on the coffee table, he let his head fall back. "Craptastic day, wouldn't you say?"

"One of the worst." She glanced around the room. "Place looks the same. Remember all the movie nights we used to have here?"

"Oh, yes, you and Miranda always wanted to watch some chick flick, when Orion and I wanted to watch action/adventure films."

She almost tossed a pillow his way but too comfortable leaning on it. "That's not true. Miranda loved all those *Lord of the Rings* movies, and I liked anything with Samuel L. Jackson in it. That's hardly chick flick material."

"Now, that guy could act. I think I liked every movie he was in."

"Except the one with the snakes in it." She shuddered.

He looked confused. "I must have missed that one."

"Trust me, you didn't miss anything." She sipped her beer. "Are you hungry? I don't remember you eating anything today."

He shrugged. "I honestly don't remember. Too many distractions."

"Want me to make you something?"

He shook his head. "Nah."

"Remember the times Miranda had us over for dinner, and I had to kick you under the table to keep you from commenting on her cooking?"

"Miranda's a great person," he made a sour face, "but her cooking...not her best talent."

Liz laughed. "Hey, it's not her fault. No one took the time to teach her properly. She was orphaned as a kid. From what I heard, her aunt wasn't much on cooking either."

"Guess not. Remember when she tried to make a few steaks and thought an eight-minute steak meant eight minutes on each side, instead of all together. I nearly broke one of my canines biting into the meat that was overly well-done."

"Sounds like her meatballs."

"Ugh, don't remind me." He swallowed more of his drink. "They were godawful."

"She did make one thing right. Miranda ever make you one of her grilled cheese sandwiches?"

"Yes, in fact, she did." He rolled his glass between his palms. "With Swiss cheese and tomatoes. Those were pretty tasty."

"Yup, we used to have them as midnight snacks when I stayed over. God, I miss her."

"Yeah, me, too. Think we'll ever see her, again?"

Liz gazed around, again. "Yeah, I do. It just might be a long while. Wherever she is, I'm sure she's where she has to be. She'll come home when she's ready."

"Probably when we least expect it." He finished off his drink and then glanced at the clock. "It's late; you want to stay over?"

She couldn't help the sexy smile that came over her face if she tried. "Show me your bedroom."

He blinked once, and then again, like he couldn't believe what she just uttered. "Why?"

She got up and straddled his lap, then took his face between her palms. "Because," she brushed her lips over his, "I want to see it."

***

In wolf form, Cyrus padded up to the precipice that overlooked The Cajun Grill and lay down. Sometimes, it was just more relaxing to wear his animal skin. Scents of Lawe's cooking still lingered in the air, and that was preferable to the smell of blood that had infused his nostrils down in the Werehaven.

Damn, that kid he'd carried in his arms, Danny, who'd looked almost angelic, had only been in his early twenties. Christ, what a fucking shame.

But he'd seen this type of thing before, not only here in New York, but also in Chicago. His old pack master, Trent, had told him when he was there last that Cyrus could be king of the Zephyrs Wolf Clan in five years when he retired. Five fucking years! He shook his head. Yeah, the thought had some appeal; he wanted to be king, could taste it on his tongue.

Even Trent said that with Cyrus' size and know-how he'd make a great king. Cyrus had agreed wholeheartedly. But a lot could happen in five years. Trent could change his mind about retiring, decide to stay on longer, or choose someone else.

Truth was, he liked New York and didn't want to return to Chicago permanently. He'd really hoped that Lizandra would have made him her king, but now, that dream was gone. He'd sent her to her beta, Gavin. A low growl emitted from his throat. It was the right thing to do, even if he'd been shooting himself in the foot. There were other clans in the Tri-state area; maybe he'd look into one of those.

He peered up at the night sky and softly howled. Still, he heard the other wolves as they returned their melancholy howls. Everyone in the clan was mourning the loss of one of their own. Maybe this death, in a way, was a good thing. The wolves would fight harder now, knowing death could touch any one of them. The males had certainly seemed more aggressive when the news had spread.

Gazing out over the park, Cyrus wondered if he'd really leave Werehaven. Central Park was one of the best parks he'd ever seen; it had been his home for years now, worth defending. War was just around the corner. He would not desert the clan or Liz before that. She needed him, so did the pack. He'd see it through to its bloody end. But after?

Well, there'd be plenty of time, then, to consider alternatives.

Chapter Nineteen

Gavin's head was spinning, and it wasn't because of the amount of alcohol he'd consumed. No, it was because of the woman presently straddled over his lap, working her hips like a fine-tuned piston, making his dick harder than it had ever been.

Liz was driving him out of his ever-loving mind, waking the beast that lay just below his skin. When he finally tore his lips from hers, he pulled her hair back and panted, "Playing with fire, aren't you?"

"We need the heat, you and I." Her face flushed, she kissed him, again. "It's been too damn long."

No arguments there, but before this went any further, he had one question. "Is this invitation of yours for one night only...or more?"

She stroked his jaw, her eyes meeting his, the desire never more apparent. "It's for whatever you want."

Oh, that pleased him; that pleased him very much. He wasn't sure what he would have done if her answer had been anything less satisfying. His fingers dug into her hips. "Good."

"Cyrus and I had a talk tonight. He knows there's no future between him and me." She snickered. "A while back, he even suggested a threesome with you."

Gavin's eyes nearly bugged out. "A threesome? With him?"

She purred, "Mhmm," then nibbled his ear.

"When pigs fly. I would never agree to that." He massaged her ass and pulled her even closer. "What did you tell him?"

"I didn't tell him anything." She began trailing kisses down his neck. "As carnal an image it is, I couldn't see it happening. I think I prefer reality over fantasy."

After all this time, she was finally coming around. But one doubt lingered. "You sure you're not doing this because Dan's death got to you? I don't do pity fucks, Lizandra."

Her eyes narrowing, she pulled back from him. "Neither do I. As well you should know."

He growled before taking her lips in a bruising kiss. "In that case, let's get this party started."

Chuckling, she reached for the hem on his T-shirt then ripped it off him as he did the same to hers. Next, he sent her bra flying. He held her close, the warmth of their bodies rubbing against each other. "God, what you do to me."

Her breaths were heavy as she unzipped his pants and slid her fingers inside. "I always liked the way you felt in my hands, like smooth velvet over steel, so tempting." She slid her thumb back and forth over the head of his cock, his pre-cum making for an easier slide.

It felt good, too damned good. Liz was right, too much damned time had passed with them being apart. He wasn't sure how much longer he'd last if she kept it up. He pulled her wrist away and dipped his head to suck one of her nipples, grazing the sensitive nub with his teeth. The sound of her groan aroused him even more. His beast was fully awake, now, wanting—no, *needing*—to mate with her.

He moved his mouth to her other breast as she slid down onto the cushions. He let her nipple slip from his lips, making a wet popping sound. "Fucking delicious." He trailed kisses down her stomach and then reached for the waistband of her jeans. After unbuttoning them and lowering the zipper, he pulled them from her and tossed them to the side.

Only her black lacy thong remained, but he wasn't ready to strip her bare, just yet. He wanted to play with her, torture her with pleasure, keep her on the edge, the way she had with him.

When she tried to push her thong off, he stopped her. "Not yet." He stroked her inner thighs, the skin there silky smooth, just as he'd remembered. Then, he trailed one finger to her thong, touching her everywhere but where he knew she wanted him most.

Her female scent was intoxicating as it perfumed the air around them. He continued with his ministrations, albeit slowly, ever so slowly so that she was squirming for him to go faster. "I bet you're hot as hell inside, wet and ready for me, aren't you?"

Her eyes were heavy lidded as she arched her back and smiled. "Why don't you stick your finger inside and find out for yourself?"

"Oh, I plan to, I plan on sticking more than just my finger inside you." He continued to massage her, now with two fingers. "I'm curious, what did you like best when we were together?"

Her eyes appeared to roll back when he found a bundle of nerves he worked ever so slowly. He was waking her beast, a creature who didn't like to be teased. Too bad. He was in a mood tonight. She could be queen anytime she wanted. But here, in his place, he was the king of his castle and would do as he pleased.

Another moan escaped her tantalizing lips. "Not sure, the way you," she bit her lower lip, "everything, just fucking everything." This time, when she went to remove her thong, he let her.

After she lay back down with one bent leg high up on the couch and the foot of her other leg resting on the floor, she looked divine, like a sacred offering.

"You waxed for me."

She winked at him. "I know you like that part of my anatomy bare. Besides, it feels better when you use your tongue there," her eyes glared at him with wicked intent, "so use it."

"Always so monarch-like, so demanding. Don't you know, sweetheart? I like to take my time."

"You can take as much time as you want, just go down on me."

"In time." He was enjoying the tease but then decided to give her some of what she asked for and used the tips of his fingers to slide across her swollen flesh. "I love the way you feel." After coating his fingers, he brought her honey to her lips. "Taste."

She grabbed his wrist and licked them clean, then sucked them into her mouth, doing that thing with her tongue that drove him absolutely crazy. He knew that move, knew how it felt when she tightened her mouth around his dick and used that unholy tongue to torment him.

If her point was to remind him of her talents in the bedroom, she was succeeding, exceptionally well.

When she broke from him, she said, "Take your damn pants off."

"Why don't you? You're close enough."

She went to her knees in front of him and yanked his pants and boxer briefs off in one fluid moment. *Impatient much?* Her eyes held mischief of the most dangerous, sexy kind as she looked up at him. "Any other requests?"

"Suck me."

She slid her hands up his thighs, her nails lightly abrading the skin there. Her tongue snaked out to lick along the seam where thigh met pelvis, then she did likewise on the other side. It was her turn to keep him on edge, licking everywhere but where he wanted her.

"Wrap those luscious lips around me." His voice was gruffer than he'd intended.

"Like this?" Liz blinked her eyelashes, hiding behind such an innocent façade when he knew the witchy woman was lurking beneath the veneer. She massaged the head of his dick with her mouth and then let it pop free. "Or like this?" This time, she took him deep, her lips tightening as she moved down and up in a tantalizing way that had his eyes rolling back.

He could barely think as he growled, "Yeah, like that."

Her hand followed her mouth, doubling the pleasure coursing through him, but when she cupped his balls and then gently caressed them, he nearly lost it. Not wanting it to end so quickly, he pulled her up to him. "You are one wicked lady."

Her grin lit her face up. "You ready to show me your bedroom, yet?"

He kissed her, tasting himself as their tongues danced with delight. He slid one arm under her knees and lifted her up. His body heated to the point of combustion; he had every intention of waiting to take her in his bed, but they only made it as far as the staircase.

Liz laughed with glee as they rolled around on the stairs. He was just as hungry for her as she was for him. Their bodies were so enflamed, so hot, she was amazed they weren't covered in sweat, but knew they'd soon be. Her body arched on the stairs, her ass in the air with him behind her. Grabbing her hips, he teased her core with his cock, stroking back and forth but not going in.

Finally, when she growled loud enough to wake the neighbors, he entered her. She thought she saw stars, blinding, beautiful stars. Why, oh why, had they waited so long for this to happen? She moaned at the intimate contact. "And you call me wicked."

He chuckled. "Wicked is as wicked does."

She smiled when she heard him grunt; the pleasure of their bodies finally coming together was nearly overwhelming. She wanted to drown in those sensations. But she didn't want to come too soon. Not here on the steps. When she felt him sliding back, she rushed forward but didn't get past the top of the stairs when he was on her, again.

"Where do you think you're going?"

"Uh, some place more comfortable."

He switched their positions so she was on top. She rested her palms on his chest as she lowered herself on him one delicious inch at a time. She'd prefer the bed, but pass up a moment to ride the greatest beast she'd ever known? *Hell, no!* With him inside, it felt like heaven, and she moaned at the sensuous beauty of their cherished connection.

"Perfect." She hadn't meant to say the word aloud, but it had slipped free before she could pull it back.

"No. Not yet, it isn't." He reached up to guide her head down to his. "But it will be." He drove into her, his tongue matching the rhythm of his thrusts. *Bliss, fucking bliss.*

Somehow, she was able to tear herself away. "Gavin, I don't want to come too soon. Let's go to your bedroom."

He grunted. "Wrap your legs around me." When she complied, he acquiesced to her request, his strong arms holding her to him as she locked her ankles behind him and tightened her inner muscles so he wouldn't slip free. Gavin carried her to his bedroom and kicked the door shut behind them.

He sat down on the corner of the bed with her straddling his lap.

She let one foot slide down to the floor for support and kept the other around his waist. "Hopefully, we won't make the bed squeak while we're going at it."

He offered her a lopsided grin. "Really think that's possible, luscious?"

Probably not. "Mmm." She used her foot to propel her upward movements as she wrapped her arms around his neck.

A drip of sweat rolled down the side of his face as he met her stroke for stroke. "What you do to me, Liz. God, what you do to me."

"Drive you fucking crazy?"

His lids opened, and he peered up at her. "Yes."

She licked her way into his mouth and enjoyed all the fervent emotions that coursed through her, sentiments too long buried. The pleasure was slowly building; she could feel it stirring, her body already glistening. She gazed at him and saw the intense passion etched in his handsome face. God, he was exquisite. When was the last time she'd seen him this aroused, so completely male?

Their breathing became ragged pants as their movements sped up. She could sense their climaxes nearing, so close, so very close, and then, she was shouting her release, his howl echoing her ecstasy. They clutched each other, as if needing something to anchor them to this world. Nothing could be more celestial. Exhausted, their bodies crashed down onto the mattress.

After moments passed, both of them could barely crawl to the head of the bed to lay against the pillows.

Gavin lifted his arm around her. "That was... That was... I don't even know, but holy shit, that was hot."

"Felt like an incendiary device going off." She laughed. "Think we woke the neighbors?"

He held her closer. "Who gives a fuck?"

She splayed her hand over his chest, loving the way the smattering of reddish-golden hairs felt under her fingers. "You're gorgeous."

He wrapped her hair around his fingers and tugged lightly. "I think you're the one who would win all the beauty contests."

She scoffed then looked down the length of their bodies. "You get so tanned from working outside. Your back, arms, chest, so much darker than your hips and thighs."

"Yeah, well not everyone can have such perfect skin like yours, no tan lines anywhere."

"I get them, they're just not as pronounced as yours. You need to lay out in the sun more with your shorts off. Naked."

"Um. We did that, remember? Out in Amagansett, when we rented that summer beach house for the weekend."

She did, indeed. It was one of the best times in her life. After a day of swimming, taking in the sun on their private porch, they'd feasted on lobsters and then made love to the sounds of the ocean waves crashing nearby. "Yeah, I didn't realize how sensitive the skin on your ass was. If memory serves, you had a hard time sitting down."

"No kidding. At least my groin didn't get sunburnt. That would have been much worse."

She stared at that particular region of his body. "Poor little guy. I'm sure it would have been painful."

"Hey, who you calling little?"

She slid her hand down his thigh. "Certainly not you. Turn over."

"I'm comfortable resting this way with you."

"Just do it."

He tilted his head to look her way. "Why?"

"Because I want to see your ass."

"I think you already saw it," he groused, but wrapped his arms around his pillow and turned over on his stomach.

Her hand smoothed down over his back to his cheeks. "You have the whitest ass."

"Well, I am Irish. Complaining?"

"No." She bent down and sank her teeth into his rounded globe, as if marking him. "Regardless of what I said before, I just wondered what you'd look like with a full body tan. But you know something?"

"What?"

"You don't need to change the color of your skin for me. I like you just the way you are."

"Why, thank you, Bridget Jones."

She laughed at the name of the character in a movie they'd watched together. "You know what I mean."

"Do I?"

"We're lucky. Skin color never meant anything to either one of us."

"Why the fuck should it? People are just people. It never occurred to me to be judgmental." He wrapped his arm behind his head. "I never really understood why some people thought differently. Where I grew up, on New York's tougher streets, we had people from all kinds of backgrounds: Asians, African Americans, Eastern Europeans, Mid-Easterners, Italians, Irish, you name it. And you know what united us all?"

They'd discussed their different heritages before, but never this deeply. "What?"

"We were all poor. I remember coming home from school and visiting with Mrs. D'Amico, who used to give me cookies. She'd have coffee with Mrs. Haveshein, who made the best blintzes. The Patels introduced me to curry. I developed a deep appreciation for ethnic foods."

"I bet you did."

"Everyone watched everyone's kids, back then; no one cared what race you were, we worked together. There was a

Black family in apartment 3C—the Careys. Mrs. Carey was a nurse who taught me how to make a tourniquet, got me interested in medicine, and her husband, Louis, always played basketball with us. The Hispanic family in 1B, the Santos, made me empanadas and helped out the elderly when they could. All the kids in the neighborhood played together. Race was never an issue with us."

"Is that what made you such a good cook, learning all those cultural foods?"

"I guess." He tilted his head. "Did our different skin colors ever bother you?"

"Never. In the beginning, I wasn't quite sure if I was a novelty to you, but you quickly showed me you were colorblind."

"Growing up, it used to bother me that we weren't as rich as some people. My dad was a carpenter, he taught me how to build things; some years were more lean than others. But, you know, I think it shaped me. I can't imagine it any other way. If I had grown up in an upper middle-class neighborhood that only had one ethnicity, I might have developed myopia, but I didn't."

She rolled on top of him. "I think you would have been open-minded no matter where you grew up. I'm just glad I found you."

"Really?" His hands slid around her. "So, where do we go from here?"

A thought crossed her mind that made her smile. "Wherever we want."

Chapter Twenty

Gavin woke feeling more relaxed than he'd felt in months, except for his cock, which stood proudly at attention. Sheesh, you'd think after last night, he'd be satisfied, but his arousal didn't think so. God, they'd gotten so drunk on lust, he couldn't even remember how many times they did it. Each time had been better than the one before. Glorious. When he reached across the mattress for Lizandra, he found her space empty.

"Oh, fuck," he muttered, feeling dejected. When the hell had she left? Doubt crept in, darkening his mood. He'd thought, for sure, she'd be there when he woke up. Was one night with him all she'd wanted? Didn't he mean more to her? She certainly meant more to him. He leaned over to inhale her scent from her pillow and groaned until another aroma hit him.

Coffee. Someone was making him coffee. And biscuits. He inhaled the buttery goodness and smiled. Then, he caught sight of the clock; it was nearly eleven a.m. He never slept that late, but since they hadn't fallen asleep until it was nearly dawn, his body had obviously needed the rest. He jumped out of bed, showered, decided to skip shaving, and dressed in fifteen minutes flat.

"Something smells terrific," he said as he descended the stairs.

"Something, or someone, *is* terrific." Liz handed him a cup of the heavenly brew, which he quickly sipped. "There's croissants and pastries in the box on the counter. I had them delivered, as well as some chicken and lamb kebobs from the Mediterranean restaurant down the block."

He opened the pastry box and chose a cherry danish, then peered into the bags. "You planning on feeding an army?"

"No. I was thinking of visiting Grandma Wells and Casey for lunch. Figured they'd like some souvlaki, hummus, and stuffed grape leaves, as well as the kebobs."

He sniffed one of the boxes. "Any baklava?"

"You know it. Gram's favorite."

After devouring his danish, washing it down with the coffee, he started on a blueberry muffin. God, he was hungry. Right, he'd missed dinner last night. Disappointment swelled that she wouldn't be staying with him, but Gavin was glad she was going to spend time with her relatives. He'd always gotten along well with the woman who helped raise Liz, and Liz's teenage daughter. "How've they been?"

She bit into one of the croissants, swallowed the morsel, and smiled up at him. "Why don't you come with me and ask them yourself?"

His stomach fluttered at the prospect. "I could do that. But I think we should be back at Werehaven before dusk."

"We will be." She pointed to the counter. "You have a couple of texts from Lawe. I charged our phones when I woke this morning. Brent and Cyrus reported everything's quiet this morning. No disturbances."

"Good to know." He checked his messages. Since nothing was pertinent, he pocketed his phone. "When do you want to leave?"

"Now, if you're ready?"

Gavin grabbed his wallet and keys from the table, then donned his aviator glasses. He carried the box in one arm as he locked the door behind them and then pointed to where he was parked. In minutes, they were driving uptown on West Side Highway. "I always liked this drive. Being able to gaze out at the Hudson River."

"Yeah, it's peaceful."

"So, why'd you pick today to go visit your grandmother and Casey? This isn't some sort of sentimental farewell, in case of 'if I don't make it', on your part, is it?"

"Of course, not." She scoffed, but her body language conveyed her concern. It was in the tightness of her muscles and the way she kept her body arched, as if waiting for an attack.

He reached for her hand and squeezed. "Everything will be all right."

"Of course, it will."

So, this was how they were going to play it. Keeping a positive outlook, but underneath, both of them knew things could turn ugly real fast when it came to the Red Claws. "We'll deal with whatever comes our way."

She looked determined, yet faraway. "We will."

He took the exit that would lead them to Gram's apartment. After circling the block a couple of times, they finally lucked out and grabbed a parking spot at the corner. Once inside the building, they took the elevator up to the tenth floor. He was looking forward to seeing her relatives, knew it would do her good.

Liz had told him long ago, she felt a tighter kinship with her grandmother than she ever did with her own mother—a concert pianist who now called Las Vegas home.

Liz had had Casey when she was so young. Grandma Wells had volunteered to watch the kid so Liz could serve in the army then get her college degree. Gavin respected the hell out of single women who accomplished so much. Life wasn't always fair; it certainly was harder for some more than others, but Liz never let much get her down. She was the most resolute woman he'd ever met. And he loved her for it.

"Gavin," Casey yelled as she opened the door to let them in. "I've missed you so much."

"Whoa, Lil' Knick. Let me look at you. You've grown so much; you're almost as tall as your mother." He'd given Casey that nickname because she loved the Knicks basketball team.

"Not quite," Grams said as she embraced first him, then Liz. "But in a few years. Come in, come in. Make yourselves at home. What are those decadent scents I smell?"

Liz answered. "Your favorites from the Mediterranean restaurant you like so much."

Grams whispered to Liz after he passed by with the box. "Those weren't the scents I was referring to."

"Grandma!" He caught Liz patting the older woman on the arm as if that would censure her brazen sense of humor. No chance of that. Grandma Wells was a straight shooter, who had one of the most delightful, dirty old lady laughs he'd ever heard. He saw a lot of Liz in her.

He laid the food down on the dining room table while Casey and Liz got the plates, cutlery, and glasses.

"Iced tea good for everyone?" Grams called out as she reached inside the fridge for the pitcher.

"Love some." Today was one of the hotter days. Even with the AC blasting in the car, he'd felt the heat from the sun on his arm while driving. "Mrs. W, you make the best iced tea I've ever had."

"Homemade, from brewing real tea bags, fresh lemons, and raw sugar, none of that artificial crap. And you call me Grams like everyone else, or did you forget?"

"I didn't forget."

After they'd consumed most of the food and stored the leftovers in the fridge, they spent some time catching up. But he could tell Liz wanted some alone time with her grandmother, so when Casey asked him if he wanted to shoot some hoops down in the park lot across the street, he said, "I'm game."

"So, you going to tell me what brings you up this way?" Grams put the cleaned glasses in the cabinet. "Glad to see you, but you usually give me more notice than a couple of hours."

"Grams, I don't know where to start." Liz finished drying the last of the plates and, after putting them away, perused the living room. She eyed the Steinway by the far wall where she'd learned to play piano and, above it, the Romare Bearden print, *Out Chorus*—featuring musicians. It was one of her favorites. On the opposite wall was a Jean-Michel Basquiat drawing that Casey liked.

"You used to love to play."

"I still do, when I can." Liz stepped back into the kitchen and leaned up against the fridge. She took a deep breath and exhaled. "I wanted to give you a head's up that the Black Stars are probably going to war with the Red Claws."

Grams' eyes bugged out as her body stiffened. "When?"

"I'd say imminently. The full moon isn't until a couple of days. I don't think he'll attack before that. All Weres need their Lunar Run."

"And why does that rat Renworth want to attack my family?"

Liz beckoned her to sit with her at the kitchen table and then, taking a deep breath, recapped all that had gone on with the pack master, including his desire to build his pavilion and Dan's death. "He was just a kid out on a date."

"With all the land he's got, you'd think he'd build the damn thing on his own territory."

"His financial advisors did a prospectus and figured they could make much more money in a centralized location."

"Central Park. That bastard." Grams went to the cabinet and retrieved two shot glasses and the apricot schnapps. She poured them each a glassful.

Liz tasted the liquor and grimaced. "How can you drink that stuff? It's super sweet."

Grams shrugged. "I like it." After she downed the rest of her drink, she moaned, "Ahh." Then sat forward. "Now, tell me the truth. Can you win this?"

"I don't know. There's no guarantee; it could go either way. His clan outnumbers mine, by a lot. But Gavin's learned battle tactics from Lord Valadon's second, so we have that on our side."

"Will the vamps help you in this war?"

"I wish. Valadon has his hands full fighting with some human extremist organization, and besides, how would it look, if I called in the vamps to help me fight a war? What message would I be sending?"

"I see your point. Clans respect strength. You'd incur the wrath of all the neighboring clans if you bring Valadon's people in. There are still some Weres who don't like vampires. Don't trust them."

"I know."

With her arms crossed over her chest, Grams seemed to be studying her. "What you need, dear grandchild of mine, are allies."

"Lovely thought, but clans stick to their own territory. They won't cross Renworth to help me out."

"What about Jenkins?"

"Who?"

"Derrick Jenkins, the leader of the Dark Moon pack. Don't you remember him? He was sweet on you back in high school, was even friends with your first husband, Trevon."

Liz sighed and pulled on the ends of her hair. "Grams, that was a long time ago. Derrick has the smallest clan in Manhattan; the Dark Moons only gather in Morningside Park. Even if he did remember me, I would need far more men than he's got."

"So sure about that?" She poured more of the schnapps and took a sip. "Derrick's expanded over the years. He united the Weres in Fort Washington and Fort Tryon Parks, then added Inwood Hill Park near the Cloisters museum to form one large clan."

Shocked, Liz felt her heart racing and quickly stood. "Why didn't you ever tell me this?"

"You never asked." She shrugged. "Besides, Derrick likes keeping a low profile. He's got some prime property up there, not far from the museum. Doesn't mess around in Mid-town like you and Renworth. Why don't you take a drive up there? You've got nothing to lose."

Rubbing her arms, Liz went to the bay window in the living room and gazed out to watch Casey playing basketball with Gavin. "I can't believe how much she's grown."

Grams came beside her. "She misses her mother, asks about you all the time."

"I spend whatever time I can with her. I can't bring Casey to Werehaven." She glanced back at the woman who helped raised her and now her own daughter. "You know what goes on there. She's too young for that."

"She's going to be sixteen in a few months. Remember what you were like, then, so ambitious to join your parents at Werehaven. I practically had to stand guard to prevent you from sneaking out. Lotta good it did me."

Liz remembered how rebellious she'd been in high school. What good friends Trevon and Derrick had been, how they'd played basketball and other sports. Good times. It was strange what triggered memories. Most were good, but some...were not.

Especially the time some blond senior tripped her on the way to class and her books and papers got scattered all over because Liz had forgot to close the zipper on her backpack.

There were lots of kids around, but no one stooped to help her.

Except for one.

"Don't give them a second thought. Rich kids think they own the school."

Liz had peered up to see a pale-faced, punked-out girl with black cropped hair and more piercings than Liz could count bending down to hand her the books. She'd worn denim shorts with black fishnet stockings and three-inch combat boots. But Liz had been frustrated and furious at the way some of the girls in the school had treated her and snapped, "What do you know about it?

Punk girl had hiked her backpack over one shoulder and stood. An imposing figure, she was nearly six feet tall and looked muscular. "Enough to know anger gets you nowhere." One side of her mouth had crooked up. "Have a nice day."

When the dark-haired girl had gotten near the stairs, Liz'd called out, "What's your name?"

She'd grinned. "Sam, I am."

Sam had climbed just a couple of steps when Liz asked, "What does?"

"Huh?"

"You said anger gets you nowhere, so what gets you somewhere?"

Sam had started tapping her hands on the railing to whatever music was playing in her mind, met her eyes, and smiled. "Talent." Then, she'd scurried up the rest of the stairs and disappeared.

Liz never saw that girl, again, until years later, when she'd seen her picture on an advertisement in Times Square for the Met. Samantha Kean was a musician. Liz's jaw had dropped, and she'd immediately googled the girl.

After high school, Sam had gotten a full scholarship to Julliard, for, of all things, opera singing. *Opera? Holy shit!* Liz remembered she'd been happy for her and had wanted to get tickets to see her, but something had always come up and she never had.

Just went to show you could never predict how some people would turn out.

"Hey, where'd you go, just now?" Grams snapped her fingers. "You looked like you were zoning out, like that crazy friend of yours."

"Which one?"

"The one that worked at the museum."

Liz grinned. "Miranda's not crazy."

"Miranda," Grams snapped her fingers, "that's it. Whenever you brought her around and I'd be talking to her, her eyes would get this faraway look, and poof," she gestured with her hands, "she'd zone out on me. That girl was touched, if you ask me."

Liz remembered when Miranda would space out at her during movie nights. Liz usually threw popcorn at her to break her trance. "She was special."

"Hmm, speaking of special, remember when you gave me that needlework over there? I had it framed."

Liz glanced to where Grams was pointing on the far wall. "The Maya Angelou poem?" One of her favorites, "Still I Rise" had affected her deeply on many levels; she'd even memorized the lines. "Yeah, one of my teachers in school gave me a copy of her book, said I could keep it. It's one of the most inspirational poems I've ever read." When she spotted the embroidery online, she'd immediately ordered it for Grams. And, now, reading the poem, again, infused her with pride, made her feel resolute.

"Maya knew what it was to face all kinds of adversity and overcome it. She never let anything get her down for too long. Neither should you."

"I won't." Liz's back straightened. "People tried to crush her any way they could. Destroy her spirit, devastate her. Wound her with their evil. Maya didn't stand for that. She sure showed them."

"She certainly did." Grams' eyes widened at her. "So, I ask, again, are you going to go see Derrick?"

Liz stared out the window again at the basketball players. "I don't know. I'll ask Gavin if we have time."

"So, you back with him?"

Liz couldn't stop the grin from spreading across her face. Last night had been beyond wonderful. It had been right. "Maybe."

"I don't think there's any maybe about it. I see the way you two look at each other. Um-hmm. I always liked Gavin. You two were good together. A lot better than the other guys you brought around. He was the only one who took an interest in Casey. You know on her last birthday he got her tickets to a Knicks game. Always sends her a birthday card with a gift card inside."

Liz stood there in shock. "What?"

"You heard me. Just because you and he split up didn't mean he stopped caring about Casey." She nodded outside. "Just look how they play together."

Liz turned to watch them. The friendship between them was so obvious. And, if she was honest with herself, she'd admit there was a bond between them. "I didn't know that."

"Well, he's a keeper."

"Once upon a time, he wanted to marry me."

"For heaven's sake, girl, why'd you turn him down?"

"After Trevon, and then Darnell, I just couldn't see myself married for a third time."

"I never liked Darnell; he thought the world owed him something. That everyone should bow down to him. I was glad when you gave him the boot. But this one," she pointed Gavin's way, "he's something else. And he still loves you."

"I know. And I...I'm beginning to think breaking up with him was a mistake."

"Well, better late than never."

At that moment, Gavin looked up at her and waved. She returned the gesture. "He makes me happy."

"Handsome dude." She snickered in her dirty old lady voice. "He'd make me happy, too."

"Grams!"

Chapter Twenty-One

After kissing Grams and Casey goodbye, and promising to visit, again, soon, Gavin hopped on the Henry Hudson Parkway that would take him and Liz north to the Dark Moon Clan's hangout. "Geez, Liz, you couldn't find anyone closer? We just passed the George Washington Bridge. How much farther?"

"Derrick said to get off at the Fort Tryon exit. Only a couple of more miles, now."

"If memory serves, we once went to that museum, up that way, the Cloisters, didn't we? That's where they had all that Medieval stuff, the artwork from the Middle Ages. Incredible architecture. Impressive archways with the statues. I liked going there."

"Yeah, I really liked the tapestries and those beautiful gardens; it was a good trip." She glanced his way. "Maybe we'll go back, someday."

Gavin hoped so, but right now, he was curious about the guy they were going to see. "So, tell me about this Derrick. Were you and he...?"

"No, we were never lovers. We met in high school; he was a close friend of Trevon's. Saw him a few times afterward at family gatherings. Lost touch over the years."

Gavin tried to place the guy. "Did I ever meet him?"

"I don't think so. He started off as a DJ, worked at a few clubs. Found out he could make good money doing weddings, even got his license to perform the ceremonies himself. We used to call him 'Preacher Man'. He was smart, invested his money well in some land up there. When he saw all the tourists going to the Cloisters and then sightseeing by the

Hudson River, he petitioned the City Council to open up a tourist shop/snack shack by the piers."

"How'd that work out?"

"At first, they balked at the idea, but when he proved to them how much money he could bring in, making sure the city got its fair share, they gave the okay."

"Tourism is big business."

"I'll say, even this far from Mid-town. After he did well with the shop, he soon expanded to a larger restaurant, then the catering hall. Want to guess what he called it?"

He thought of the clan name. "Dark Moon Hall?"

She laughed. "Not quite, but good guess. Originally, he wanted to name it Moonshiners, but he wanted a family-oriented place and felt some people wouldn't want to bring their kids somewhere that sounded like low-grade booze."

"I can see his point. So, what did he decide on?"

"Moon River. They play it as the last song of the night. He's done quite well for himself."

Gavin checked the exit signs and continued driving. "Has he?"

"Yep. Got his friend who did all the wedding photos to shoot around the area and make postcards, picture books, things like that. Hired some fledgling company to manufacture all the stuffed toys, coffee mugs, key chains, stuff like that. Tourists spend a fortune on souvenirs."

"I know."

"Y'know, I don't get tourists, really, I don't. The millions that flock to the city, most stay within a certain radius and don't venture out much further, when there's so much more to explore in the outer boroughs."

Narrowly dodging a pothole, Gavin recalled all the places they used to frequent. "Like the Brooklyn Aquarium and Botanical Gardens."

"And the Bronx Zoo and the Science Museum in Queens."

He was glad she remembered all the wonderful places they'd visited; they were good memories. "Don't be too hard on them. Many are foreigners and don't know how to navigate outside Manhattan. They want to see the Statue of Liberty, the Empire State Building, Times Square—the usual."

She shook her head. "Anyway, this far north, Derrick got the idea from the gorgeous scenery that wedding photos would look great up there, especially in the spring when the flowers are in bloom. Says he does a better business in the fall, when all the leaves are turning colors."

"I'll bet." Gavin put his directional on for the exit they were taking. "One thing he's got in his favor, not too much traffic up here, at least not like Mid-town. It's up ahead."

Once they parked the car, Gavin surveyed the area, then they walked down to the pier to the riverside restaurant. They were met by two of Derrick's guards who escorted them inside.

If Gavin was impressed with the elegant exterior, he was even more amazed at the chic grace of the interior. Blue drapes lined the windows that overlooked the river. The floral arrangements were nothing less than stunning. At the far end was a massive fireplace that probably heated the whole expanse in winter. He could see why couples would want to be married here. The view at night must be extraordinary.

They were ushed into a spacious corner office with a spectacular view of the river and trees, then asked to take a seat. He could hear someone talking on his phone, even though the chair was faced away from them.

When the guy turned their way, Gavin immediately thought Derrick reminded him of Laurence Fishburne, more from the *Matrix* movies than the *John Wick* ones. He half-expected the guy to don his sunshades. Despite what anyone thought, Reeves and Fishburne really knew their martial arts moves.

Derrick finished his call, swiveled his chair, and smiled. He stood and came around to shake his hand. "So glad to meet you."

Gavin rose. "Same, Mr. Jenkins."

"Call me Jenks; everyone around here does." Their host grasped his shoulder. "Grandma Wells had nothing but high praise for you. Any friend of hers is a friend of mine."

That was certainly good news to hear. Gavin felt a good vibe emanating from Jenks and decided he liked the guy already. "Nice place, you've got here. I think you have a better view than any of the offices in Mid-town."

"I like it." His eyes swiftly moved to Liz. "And you," Jenks pulled Liz into a tight embrace, then quickly released her, "it's been way too long since I've seen you."

"Leading a clan can be time consuming, as well you must know."

"I do at that. You're looking well," he brushed a strand away from her face, "maybe a little tired."

She resumed sitting. "You know the big city; something's always going on."

"Oh, yes." He retreated back to his chair. "That's why I moved up here, to get away from all the nonsense. I never thought Moon River would take off as well as it has. I recently leased a couple of boats for the married couples to plan a quick getaway. The wedding parties love them. Enough about me; how are things in Central Park?"

Liz reclined back in her chair. "I suppose you've heard of the difficulties Renworth is making for me."

"Renworth, that cocksucker. He wasn't satisfied with his own territory, tried to reach beyond the GW Bridge, but we threatened him with quick retaliation if he tried to cross over."

That perked up Gavin's ears. "You've had confrontations with Renworth?"

"A few. Man thought he could have all the territory on the western coast of Manhattan. Ambitious fucker. We had to file multiple complaints with the Commissioner of Clans to get him to back down."

"They censured him?"

Jenks shook his head. "No, no. The only thing that motivates him, besides his overly big ego, is his greed. I suspect his financial advisors assured him there was no gain here, no potential for financial advances, at least not the kind he could make elsewhere. He eventually backed off and started scouting other interests."

Liz leaned forward. "Grams tells me you united the smaller clans of Fort Washington and Fort Tryon Parks with Morningside."

"Sure did, also with Inwood Hill. Consolidated everyone, safety in numbers and all that, so we don't have to deal with trash like Renworth. We're so far up north, no one really bothers with us." Jenks picked up the pen from his desk and started twirling it. "We like it that way."

"Renworth expressed interest in building a sports pavilion in Central Park. I politely told him no. He doesn't take rejection well."

"I heard he proposed marriage to you." Jenks smirked, swiveled in his chair. "After the primest of the prime, *mhmm*." He turned his attention Gavin's way. "At one time or another, all the clan leaders were interested in Lizandra. But she only had eyes for one."

Gavin liked that Jenks' eyes landed on him. "Liz doesn't have interest in marrying, again." He took her hand in his. "If she did, we would have been married a long time ago."

The Dark Moon leader leaned his head back and laughed. "I think so, my man, I think so. She ever tell you about the Halloween party I threw at one of the clubs I worked? The theme was to go hand in hand with Michael Jackson's *Thriller* video; everyone was supposed to dress up as zombies or some sort of monster. This one here," he pointed Liz's way, "prances in wearing some goth number: leather pants with boots five inches high—the kind that laced in front, a top with zippers and chains all over the place, leather bracelets and a necklace with studs in them."

Liz grinned. "We were just kids back then."

"God, you had so many piercings, I thought you'd gone completely crazy until I realized they were the clip-on kind."

"Most were."

"Good memories, good memories. So, what brings you to Moon River, Lizandra? I know you didn't come all the way up here for my sparkling personality."

"If there's a war between the Red Claws and us, can the Black Stars count on the Dark Moons helping us out?"

Jenks looked first at Liz, then Gavin, and back at Liz. "If Renworth declares war on you, you're gonna need more than just help." He tossed the pen back on his desk and scoffed. "A miracle more like it."

Gavin said, "But you've tangled with them before."

"Yes, to defend my own territory, and it wasn't a war exactly, more like a skirmish or two. Renworth's got the largest pack in this region. He makes war on you, it's going to be a bloodbath."

Liz sighed. "So, you won't offer us any assistance?"

"I didn't say that." He swiveled, again, eying them both. "What's in it for me?"

She stared him down. "What do you want?"

A hungry, lascivious grin stretched Jenks' mouth, the wolf sighting prey as his eyes traveled leisurely over Liz's body. Before he knew what he was doing, Gavin was up and out of his chair and throwing a punch that had Jenks crashing to the floor. Within seconds, his two bodyguards restrained each of Gavin's arms. "Don't ever look at her that way, again."

Jenks waved off his guards, who resumed their spots by the door. "Damn, man," he rubbed his jaw, "I wasn't making moves. What I was thinking was something else."

"What?" Gavin and Liz demanded.

Jenks sat back in his chair and smiled. "Your voice."

Liz looked stunned. "What?"

"You heard me." The Dark Moon King eyed Gavin. "Back in the day, this one used to sing in our church choir. She hit notes nobody else even came close to. Like some sort of angel, gospel songs. She had us all mesmerized. When we graduated, I had all these dreams of managing her career, soaring to the top of the music world, but Liz wanted to go to college and the army. I was so disappointed." He turned toward her. "What I wouldn't give to hear you perform one night at my restaurant. The clientele would go nuts."

"One night?"

He nodded.

"We might be able to work something out. Then, you'll lend me some men?"

"Not quite." His gaze shifted, again, to Gavin. "Two people came requesting my help. Two people should make offers."

Suspicion gnawing at him, Gavin's eyes narrowed. "Such as?"

Jenks' hungry wolf smile returned. "A competition."

After Jenks said to follow him outside, Gavin was hesitant to leave Lizandra alone, but Jenks assured him she'd be safe with his guards. And, besides, she'd be sitting in one of the Adirondack chairs on the patio with a carafe of coffee and a selection of desserts from his Viennese hour—clearly in sight of him and Jenks on the rear deck of his boat docked at the pier.

Jenks retrieved two beers from the mini-fridge and handed him one. Once they were comfortably seated facing each other, Jenks reached below the cabinet separating them for a box with squares on it. He unfolded the chess board then set up the pieces. "You do know how to play, don't you?"

Not quite the competition Gavin was expecting, but okay. "Yeah, actually, I do."

"Now, tell me the truth, can you win this war?"

Ah, so this was why *Preacher Man* wanted him away from Liz. "We're going to do our best."

"Not the answer I was looking for, my man." He gazed back up at Liz. "She's special. A fine woman, well-respected by all the other clan leaders. It would be a damn shame if any harm came to her."

"I would lay down my life before I let that happen."

"Good. Now that we got that settled," Jenks brought the bottle to his lips and threw back some of the brew, "check out the board. Which piece would you say is the most valuable?"

Gavin hadn't played since college days but knew the basics. Since the whole game was based on protecting the monarch, the one who called the shots, he said, "The king."

"Nah, nah. The king sits on his fat ass throne and sends all his people out to play." He snickered. "Kinda like Renworth. The king's pretty much useless, can only move one square at a time." Jenks tapped the piece nearest the king, "The queen." His eyes shifted to Liz. "She's the most powerful, can move in any direction. Renworth will send all his pawns her way, see what damage he can cause."

Gavin pretty much assumed that and sipped his beer.

"Now, imagine this board is Central Park. You have the north here, the east and west here, and then the south. Which direction do you think he'll attack from?"

"If I understand tactics correctly," and after conferring with Remare, Gavin was pretty confident he had a good handle on it, "they'll attack us from all directions."

"Too true. Expect the unexpected. Look at the board, again, he...or she who controls the center of the board usually wins the game. Central Park? Whoever controls Werehaven wins. If Renworth gets his men inside," Jenks raised his brows and widened his eyes to make sure Gavin was paying attention, "checkmate, my friend."

"He won't get inside." Gavin would make sure that never happened.

"I hope not." He pointed to the back row of pieces. "I'm betting you already know who all his key players are."

"We made it a point to find out."

Jenks tapped the white queen. "Renworth's most important piece, his second, Victor. Intelligent, cunning, shrewd bastard, doesn't fight in the cages from what I hear. Renworth doesn't need him for that, requires him as his advisor so I don't expect him to engage."

"You fought Renworth before; who were his best fighters?"

Jenks tapped the knight. "Curtis is one mean-ass motherfucker. Has muscles on top of muscles. Super strong. From what I hear, no one beats him in the fighting ring. Ever."

"We've heard rumors that the Red Claws may be taking steroids."

Jenks blew out a breath. "I wouldn't be surprised. He's got some feral wolves there; I mean, more than the usual." He took a long deep swallow of his beer. "It's in the eyes—they turn red. Now, you know that ain't natural."

No, it wasn't, Gavin agreed.

"Your alpha as strong as the rumors suggest he is? He's going to have to be to take down Curtis."

Gavin nodded, gulped down more of his beer. "He's strong." Not wanting to dwell any more on Cyrus, he asked, "Who else?"

Jenks slid his finger down the bishop. "His lawyer is a slithering snake, Alexa Cantrell. She tried to seduce me into seeing things Renworth's way. Calculating little cunt. Beautiful and dangerous as they come. Don't expect her to fight fair. She won't."

Gavin's immediate impression was that she had player written all over her. "When I first saw her, I thought she was a shark."

"She is." Jenks tapped both rooks. "Keep an eye out for Sinclair, or Sin, as he prefers, and Ramos. Both are excellent fighters, no hesitation; they'll go for the kill first chance they get."

"Will do."

Jenks seemed to be studying the board. "I don't believe Renworth will hit you all at once. More likely, he'll send wave after wave of his men. Try to wear you down." He moved all the pawns to the center of the board. "Then, he'll send in his top guns. I wouldn't be surprised if they each attacked from all four directions. What I just showed you here? You know Renworth's got the same logistics on you and yours. He knows who all your key people are."

"Of course, he does."

Jenks' expression turned serious. "He won't show any mercy."

"We don't expect any."

Staring out over the river, Jenks leaned back in his chair and laced his fingers over his stomach. "Now, the last of my unsolicited advice: If I was planning an offensive, I'd save the major battles for where the humans congregate the least. No blood near the zoo, the carousel, the restaurant, any of the touristy areas. Humans come across a dead body in the park, they'll freak out, bad for tourism, bad for business, and the city council members will rain hell down on you. My thinking is he'll attack at night, probably late, but early enough that the fighting will be done by dawn. Weres gotta retreat by daybreak—no evidence left to be discovered."

"I agree." Gavin regarded the board and could easily see how it would play out as Central Park's battleground. "It all depends on how arrogant Renworth is. If he thinks we'll be easily defeated, he'll attack late; if he leans toward the side of caution, he'll strike earlier."

"That he will." Appearing reflective, Jenks nodded in Liz's direction. "Her parents had her take karate when she was just a kid, made sure she knew how to protect herself, same with her brothers. Sam and David always respected the fact that the Black Stars is mostly a matriarchal clan. I never saw any jealousy between them, and I've been friends with the family for over twenty years."

"You think there're members of the clan who don't share that respect?"

"I'm not saying there is. Just not all people share the same beliefs. Lotta backward thinking people out there; some don't believe queens should have that kind of power, that only kings should rule."

Yes, Gavin had met some of them. "Can you imagine just how much more fucked up this world would be if that were the case?"

Jenks threw his head back and laughed. "Ain't that the truth." After a moment, he said, "You consider any insurance?"

"What do you mean?"

"Stacking the cards in your favor. Renworth outnumbers you; you need a trumping card, an ace up your sleeve."

"Such as?"

"Take away something he values; something he loves."

Gavin scrutinized him. "From what I hear, he harbors no sentimental feelings for any of his ex-wives or lovers. If you're suggesting we kidnap one of his kids, forget it. I won't bring a child into this."

"You don't think he's considered that with Lizandra?"

Gavin's heart lurched at the thought. "You think he'll try to go after her family?"

"He might. I think she's been wise staying away from them as much as she has. Breaks her heart, but she has to do what is right by them: keeps them safe by keeping away." Jenks gestured his way. "Anyone sees you two together, sees the way she looks at you, they're gonna know you're her weakness; they'll pounce on you."

"I can handle myself."

Jenks rubbed his jaw as he rose. "Yeah, I think so."

Gavin stood. "One other thing, did you ever hear of a Red Claw named Bali?"

Jenks seemed to be searching his memories. "Can't say that I have. Why do you ask?"

They walked, side by side, up the hill to where Liz was waiting for them. "She or he, unidentified gender, is the one that killed one of our packmates."

Jenks' eyes widened, and he tilted his head. "You don't know?"

"Dan wasn't real big on sharing details before he died; he was too butchered to be coherent."

Chapter Twenty-Two

Brent looked up when Quint opened the door to their room. He'd been studying for a while now and welcomed the needed break from the volumes on their bed.

Quint scanned the titles. "Interesting reading, *The Art of War,* by Sun Tzo, *Conquests during the Roman Empire,* Sherman's *Principles of Strategies,* learn anything new?"

Brent shook his head. "I thought I'd reread certain passages."

"How long have you had those books; they look really old?"

Brent shrugged. "Seems like forever." One had been a gift from someone he highly esteemed, someone he wished he could...

"You've been glued to the laptop for the last few months, analyzing every conceivable war strategy from Genghis Khan to Napoleon."

"Don't forget Rommel and Hannibal. Those men excelled at tactics and strategies."

"Yes, I know." Quint removed his shirt and then grabbed a fresh T-shirt to pull over his head. "Gavin made sure we studied their maneuvers and battle plans." He sat beside Brent on the bed and kissed his cheek.

He closed his laptop and rubbed his eyes. "Speaking of which, have Gavin and Lizandra returned, yet?"

"Yes, they've been spending quality alone time. They're up top, walking along the trails, where you and I should be."

"Did you talk with them?"

"Not yet."

"Okay, let's go, then." Brent rose from the bed. "I want to discuss a few things with Gavin."

***

After returning to Central Park, Liz and Gavin strolled the wooded path where the flowers were in bloom. Holding his hand in hers sent a thrill through her. And, from the slight smile on his face, she knew he was feeling the same. When was the last time they walked together in the sunlight, just the two of them? She couldn't remember. But she knew she was immensely enjoying the moment, and that it wouldn't last.

Gavin stopped when they neared Bethesda Fountain. "So, what did Jenks say to you when you had me put the dessert platters in the car?"

Liz smiled, knowing he would ask her that question. She pointed to one of the rock formations that were scattered throughout the park. "Let's go sit up there."

When they were situated high up on the precipice, she looked over the terrain. Certain they wouldn't be overheard, she said, "Jenks told me he would not order his men to defend our territory but would ask for volunteers and text me how many men he'd lend us."

Gavin removed his sunshades. "He's confident some will actually step up?"

"Jenks said he would make it worth their while."

He leaned back so his face could absorb the sun's rays. "But he, personally, won't help?"

"No, he said it's better his presence isn't noticed."

"Being careful."

"Yes, he is."

Gavin stroked her hand. "Speaking of being careful, what do you think of the idea of asking Grams and Casey to leave town for a while?"

"I already have. Grams is going to take Casey down to Virginia and stay with relatives for a while. Until I call and tell her it's safe to return."

"Good. That was weighing heavy on me. I think that's the right thing to do."

"I'm reasonably sure even someone like Renworth wouldn't go after children. But I'm not taking any chances, not after what was done to Dan. I'm also having Sam track down Dan's girlfriend Lisa, see if he can get a bead on her. If she checks out, Sam will offer assistance."

She no sooner uttered her words when Max strode up to where they were sitting. "Hi. How are you guys doing?"

"We're fine." Liz motioned for Max to sit beside them. "What's up with you?"

Maintaining her Peter Pan pose with her legs positioned apart and her hands on her hips, Max said, "Dr. Farraday okayed Dan's body for transport back to California. Drew said he wanted his brother to have a proper burial, one that his family could attend, so he's flying back."

Liz nodded. She'd expected as much. "Is Sasha going with him?"

"No." Max exhaled. "Drew said it wasn't a good time for her to meet his parents and to wait for better circumstances."

"I can understand that, but still, I don't like the idea of him going alone."

"He's not alone. Granger didn't like the idea of him flying solo, so he decided to go with him. Their flight left this afternoon."

Liz was grateful for that. Granger had endured enough by the Red Claw attack.

"When Cyrus heard what they were planning, he volunteered to pay all transportation costs. Said he recently got a bonus at work and that he could afford it. He even took care of Dr. Farraday's fees."

Mildly surprised, Liz was grateful for Cyrus' initiative. If he hadn't settled all finances, she would have. "Where is my alpha, now?"

"He's helping Lawe in the restaurant."

"Anything else I should be aware of?"

Max gazed out at their surroundings. "Not really, I just thought you should know."

"Thank you for telling me."

Max nodded. "If you need me for anything, I'll be down at the bar."

"Go. Enjoy what's left of the afternoon."

Liz watched as Max scurried away. "I don't want Max or Sasha around when the fighting starts."

Gavin looked over his shoulder. "Max can handle herself. That girl has moves, despite her short stature."

"I know, but she's young, too young."

"I can order her to stay inside Werehaven, but knowing her personality, she'll defy my mandate and sneak out. Better if I put her somewhere where she'll be reasonably safe."

Liz raised a brow. "And Sasha?" That girl was one of the most feminine women Liz had ever met and had suffered miserably when she'd been a Red Claw for being the weakest in the pack.

"I planned on having her in the communications room. I don't want to think what the Red Claws would do to her. Anyone who leaves their pack to join another is seen as a traitor. They would be merciless."

"Good, I want her as far away from the battle as possible. Make sure you tell her it's a directive."

"I will." Gavin laced his hands behind his head and reclined back. "Were you surprised by Cyrus' actions?"

"Not really. Despite what people think, he's a good man."

"A little rough at times."

"Because he needs to be." She glanced down at him. "You never really warmed up to him, did you?"

"Do you blame me?"

No, she couldn't. She knew Gavin was still sore at having been made beta after so long as her alpha but had thought those feelings would abate over time. "I had hoped you two would learn to get along better."

"We tolerate each other. That's about as much as you can expect."

Before she could respond, Brent and Quint approached. She gestured for them to join her and Gavin. "What's new, guys?"

"I was just going to ask you that." Brent sat across from them.

Liz folded her arms over her knees. "We may have snagged an unexpected ally. Met with Derrick Jenkins of the Dark Moon Clan. He may be lending us a few men."

Quint shrugged. "We'll take who we can get, but more would have been better."

Brent asked, "Did he say how many?"

"He'll let us know."

"It's going to be the full moon in a couple of days." Brent rubbed his jaw. "Do either of you think Renworth will attack, then?"

Liz glanced at Gavin. "Under different circumstance and with anyone else but Renworth, I'd say no. But the Red Claw King has no regard for anything sacred. The Lunar Run has always been one of our most revered traditions, the same in all clans. The Red Claws should run along the paths near the Hudson River as they usually do, but expect the unexpected."

Brent sighed. "If he attacks in wolf form, it will be much worse."

Gavin said, "I can't see him leading a wolf pack through Manhattan's West Side. Humans would lose their shit. If he does attack, he'll haul his men in vans or moving trucks."

"I agree." From the look on Brent's face, she surmised he wanted to discuss something with Gavin. Liz looked Quint's way. "Would you escort me down to the restaurant? I want to see how Lawe's doing."

"My pleasure."

Gavin watched as Quint took Liz's hand and led her down the boulder.

Brent seemed to be studying him. "Is everything all right?"

"No." Gavin resumed basking in the sun.

"I thought you and Liz were..."

"A work in progress."

"But better than it's been?"

Gavin shaded his eyes. "Since when have you been interested in my love life?"

Brent smirked. "I'm not. But I always thought you and our queen made an awesome couple. I enjoyed serving you and her before..."

That got Gavin's attention. "Before?"

"Before the White Wolf made an appearance in our humble clan."

Gavin muttered, "That makes two of us."

"But you are back with her?"

One of his best lieutenants, Brent was loyal to him and was just trying to be a friend, but the subject matter still grated. Gavin raised up on one elbow. "What's your thought about Cyrus? And don't bullshit me."

Brent brought his knees up and circled them with his arms much the way Liz had. "I don't like him."

Gavin felt vindicated in his feelings about the alpha, until Brent said, "But he is a good commander. Precise, direct, and ambitious."

The words were out of Gavin's mouth before he could stop them. "And I'm not?"

If Brent were trying to conceal his grin, he'd failed in the attempt. "You are, by far, a more desirable male."

Now, it was Gavin's turn to smile. "Really?" The two of them were comfortable enough in their sexuality to be able to jest every now and then. They'd traded innuendos many times over the years.

As if reading his mind, Brent said, "I mean that in the best possible way." He looked in the direction Liz and Quint had gone. "And I believe our queen shares that opinion."

Gavin was beginning to believe that, and it was that belief that had him asking, "You didn't come up here to discuss my relationship, so what's on your mind?"

"I've been perusing some old texts on battle strategies. Do you remember according to *The Art of War,* what the first principle was?"

He knew that book well. It had been a favorite of Remare's. "Deception."

"Precisely. I don't believe Renworth will telegraph his intentions. He'll attack when and where he thinks we least suspect him."

"According to the 'Military Calculus', it's vital to know any and everything that could occur and plan for it. Speaking of which, have you heard any more from your spy in Renworth's clan?"

Brent nodded. "Renworth is keeping his plans to himself. He has this model of Central Park that he's become obsessed with, studies it daily, but has not given his commanders any set date for an attack."

"Is your spy safe?"

"He believes so but relays tensions run high in Castle Renworth. His men have been prepped as well as ours."

"I know."

"One of the best things any war commander can have is unity. Our people are united behind you and Liz. And Cyrus.

The tension between you two has been noted. I think that unity would be stronger if they believed you two shared a common goal."

"We do."

"Then make it apparent. Our people have always revered you. They respect Cyrus, but they don't have the level of trust for him that they do for you."

"I understand." And he did. Division among the ranks was never a good thing. "I'll try harder to keep my personal feelings under better control."

"Good. Now, I'll go see where Quint has disappeared to."

As Brent descended, Gavin regarded him. There always something different, something otherworldly about him Gavin could never put his finger on. Those startling blue eyes that turned a darker shade of gray whenever he was thinking too intently.

But Brent had always been trustworthy, despite never giving up his spy's name, something that still bugged Gavin. He shrugged. Probably best, he thought. He could understand the dangerous position the agent was in and what would happen if his identity was ever discovered.

Gavin made his way down to the restaurant. He wanted to confer with Lawe. And see where his queen had taken off to.

And if she was still alone.

Chapter Twenty-Three

It was already dark out when Liz heard someone knocking at her door. Reclining on her sofa, she turned to see Gavin entering and locking the door behind him. Ever since she'd spent the night at his place, her body reacted sensuously whenever they were in close proximity. Besides the clusters of butterflies taking flight in her lower belly, her skin became clammy, and her heart thudded loudly in her chest.

She wanted to blame it on the upcoming full moon, but that would be a lie. All those emotions, all those needs she'd buried long ago, were, once again, clawing at the forefront of her reality. What was now awakened refused to sleep, or even nap.

A force to be reckoned with, he leaned sinuously back against the door and seemed to be regarding her with a profundity she'd never seen before. "I just came from meeting with Cyrus."

Bending one knee, she lifted one foot to lay it on the coffee table. "And?"

"I appreciate him paying for the transport for Drew and Granger. But I want to pay for the casket and burial. I think it's the least I can do."

"I believe, as queen, the Black Star Clan should cover all funeral expenses. I've already sent a sympathy card to his family and will order wreaths of flowers to be sent once we know what the final arrangements are."

He continued staring at her, and she used this opportunity to really study him. Those damned whiskey-colored eyes of his always held her prisoner within their depths. Finely chiseled cheekbones, full lips that felt like soft petals whenever he brushed them against her skin. And that reddish-brown hair that grew so fast he let it grow long in the back. She loved running her fingers through those thick, luscious waves.

Liz couldn't remember ever meeting any male who was more handsome, more desirable, but his appeal was so much more than that. His emotions ran deep, like hers. Gavin was a man of passions—for life, laughter, and especially for her. For so long, he'd sealed part of himself away because of her. She now realized she was the key to his lock, the cause of so much pain, so much suffering. Her denial of him had sentenced him to a hell he never deserved.

"Fine, but I, personally, want to pay for his coffin." He stepped in her direction. "I don't want the clan to pay for that."

She rose to meet him and was aware of how his eyes traveled over her like a lover's caress. His need was a visceral thing, so strong, so resolute. It was as if the attraction between them intensified in its palpability. She pushed his hair behind his ear. "As you wish. We'll handle it, together."

His hands stroked up her arms, his thumbs massaging her biceps. "I'm staying here tonight."

"Oh, yes." Her lips skimmed seductively over his. "All. Night. Long."

Then, she crushed her mouth to his as his arms slid around her and pulled her tightly against him. *Yes, this is what I need, what we both need.* Somehow, with their bodies wrapped around one another, she felt as if she absorbed his strength, his warmth, and all that was good about him. She kissed him with a fervor she wasn't sure she'd ever thought possible. Lips, teeth, and tongues rubbed together, arousing, demanding more.

Gavin tore his mouth away to lift her up in his arms and carried her to the bedroom, using his foot to slam the door shut. He tossed her on the bed, his face taut with heated desire. Gavin was a man who would not be denied. She was his, and he looked as if he planned to brand her that in every way possible.

He reached down to peel his shirt over his head and tossed it aside. How she loved his masculine chest with the smattering of hair and well-defined muscles.

As he undid his belt, she ran her hands up past her ribs to cup her breasts, knowing he needed no teasing tonight, no seduction. Words weren't even necessary. They knew who they were, knew each other better than anyone else ever would.

A growl tore from his throat. "Get naked."

She shed her shirt and then her bra, her eyes never leaving his. As he stood gloriously naked before her, she wanted to taste every inch of him. Run her tongue over his abs to his pecs, drive him wild with lust. Laying back down, she lifted up and removed her jeans and thong. Their scents of arousal perfumed the air. She lifted up on her elbows, enamored of his physique, how toned he was. "Perfect."

"Yes, you are. You always were." That was all the warning he gave as he prowled up the bed to cover her with his body. Holding himself above her, he fused their lips together in a kiss that had her head spinning. She wanted to maintain control tonight but knew it would be impossible. Gavin wanted her complete surrender, and there was no way she would deny him. Not ever again.

When she tried to reverse their positions, he fought for dominance. She may be a queen to the clan, but in this bedroom, he was her king, and it felt so damn wonderful to just let go, let someone else take charge. She slid her hands around his neck and down his back, raking her nails along his flesh.

The snarl that broke from him sounded like a pissed off lion, but Gavin wasn't irate. He was as turned on as she was and nuzzled her neck, taking tiny bites along the way. He sucked her lobe into his mouth, a move he knew drove her insane. When he finally lowered his body against hers, he rubbed his erection between her thighs, making her hotter than she already was.

She felt drunk on the passion he was building in her. How she loved his larger body possessing hers, proving how deep his desires were. Gavin had always been a spectacular lover, experienced enough to take his time to make love with flawless expertise, make her reach heights she'd never imagined, make her want him as much as he wanted her.

Her breaths became ragged as the hunger increased. Grateful, so damned grateful for him, that she had him in her life, her bed. He was a part of her very fiber, part of her soul. He already owned her heart; he had since the day they met. But it was times like this when she felt she wasn't alone in the universe, that there was someone else who could ride through the cosmos beside her.

"Gavin," she uttered his name as if it were a prayer.

His gaze caught hers as he slipped his hand down to massage her inner thigh. She knew what he was asking, but she didn't need foreplay tonight. She needed him. She shook her head as her eyes began to close. "I need you inside me."

Gavin's lips curled up on one side. "That's the plan." His palm slid to her core, and his touch made her feel as if she was on fire. As he stroked her most delicate flesh, she arched her hips up, wanting more of his touch. Her skin became coated in a fine layer of perspiration, just as his was.

She wrapped her fingers around him and caressed his cock, so thick, so vibrant in her hand, and reveled in the way he threw his head back, his pleasure evident in the way he ground his teeth together. "Now, Gavin, now."

His lips met hers as his tongue leisurely explored her mouth. He wanted to make this last; no rushing like the last time they'd been together. No, tonight, they both wanted to savor the moment, memorize the way they felt, bask in the rapture of their mating.

He spread her knees farther apart and lined his cock up with her entrance, careful to coat her with more of his pre-cum to make sure she was ready for him. She was. She'd been ready from the moment he first stepped foot in her apartment.

As he slid inside her, one delicious inch at a time, Liz thought she saw stars. He smiled down at her, as if he knew exactly the effect he was having. It was all male, all possessive. In that moment, he owned her; she was his, totally and completely. There was nothing she wouldn't do for him.

He bent down and brushed his lips over hers. "Mine."

"Oh, yeah, mine, too." She moved her hips up to take more of him inside, their thrusts in perfect sync. And she knew, somehow, she'd get these feelings down on paper, compose the song that had been burrowing in her heart. So caught up in the ecstasy, she couldn't voice all the things she wanted to tell him, but she could do it through her music, and she would. He was hers and always would be.

When the intensity between them had them both on the fine edge of completion, so very close, they existed in a place removed from the world they knew. It was electric; it was heavenly. She stared into those gorgeous eyes of his, and a tear escaped her. Emotions were flooding her: hunger, desire, and the soul-searing need to claim what was theirs.

He must have been feeling the same because he sped up his movements. She could feel him growing thicker inside her, sending sensations that had her soaring to new heights of pleasure. A drop of sweat fell from his face onto hers. She wanted to lick at it, but it slid down the side of her face. Suddenly, the room felt like a blazing inferno, so intensely hot the world faded from view, and there was only Gavin, her lover, her mate.

When they came, their roars reverberated off the walls. The muscles strained in his neck as he clamped his jaws together. He was never more beautiful than in that moment. Then, he crashed down on her, but she didn't mind his weight, knowing he was too swollen inside to slip free. And she wanted to hold him close to her, not ready to let go, not just yet.

Just one more moment.

Time drifted, and she had no idea how many minutes passed before he pulled away and rolled off her. He tugged her to his side, and she knew sleep would soon claim her. Exhaustion clawed at her, and not just from their lovemaking. Her mind was whirling with all that had taken place in the last few days. Not tonight, she thought. Tonight, she would find solace in the arms of the only lover who had ever made her feel safe, feel alive.

She was dreaming; she knew it because the otherworldly landscape was unlike anything she'd ever seen before. It was snowing, a winter wonderland, and everything around her was white, including the birch tree with an owl perched high up on the branch. Even her clothes were white, a color she hardly ever wore. Long, gossamer skirts trailed in the snow, and she was barefoot. Why was she barefoot in the snow? And yet, she wasn't cold. It made no sense.

As she walked silently in the woods, an inexplicable mist greeted her; it felt like she was walking on clouds, so very peaceful, so very quiet. When she emerged into the clearing, the warmth of the sun caressed her face and beckoned that she continue on her path.

Up ahead, she saw an ice structure that seemed to summon her. The light shone brightly on it, illuminating the shiny surface. Drawn to the enigmatic edifice, she walked toward it. When she reached the ice wall, she brushed the snow away from the facade and was immediately met with a powerful surge of energy, an intensity she'd never felt before. She kept her hand on the ice until a figure seemed to manifest on the other side. Cloudy swirls of light appeared, shimmered, and then, slowly, ever so slowly, a face materialized.

Her hair was made of a thousand shards of iridescent crystals; her face paler than Liz had ever seen it. The woman was smiling, waving to her. Liz was captivated by the serenity radiating from her, an expression she'd rarely seen in anyone. Her heart pounding in joy, Lizandra returned the gesture, overcome with gladness to finally see the one she'd shared so much with, the one she laughed and cried with, missed so very dearly, her friend, Miranda.

Liz quickly looked for a door to open to let her out, searched all sides of the exterior that seemed to stretch out to eternity, but despaired when she discovered there was none.

When Liz gazed back at her, Miranda's visage seemed to emanate a profound sadness, a bittersweet goodbye, and the wave hello from before, now seemed to be a final farewell. "No!" Liz shouted. "Wait, please wait!" But the figure slowly dissipated, and abruptly, Liz woke, shaken, her body cold to the touch.

"What is it?" Soothingly, Gavin stroked her arms. "You look like you've seen a ghost. Your skin feels like ice."

Still riveted, Liz clasped his biceps and, when she could speak, said, "I dreamed I saw Miranda. Oh God, Gavin. I think she's dead. She waved to me. At first, I thought she was saying hello, but the look on her face... Oh God, my God, she seemed ethereal, not of this plane of existence. I think she was saying goodbye, forever." Liz's body was wracked by tremors of sorrow. "It terrified me."

He held her tightly to his side, his heated flesh a soothing balm. "You just miss her, that's all. Too much has been going on." His voice was gravelly with sleep. "It was just a dream, just a dream. You said it yourself—she'll return when we least expect it. When she's ready. Sleep, now."

Oh God, she hoped so. Chilled to the bone, Liz settled more securely into his side, clinging to the warmth she seemed to have lost. That had to be one of the eeriest dreams she ever had. She sighed. Gavin was right, it was just a dream, but she couldn't help but think it was some sort of a portent. And, a dangerous one at that.

Please let Miranda be all right, Liz prayed as she was lulled by the cadence of Gavin's breaths, and soon sleep, once again, overtook her.

Gavin woke with a pain over his right eye. When he rubbed it, he found a slight swelling. "I think you elbowed me sometime in the night."

Liz was wearing her robe and pacing. "I hit you with the clock."

Shocked, Gavin asked, "Why, for God's sake?"

"You were moaning Miranda's name in your sleep."

Offended, Gavin scoffed. "I was not!"

"Yes, you were and loudly, as if she were stroking your dick."

He shook his head, not sure he was hearing her correctly. "You must be joking."

"No, I'm not. You had sex with her, didn't you?"

"With Miranda? Never. What's gotten into you?"

"You. I never knew you had the hots for her."

"I don't." He tried to shake off the last vestiges of sleep. "Listen, Liz, if I mentioned her name in my sleep, which I still don't remember, it's because you woke me in the middle of the night with your nightmare about her."

"Hmmp." She stopped pacing and faced him. "Just tell me the truth. I'm not mad; I just want to know. Did you sleep with her?"

"What?" He couldn't believe they were having this conversation. "She's Remare's wife. Why would I sleep with one of my best friends' wives?"

"You tell me."

Anger started to build in his gut. "I wouldn't."

"Not ever?"

"Never."

"What about the time she visited here and you drove her home? You never came back that night."

Amazed she would even question him about this matter, he said, "I slept on her couch. She slept on the other. All we did was talk."

Her nails dug into her hips. "And, when you were in Japan with her? You told me you were going to be Valadon's bodyguard, but somehow, you wound up sleeping in her hotel room."

"I did go as Valadon's bodyguard. When we got to Tokyo, he assigned me to Miranda, as Orion and Bas were already there. When we got to Sapporo, we checked into a hotel suite. She had her own room, and I had mine. Nothing went on, I swear it. You know she only has eyes for Remare." He watched as she avoided his gaze. *Why is she bringing this up, now?* "And you, did you ever sleep with Remare?"

She resumed her pacing. "If I did, it was before I met you."

"If? *If?*" He was stunned. They'd known each other for years, and she'd never mentioned it. "When exactly was that? We knew each other for the better part of a decade."

"Long ago. When I was a young queen. I knew I needed allies, and becoming...acquainted with the vampire king seemed like a good idea."

"Acquainted? Is that what they're calling it, now?" He got up and drew on his pants. "Did you fuck Valadon, too?"

She rolled her eyes at him. "No, but I might have. When I requested a meet and greet, he sent Remare here to solidify our good will. It only happened once. I'm sure he's forgotten it by now."

"Really? Does Miranda know?"

"No. I saw no reason to tell her, and I expect you not to, as well." She glared his way. "I'm not sure why you're getting so upset. It was before we became involved. I'm sure you had your share of lovers back then, as well."

Gavin rubbed a hand through his hair. He hadn't slept well last night. After Liz had her nightmare, she'd tossed and turned all night, so had he. "Can we drop this, now?"

"Certainly."

Something else that had been on his mind, for some time now, surfaced. "When are you going to reinstate me as alpha?"

"What?" She seemed genuinely surprised, as if it were the last thing she expected.

"C'mon, Liz. I'm sick of being beta. Either we're together or we're not. If we are going to resume our former relationship, I want to work beside you, not behind you. I want to be alpha, again."

She stared at him for a moment. "I'm not sure now's the best time to discuss this."

"Will there ever come a good time?"

"We're on the brink of war with the Red Claws," her voice heightened, "and you ask me this, now?"

His voice was louder than he intended. "I was your alpha for years; I protected the clan and you. That hasn't changed."

Her eyes narrowed. "Cyrus wanted to be with me. He did everything he could to impress me, earn my love and respect. That's why he undertook so many ventures in the park. He knows I'll never be his. He's already lost me; I can't take away his status, too."

Gavin returned her stare. He was surprised just how raw his emotions were, but these were issues that had been brewing for years, issues he'd kept buried because the clan was vital to him. Just hearing Cyrus' name irked him, set him off. "But you could do it to me. Humiliate me in front of the entire clan. That, you could do."

"I didn't humiliate you. You are the second highest ranked male in the Black Stars." She cupped his cheek. "And, you have me."

He circled her wrist and pulled her hand away. "And, you have Cyrus."

She stepped back from him. "We need him, Gavin. This war is about to get ugly; Cyrus is crucial to our success."

His stomach roiled the more she spoke Cyrus' name. "And I'm not? Yes, Cyrus is strong and larger than any other Were, but who learned strategies and tactics, who's been at your side far longer, who's trained our people to be at their best?"

"Don't put this on me, Gavin, not now."

"It's time for you to make some hard decisions, Lizandra. You want me in your bed? Then, elevate me."

Her temper flared. "Don't give me ultimatums, Gavin. I'm still your queen."

Before he said or did something he'd regret, he grabbed his shirt and reached for the door. Turning back to her, he growled, "Then, act like one."

Chapter Twenty-Four

Gavin unlocked the door to his apartment and was halfway up the stairs to his bedroom when he heard someone knocking. After his gut-wrenching argument with Lizandra, the last thing he wanted was company. *Not really in the mood for socializing.* What he needed was a couple of hours of peace and quiet, maybe even some sleep, which he, obviously, needed since he didn't get much last night.

He rubbed the back of his neck. God, last night had been incredibly sensual. The connection between them powerful. Just like it had been when he and Liz were a couple. He could still feel her hands along his back, her nails lightly abrading his skin while he'd been inside her. Magical, that's what it had felt like, at least that's what it had been for him.

Gavin shook his head. He'd been so sure she'd shared the same passion, the same need. He groaned at the depth of their desires—something a man could drown in. He'd been certain she would have elevated him to her alpha. Boy, had he been wrong.

The knocking started up, again, louder this time. *Geez, buddy, can't you take a hint?* Afraid the person wouldn't leave, he reversed direction and went to open the door, thinking it might be some sort of delivery. Not for him, he hadn't ordered anything, but maybe his housemates, Max or Sasha, had.

He was shocked to find who was standing there.

"Well, hello there, handsome, going to invite me in?"

"Alexa Cantrell." He crossed his arms over his chest and leaned against the doorframe. "What ever would bring you to my doorstep?"

Dressed to kill in one of her power suits that hugged every curve, she smiled flirtatiously. "I thought you might want to have lunch with me."

His stomach took that moment to growl. Figures, he was starving, having missed breakfast because he'd woken up later than usual. "Now, why would I want to do that?"

Alexa chuckled. "Because you missed me as much as I did you."

"What have you been smoking?"

She laughed, again. "Nothing ominous, I assure you. C'mon, Gavin. We met for a drink, and no harm was done. Just lunch, I promise. My treat, what do you have to lose?"

He casually peered down the block both ways to see if she was alone. "My neck. Does your boss know you're here?"

"I don't share everything I do with him, especially things concerning my private life."

Gavin sized her up. "How did you even know where I lived?"

"Seriously. You think there's anyone we couldn't find info on if we looked deep enough?"

Right. Stupid on his part to even ask. His stomach rumbled louder.

"I'd say you're hungry. Wish it was for me, but since we both know that's not true, and isn't that a pity?" Her smile grew larger. "May I suggest that cute little Mediterranean place I saw up the block?"

Oh, hell, no, he was not going somewhere where she might have others of her pack waiting for him. "Your treat, huh?"

"Yes, anywhere you want."

He couldn't imagine what they might have to say one another. But there was one thing he wanted to know, and if she was feeling chatty, it might be worth his while. "You have one hour. Let me grab my jacket."

Once seated at a café the university students frequented, he chose the booth by the large windows so he could keep an eye out. He scrutinized the place and felt reasonably safe with the heavy foot traffic of people going in and out. After placing their orders, he relaxed back into his chair and considered Cantrell. "Okay, I'll bite, want to tell me what I did to warrant your attention?"

She sipped her drink then placed the glass down. "The last time we spoke you were irate with me."

"One of my men was killed."

She leaned forward and kept her voice low. "Which I had nothing to do with. I tried to reach you a couple of times, but you refused my calls."

"Do you blame me?"

"No, I don't. Renworth can be...unpredictable, ruthless. But I thought, if we talked, we might find a way to mend some fences. Call a truce, maybe."

Gavin thought that highly unlikely as the waitress served him his cheeseburger and Alexa her Caesar salad.

"Will there be anything else?"

After shaking their heads, the waitress left to attend to her other customers. Cantrell moved her food around with her fork. "Thank you for meeting with me." She covered his hand with hers. "I am sorry for the loss of your man. But you realize we lost one of ours, too."

"Oh, really?" Gavin bit into his burger.

She seemed to be studying him. "You didn't know?"

"Know what?"

"One of our younger members, Robin, met with an unfortunate accident, tripped and fell down a flight of stairs. Broke his neck in the process, died instantly." Her eyes met his. "Same one that tangled with one of your guys and...allegedly was photographing certain members of your clan."

Gavin stopped eating. "What?"

"No one believes a Were could be that clumsy," she bit into her salad, "but the timing is somewhat suspicious, don't you think?"

"If you're implying one of my people took vengeance into his own hands, you're dead wrong."

She shrugged. "I guess we'll never know since there were no witnesses. In any event, it's over, now. I was hoping we could discuss ways of opening channels of communication between our clans. Perhaps a way to garner understanding, promote goodwill."

"How do you propose we do that?"

Her eyes glinted. "You kill Renworth and make me queen. I'll make you my alpha."

Gavin nearly sputtered his water. "Nice pipedream you have there; any other fantasies you want to share with me?"

Grinning, she licked her lips suggestively and moved in closer. "Oh, I think I can come up with one or two."

"Stop." He raised his palm. "Don't even go there."

She chuckled and leaned back. "You asked."

Gavin sipped his water. Alexa seemed determined to at least make an effort at improving relations between the clans, but whatever her endgame was, was anyone's guess. He took another bite of his burger, chewed, and swallowed. "I want to know one thing."

"You can ask me anything, Gavin."

But will you tell me the truth? "Who's Bali?"

Her eyes widened in surprise. "Excuse me?"

"One of your Red Claws. I believe she's a woman, the one who killed Danny."

Alexa looked down and had the grace to look repentant. "Bali Malahani."

"Sounds Polynesian."

"She is. I never liked her much."

"Why's that?"

Alexa peered out the window and stayed quiet a moment, then said. "Her scent. Something's off about it. I was never quite sure about it." She huffed. "Never quite sure about her being a her."

That was similar to what Dan had said. "Why do you say that?"

"Most women have a care about their appearance, care about something. I never got that sense with her. She's both masculine and feminine, like she can flip a switch and be either."

"That's strange."

"It is. Anyway, a couple of years ago, Bali showed up on our lands, asking to become a member of our clan."

"And?"

"Renworth took one look at her diminutive size and dismissed her. Before he had her thrown out, Bali told him she could beat any of his warriors. Edgar laughed at that, said it was impossible, but if she wanted to provide the night's entertainment, she was welcome to try."

"What happened?"

"She kicked major ass. Renworth and the others thought Bali wouldn't last two minutes. She downed the first two fighters he put in the ring with her. She moves incredibly fast, like a cobra, shows no emotion. They started calling her Ladycobra."

And that was the reason he agreed to have lunch with Cantrell. "Can you describe her?"

"Gavin, if war does happen between our clans, avoid her at all costs. She's lethal."

"Aren't all members of the Red Claws?"

"No, some are worse than others."

"What does she look like?"

Cantrell shrugged. "She's short. Large eyes, dark. Keeps her hair buzz-cut short. Doesn't wear much makeup, except for purple lipstick. She has gymnast-type moves. Very flexible, likes showing off her backflips."

In truth, Gavin hadn't expected Cantrell to be this forthcoming. As soon as he got home, he would download everything he could find on Malahani. "If Renworth knew you were sharing information with an enemy, it wouldn't go well for you."

"My personal life is my own, and...like I said before, I missed you. You're like a refreshing breath of air. I wish you could trust me, but I know you don't. At least not yet."

"And that doesn't bother you?"

"Trust is earned, not easily given." She twirled a strand of hair around her fingers. "All right, I told you about one of mine, tell me about one of yours."

He wondered what she was really after. "Who?"

"That adorable blond lawyer of yours, the one we met at Bryant Park, Quint."

"Adorable, huh? Sister, if you have any designs on him, you're wasting your time. He bats for the other team."

"I suspected as much." She grinned. "He's too beautiful to be straight."

"You don't look disappointed."

"I'm not." She shrugged. "I'm more interested in the one in front of me." Her gaze traveled all over him. "He intrigues me, and I like the way he speaks, the sound of his voice."

"Don't be so interested, Alexa." Gavin gulped down some water. "He'll only disappoint you."

"Maybe," she wiped her mouth on her napkin, "maybe not." She winked his way. "All good things in time."

If only that were true. When she lifted her water, he tapped his glass to hers. "I'll drink to that."

***

Renworth looked over the latest batches of reports and sighed. Death, he could deal with. Robin had been a loyal pack member; his death was unfortunate, but Renworth didn't believe for a minute he'd had an accident and had fallen down a flight of stairs in his apartment building after slipping on someone's spilled coffee.

Weres had incredible balance, much more than that of humans. And Robin's reflexes were solid. No, Renworth deduced as he swiveled behind his desk, he'd had a little help. Retribution for that young blond Black Star who had died.

As much as he regretted Robin's untimely death, he accepted it. In war, there were always losses. But what he couldn't accept was betrayal. Someone in his organization had betrayed him. Had given classified information to the Black Star Clan. And that he would not forgive.

"You sent for me?" His second, Victor, entered his home office, escorted by two of Renworth's strongest men. Best to have his guards present if any unpleasant business ensued.

Over the years, he'd trusted Victor the most. Oh, how it grated that one of his own, one he felt closest to, would deceive him so dramatically. "Yes, I wanted to speak to you, in person."

Victor tilted his head as if to say, "And?"

"It seems we have a traitor in our ranks."

Appropriate anger marred Gren's handsome face, his face taut with stress lines. "Who?"

Renworth kept his gaze on him. "One, I've trusted for some time, one I've had complete trust in, until now."

Victor's eyes narrowed as if he were trying to comprehend what Renworth was thinking, and more than likely, sensing his restrained rage.

"I'm surprised you haven't figured it out by now. You're usually good at staying on top of things." Renworth waited a moment then pushed the damning photos his way, the truth obvious about who had been meeting clandestinely with a prime member of the Black Stars.

Victor licked his lips then perused the images and sighed, his shoulders visibly lowering. "What are you going to do about it?"

Renworth grinned. "You show no hint of surprise. Aren't you curious about what first piqued my interest?"

"I'm sure you had your reasons."

"I did. Phone calls from my wing. There are only a few who have access to my private offices, and fewer who have the passwords to use my computers."

Again, Victor cocked his head in question.

"You've been careless, my friend. This happened on your watch."

"If it had been I who betrayed you, you would never have discovered my duplicity."

"Think so?" He considered the reasons why Gren might possibly sell him out, but his second showed no reasons for disloyalty, no weakness for either gain or passion for another. Unlike his traitor, who was known for indulgences.

"I was in the middle of an important conference call." Cantrell entered and seemed pissed that her work had been interrupted by being summoned. Even if it was for an audience with her king. She looked wantonly beautiful, as was her usual. Teal suit, hair and makeup perfectly administered. Nails painted red. She'd been fantastic in bed, as he was sure a member of the Black Stars now knew firsthand.

"Have a seat, Alexa. This won't take long."

She glanced between Victor, who stood with his arms crossed over his chest, and Renworth. "I hope not. I have a desk loaded with work that needs my attention."

He pushed the photos to her. "Have a gander."

She glanced briefly at them then rolled her eyes and affected a bored pose. "So what? I told you I was going to have a bit of fun with him when we left Bryant Park."

He saw what she'd refused to acknowledge. The heat reflected in her eyes was more than just fun. Alexa had the look of a woman who was infatuated. "It appears you've been indulging yourself. Do you know what this says to me?"

She met his stare dead on. "What?"

"You desire that Were, lust for him, and now, you've stupidly made yourself vulnerable."

She tried to brush it off. "No way, he's nothing to me."

His eyes sharpened in his scrutiny of her. He'd always prided himself in being able to assess the strengths and weaknesses of others. Alexa was no different. "I've monitored your phone calls," he waited a beat, then added, "and your emails." What he didn't tell her was that he'd listened to a tape of her conversation, the one where she was conspiring to have him killed.

Outraged, she stood, forgetting for the moment whose presence she was in. "Why? I've done nothing wrong."

"How many times have you met with him?"

Her voice heightened. "Once or twice, what difference does it make?"

"What did you tell him about our planned offensive?"

"Nothing! I did not betray you. Gavin means nothing to me; he's just a mark."

It was her duplicitous scent that gave her away. Did she forget he could smell a lie?

"You have to listen to me." Her eyes were now panicked. "I did nothing wrong. Ask Victor, he knows I was just playing Gavin when I met him at the Plaza."

Now, it was Renworth's chance to rise and loom over her as indignation laced his voice. "You're sleeping with him?"

"No." She turned to his second. "Tell him, Victor."

"I know no such thing." He calmly uncrossed his arms.

Shock lit her eyes up, and she shouted, "You were there; you know the truth. Tell him."

Sympathy stirred then quickly vanished as Victor negated her demand. "I won't be a party to your lies."

When she growled and lunged at him with her claws, Victor quickly restrained her so that her back was to his front. His voice was menacing as he whispered, "Tell him the truth, Alexa. It will go badly for you if you don't confess, now."

When she tried to headbutt him then bite Victor's arm, Renworth signaled for his guards to take her. "If she likes to fight so much, throw her in the cage."

Real fear lanced her face as they took hold of her arms. "No, not that, please, Edgar, don't do this to me," she screamed as the guards led her away.

"I'd save her for the battle, but I'm not sure she wouldn't turn on one of our own." When Renworth glanced up at Victor, he said. "You'll be joining the fight."

"You've always kept me at your side during any kind of altercation."

"And so, I have, but you will fight for me." He pushed another photo across his desk. "When the battle begins, I want you to eliminate him."

Victor seemed surprised. "He's Lizandra's accountant, Brent. Why him?"

"Because he's the motherfucker who interrogated Robin and had him tortured. Robin told me so before his untimely demise." With that, he gestured for his second to leave, then added ominously, "One other thing, make sure he suffers."

Chapter Twenty-Five

The days leading up to the Lunar Run passed quickly. After arriving home from his lunch with Alexa, Gavin had downloaded all he could find on Bali Malahani. He asked Sasha to work with their tech guys to learn more and to have her picture circulated so everyone knew exactly who she was and what she had done. The next thing he did was call Lawe, explained why he met with Cantrell, and requested he inform Liz of all he learned.

That was two days ago, and still, Liz treated Gavin with disinterest. And that bugged him to no end. Apparently, their argument was still cause for hurt feelings. Liz didn't like being challenged, and his request to be alpha again, was, evidently, seen that way. The thought that he was good enough for her bed, but not good enough to rule the clan alongside her, aggravated the hell out of him. Perhaps it was time he made a peaceful overture.

The Weres were standing around The Cajun Grill socializing and waiting for the command from Liz to start the run. With the full moon shining brightly in the night sky, all the Weres were restless, wound up tight, their animals itching to be break free.

No one was expecting any acts of aggression from the Red Claws; tonight was the most sacred time for all Weres. A time when they celebrated their heritage, their wolfen natures. Even Renworth wouldn't have the audacity to attack during this time. But Gavin had no doubt it would be soon.

He inhaled deeply; there was something cloying in the air, something he didn't trust. He liked it better when the night's breezes blew, cooling off their heated bodies. Naturally warm-blooded, when they ran, they got even hotter, but with the full moon, the blood in their veins was like molten lava, and they needed the run to burn off the excess heat.

But the air was stagnant tonight, no winds ruffling the trees, not even a hint of a breeze. This whole summer had been more humid than usual, making people more irritable and short-tempered.

"She still not talking to you?" Lawe sauntered up to where Gavin was leaning against one of the trees.

"Only when she has to."

"And, here, I thought you two patched up whatever had gone wrong with your relationship."

"We see eye to eye on most things." He frowned. "Just not the important one."

Lawe's gaze shifted to the outside table where Liz was talking with Max and Tia. "Man, you should have seen her when I told her you met with Cantrell. Her eyes nearly popped out of her skull. She thought you had something going on with the Red Claw until I talked her down from that cliff."

"As if," Gavin scoffed. "It was a fishing expedition. I was only there for info gathering."

"I know, but females have a way of reaching different conclusions. That is, until they calm the fuck down and realize what's truth and what isn't."

Gavin rubbed his jaw. "What'd she say when you told her?"

"She thanked me kindly for relaying the info, then had a powwow with her girlfriends at that same table they're sitting at now. I went back to tending bar, but I'm pretty sure I heard your name mentioned a couple of times with some choice words you never hear a minister say while addressing his congregation."

"That mad, huh?"

"Oh, yeah. You're gonna have to do some smooth-ass talking, my friend, if you want back in her...good graces."

"Tell me the truth, Lawe. Do you think I should be alpha?"

"Slippery slope, *mi amigo*. Cyrus is bigger than you, and stronger. Most Weres only respect strength and size."

"Even with my training with the vamps of House Valadon?"

"Now, there's your trumping card. When it comes to know-how and trust, you got him beat by a mile."

"I can run this clan ten times better than he can." Gavin kept his simmering temper in check.

"No argument there from me, brother. Hell, you've got my vote." Lawe glanced back at their queen. "But I'm not the one you have to convince."

Gavin nodded. "I know. You think Cyrus would be satisfied being beta?"

"Men like him," Lawe shook his head, "they need the applause, the recognition. He'd fight you for it, if he thought you'd challenge him."

Gavin's spine straightened at Lawe's last words.

"Now, I *know* you're not considering something as foolhardy at that."

A smirk twisted his lips. "You did say I should convince her. What better way than proving to her I can take him."

Lawe's eyes widened in shock. "Have you lost your ever-loving mind?"

Before he could answer, Liz climbed atop one of the boulders to the side of the restaurant and called the clan to her. After everyone surrounded the queen, she addressed them. "The full moon is upon us. Tonight, we celebrate who we are, what we are." Shouts and applause greeted her. Everyone was stoked to begin the run, anxious for the relief it would provide. The excitement palpable all around them. She eyed them all, until her gaze fell on him. "Tonight, we unleash the animal within, take pride in our true natures. Tonight, we run."

More bellows of approval rang out, and she raised her hands in a majestic manner that silenced the clan. "Tonight, we will alter the course of the run. I'm in the mood for something different, something unpredictable. Cyrus?"

"Yes, my queen?" Cyrus ventured closer to her.

"I want you to take the northern sector. Lead your unit along the eastern trails near the Metropolitan Museum up toward the reservoir, pass it, circle round the Great Hill, then use the western trail and bring them back to Cleopatra's Needle."

"As you wish, so it shall be done." Cyrus smirked then winked up at her.

Gavin wanted to barf at his obsequious overtures. "Give me a fucking break," he muttered more to himself, but Lawe heard him and grinned.

"Gavin?"

He half expected her to call him her beta, reminding him of his place in the pack. "Yes, Lizandra?"

"Take your people south on the western trails passing Belvedere Castle, Bow Bridge, Strawberry Fields, and then round Bethesda Fountain. Wait for me there."

"I will." He raised his fist over his heart and nodded. After the silent treatment he'd received, that was the best she was getting from him.

"Tonight, I will lead the run farther south past Sheep Meadow, Wollman rink, to the carousel and around the zoo and up to the fountain. Everyone, go to your commanders. The run will commence when you hear my howl."

Gavin knew why she was doing this. In the off chance that Renworth did attack, he would choose the path of least resistance—the least populated area around the reservoir—

and that's why she sent Cyrus there. His unit was the largest with some of the strongest fighters.

She chose the path where the humans usually congregated the most. If war did occur, the Red Claws would not want blood to stain the ground and most likely avoid the area. Gavin's section was in the middle halfway between the two.

But there was another reason she chose to split up the clan. The message was clear to him as it was to everyone else. She was trying to assuage his injured pride, by reminding the clan, that there were three commanders, not two, and that he was as capable of leading as Cyrus.

He wondered if she specifically split them up because she'd overheard what he said to Lawe about challenging Cyrus and wanted to keep them apart.

Well, they'd just see about that.

***

Liz had had time to cool down, especially after talking with Max and Tia, who tried to get her to see things from Gavin's point of view. She had to remind them, a couple of times, she was queen, and her decisions final. It was Max who stated she was queen in all things, except in her relationship with Gavin, and if she truly loved him, she would understand where he was coming from.

"God save us all from male egos," she'd muttered. But Tia had heard her and said men's egos were a major part of who they were and reminded her that he'd loved her for years, and that kind of injury never really healed. That she had demeaned him in front of the whole clan by making him beta.

It was to protect him. Cyrus, because of his size, would attract all challengers and was strong enough to best any of them. But men had egos the size of Texas and felt the need to prove themselves. *Like I need this now.* Both Max and Tia had offered their support when they saw how conflicted and torn she'd been.

Couldn't Gavin be satisfied with their relationship? He had her, after such a long time apart, and they were finally together, united in all things, a couple. Why couldn't he just accept that? *Because that's not who Gavin is.* All right, she'd find a way of repairing the harm she caused. But not tonight.

Tonight is a time for celebration, and her skin was itching something awful. She regarded her people as they disrobed and began their transformations. Was there anything more beautiful in the world than watching how they morphed into the magnificent beasts they kept caged?

The moon's heat was pulling at her as she shed her clothes. Her black pelt began erupting from her skin, first her arms, then her torso and legs. Her nails became lethally long claws that scratched against the hard stone beneath her.

As she eyed the others, she noted how fluid the change was for the more mature members of the clan. How graceful, how glorious. The younger ones took longer, their snouts protruding slower, their shifting requiring more effort. God, she loved her people, all her people. Would fight to the death to keep them safe, protected. She'd do anything to make sure the clan endured.

Maya Angelou's poem, "Still I Rise", flashed before her— a symphony of resolve urging her on to meet what beckoned. No matter what, they would rise to any and all occasions.

Once transformed, the wolves howled, their music melodious, sounds only heard in nature. No human could ever understand the avowal, the affirmation of release of restraints, to free the creature who relied on instinct to survive. Primal, age old, the need to run free and be unfettered. This was what it meant to be truly alive. Pointing her snout at the moon, she howled loud and elegantly, a sonata of unleashed exhilaration.

The pack answered her herald with their own howls, and when she jumped down to lead her part of the pack south, they followed, loping along the trails, jumping over park benches and flowerbeds. The longer they ran, the more in tune with nature they became, their awareness sharpened, their senses heightened.

She could hear the cawing of the birds high up in the trees, smell the bouquets of the flowers. Her vision was more acute than ever, sighting the terrain of the meadow and the area that housed the carousel. Her muscles felt rejuvenated, her heart pounding loudly as she challenged herself to go faster and faster.

As they rounded the carousel, she stopped to regroup, allowing the slower members to catch up and take a breather. No one was ever left behind, not on her watch. Satisfied everyone was still with her, she continued toward the zoo. Instincts had the wolves howling to announce their presence. The seals barked their response, the polar bears growled loudly into the night, and the monkeys' shrieks rent the air. If she were in human form, she would have laughed at the pure joy of feeling alive.

When they passed the bandshell, she eyed the area and trotted slower to Bethesda Fountain. She must have outrun Gavin, because she got there first. She loved this part of the park and stood mesmerized at the angel on top of the fountain. During the day, this place was littered with tourists, but this part of the night, the fountain beckoned. There was something otherworldly about the night, something hauntingly beautiful in its peacefulness.

The other wolves came beside her and howled gloriously into the night. It was definitely magical. But where was Gavin? He should have been here by now.

Her answer came in the form of vicious growls and loud barks coming from the direction of Cleopatra's Needle. That's where Cyrus was supposed to be. She knew Weres this time of the month were restless, more high-strung than usual and the cause of many fights. She signaled for her pack to follow as she went to discover the source of the cacophony.

As soon as she made it to the clearing near the monument, she saw the reason for all the dissonance: two wolves were fighting—not unexpected. But what she hadn't expect to find were who those two wolves were as they circled one another with their fangs bared. The larger wolf had a white pelt, the other red.

From the streaks of blood on both, Cyrus and Gavin had been at it for a while. *Motherfuckers.*

Enraged, she morphed into her human form, intending to put a stop to this madness, when Lawe sidled up to her. He'd already changed so that he could speak to her. "I would let them fight."

"You would, would you? I don't have enough to deal with?" Heated anger made her voice rise. "This bullshit ends, now."

"Lizandra, you can't really be surprised, are you?"

She watched as Cyrus lunged with his claws extended, but Gavin was able to avoid being gutted. Cyrus was more powerful, but Gavin was faster. The snarls that reverberated around them revealed the bitter animosity between them. "Tell me the truth. Have they done this before?" She demanded, "Have they?"

"Not to my knowledge. But it's been festering for some time. Gavin's always kept his emotions in check, but tonight..." Lawe shook his head.

"What set him off?"

Lawe gave her a look as if she'd grown two heads. "You, of course."

"Me?"

He rolled his eyes. "Gavin's been in love with you since I can remember. Do you think it was easy for him watching you with Cyrus?"

"But I haven't been with him in…" Just then, the two wolves fought for dominance as one dragged the other under and they rolled. Gavin was on top, then Cyrus, and so it went. She knew both were stubborn mules, and neither would relent.

"Doesn't matter. He sees Cyrus as a rival. Felt he had something to prove."

She hissed, "He has nothing to prove."

"Apparently, he thought he did."

The fight became fiercer as Gavin tried to snap Cyrus' leg as Cyrus sank his fangs into Gavin's back. Enough, she thought. It was amazing one hadn't offered the other his neck in a show of submission, but neither would ever concede defeat. They were going to kill each other if she didn't end this.

Liz strode closer to them, certain neither would attack her. If one did, the other wolves would assail the aggressor.

She raised her hand for silence and was about to admonish both for fighting when more rumbles, louder, this time—came from the direction of Werehaven. It sounded like hundreds of wolves snarling and hissing. Then, the sounds became vociferous and seemed like thunder along the whole western side of the park.

"They're here," she growled. No need to specify who, everyone knew who had arrived. It was during the bloody full moon that Renworth decided to launch his offensive. *Sonofabitch!* No regard for the sanctity of their most sacred time. A time for celebration had, just now, been violated and turned into something ugly. He'd done the unexpected and waged war while they were at their most fierce. No mercy would be shown tonight.

The Red Claws were out to conquer.

The Black Stars would defend their territory to their last dying breath.

"Bring it on, you bastard." She turned to Gavin and Cyrus, still in wolf form, and issued her orders for the counter offensive. They'd been planning for this for some time. The son of a bitch wanted a war?

She'd give him a war he'd never forget.

Chapter Twenty-Six

Liz didn't get far when Brent, panting, ran up to her. "It's a recording, a ruse. We could see the speakers on surveillance. He's fucking with us. Renworth wants us to think he's attacking from the west, but his people are along the eastern perimeter. And, I suspect he's got people on the northern and southern borders. We just haven't seen them, yet."

"Who's in the tech room, now?" They had designated the tech area and adjacent conference room as war central with all the camera feeds reporting in. The large, clear, vertical board would highlight the advances and retreats of the packs. Besides all the monitors, they had models of Central Park's terrain laid out with miniature opposing armies.

"Kael, Mila, Jaxx, and Sasha."

"Good, you go there. Send Kael out with our ear monitors for the Prime members." After they'd declined armaments, some of the generous toys ValCorp had sent her included specially made ear devices that would wrap around the neck of a wolf with the tiny microphone at the end positioned closest to the ear. The cord was so thin, the wolves' thick pelts would easily keep it concealed. This way, her commanders would be able to communicate with the war room and be kept updated.

"Why not me?" Brent looked confused then offended. "I'm an accomplished fighter. Gavin can tell you, I'm ready for this. I want to fight."

"No. I want you in the war room. You know war maneuvers, can spot deceptions better than anyone. That's where I need you."

"But—"

"No buts. That's an order."

After he grunted and reluctantly left, she faced Gavin and Cyrus. "Either one of you let me down, I will fry your balls in Lawe's kitchen and eat them for dinner."

Gavin howled, which sounded more like a laugh, and took off running, leading his pack to the eastern gate. Cyrus knew his orders and nodded, then dug his claws in and sprinted to his designated area. Her brothers, Sam and David, would stay beside her, acting as her guards. She scrutinized the eastern wall and sniffed the air. The Red Claws must have been using scent blockers because she could not detect them.

She wondered how long they had been there and if they had studied Black Stars' patterns with their Lunar Run. Her people had cameras installed along the western wall closest to Werehaven and would have picked up their approach. Renworth must have realized that with the spy he had photographing the area, and had his vans and trucks circle the area to attack from the east.

"C'mon, baby, send me your pawns. Show me what you got."

Unlike the Were King, who would stay safely out of harm's way, she would fight along with her clan. Renworth was probably in his own version of a control room set up in a van parked somewhere off Fifth Avenue. But where? Central Park stretched nearly fifty city blocks; he could be on any one of those streets.

When Kael arrived with the ear devices, she quickly wrapped one around her neck. "Make sure the other Prime members have these, then radio Brent, tell him to check the cameras. See if any suspicious vans or trucks are parked along the eastern corridor. Tell him to dispatch one of the drones."

In his meetings with Remare, the vampire had suggested Gavin borrow a couple of their surveillance drones. After testing them, they discovered those black beauties were undetectable in the night sky and stealthy as they ran silent. Apparently, ValCorp had incorporated some sort of cloaking device. *Thank you, Remare.*

"Yes, my queen." Kael bowed and took off running.

She returned her gaze to the east and whispered, "Where are you? Come out, come out, wherever you are."

Ear-splitting yelps shattered the night as enemy wolves must have discovered their snares. "Welcome to the neighborhood." She grinned as she started morphing into her wolf form.

It didn't take long for the Red Claws to reveal themselves. They stood high up on the wall, peering down on them. In unison, they howled, their roaring designed to instigate fear.

It was going to take a helluva lot more to get her hair to stand on edge. *Bring it.*

The first wave of wolves barreled down on them, their eyes a peculiar and haunting red. Renworth must have loaded them up on the steroids or other performance-enhancing drugs they'd heard whispers about. Her wolves rushed them, and the fight was on.

Snarls and growls resonated all around them as the ground vibrated under them from the clash of bodies. These wolves were feral, but her troops were well-trained and fought admirably.

Wave after wave assaulted them, and they fought them back. More howls reverberated around them. She saw Sam sink his teeth into a Red Claw and then fling him hard against a tree. David had an enemy under him and was digging in deep with his claws.

She wondered how Gavin was doing in the northern region. That was one area they were most concerned with.

Far less populated up there and farthest from Werehaven. It should have been the last place they would attack.

But Renworth enjoyed his surprises, and if he was going for stealth, that's where he would invade. She knew Gavin was an experienced fighter; he'd brawled before in skirmishes with the Red Claws when they'd tried to poach on their lands. And he always emerged victorious.

She prayed he would, now, too.

***

Gavin had his troops spread out between the Great Hill and the Meadows. It would be just like Renworth to attack in the place where Granger had been mauled by that Red Claw. Gavin kept his gaze on the wall and gates separating the park from the outside.

It was quiet, now, but he knew it wouldn't stay that way for long. He looked down at his chipped claw. The fight with Cyrus had been brutal, both giving and receiving hits in equal measure, but he'd needed that. His beast had grown complacent, had rested too long, and needed to awaken.

He had with startling results: His speed was faster than it had ever been, his instincts sharpened to a point he couldn't remember ever having. He'd always considered his wolf a part of him that lived in harmony with his more civilized human self. But that was only a theory.

Once the wolf was unleashed, he gloried in his new strength, the power that rushed through his veins. He thoroughly embraced it, relished it, and made sure all those around him knew who he was—not a beta, but an alpha of the highest order.

Liz would give him hell for it, probably rip him a new one, but it was worth it to prove himself.

Gavin glanced around his surroundings. The hardest part of any war was the waiting. It took a great deal of patience to stay hidden when all he wanted to do was demand the enemy show themselves. Face the inevitable. He knew they were there, waiting. He didn't have to smell them; he could sense them.

What are they waiting for?

He didn't have to wait long as the first group of wolves scaled the wall and jumped down the embankment. They approached slowly at first, their eyes glistening red, teeth bared. Then, low growls were emitted before they rushed them.

Wasting no time, Gavin jumped high and landed on the back of one of the larger wolves, crushing the shoulders of his adversary. He looked up to see Lawe circling his opponent, and then, they attacked each other with amazing speed and force. It took Lawe only moments to grievously wound his prey.

As Gavin inspected the others, all he could think was these were not Renworth's prime enforcers; these wolves were smaller. *This is a decoy. And, if so, where are Renworth's main fighters?*

***

Brent was aggravated at having been benched. Lizandra needed him on the field of battle, not stuck in the tech room. But, admittedly, she was right. He'd discussed war strategies with Gavin, and his former alpha must have conferred with her about his studies.

He glanced up at the large clear polymer board in front of him. He could see perfectly how this was playing out. Renworth was sending in his secondary troops. *Most likely to cause battle fatigue, exhaust Black Star fighters. He's testing us, seeing where our strengths and weaknesses are.*

Brent scrutinized the various camera feeds where the fighting was taking place. When he communicated with the Prime, he informed them where the enemy was attacking, but it was difficult with the cover of night and the shadows the trees provided. Even with the two drones circling, they couldn't be in all regions at all times, but he was grateful for what they did report.

Over time, his animal grew increasingly restless, wanting to be out there with the clan, breathe the fresh air, flex his muscles, defend his tribe. Brent could do so much more out in the field. His instincts would have kicked in, his beast much stronger out there in the wild than the domesticated animal he now held leashed. His ability to predict movement would have been that much sharper.

Brent looked up at the clock. He'd been here for hours. Suddenly, he caught a figure on the screen, apart from the others and studied his movements. A solo agent. Not one of theirs, he suspected. This wolf moved differently, stealthily, cunningly. A breed apart from the others. "What are you up to, my friend?"

Liz had ordered him to the control room. But she hadn't said he had to *stay* there. He could slip out, leave Kael in charge and investigate for himself who this lone wolf was.

***

Cyrus stood guard with his troops outside Werehaven and eyed the terrain. He knew this would be the deciding moment in the battle. No way were they getting past him or any of his men. Werehaven was their home, their sanctuary, their sacred place to celebrate their Were heritage.

No one was going to take that away from them, *no one*. Lizandra and the other members of the Prime knew it would all come down to this. That's why she'd chosen him to protect it; she knew he could hold it, better than anyone, even Gavin.

He rubbed his sore side. Son of a bitch had a sharp set of teeth. He still couldn't believe his beta had challenged him. True, they'd mouthed off to one another from time to time. Cyrus had to admit there was something depraved in his personality that he enjoyed biting sarcasm. He must have said something in passing, something he hadn't even considered offensive that set Gavin off. *But what?*

No matter. When you were alpha, there were always those who thought to test you, those who had something to prove. Whoever said jealousy was a female thing didn't know squat about males and egos.

But, by now, Gavin should have known Cyrus had backed away from Lizandra. In actuality, they hadn't been a couple in quite some time. Hell, he was the one who told her to pursue Gavin. So, why the smackdown? The rumors suggested Liz was back with Gavin. They seemed happy, for a while.

Did something happen between them that Cyrus was unaware of? He rubbed his chin. Now that he thought about it, they did seem at odds. *Lovers' tiff, so quickly?* He snorted. Whatever, he was sure he'd find out eventually.

He paced along the trail, wanting this night to be over. "C'mon, you cocksuckers. You want our lands so badly, fight for it," he muttered to the night. The Red Claws were playing fucking mind games, psychological operations like the army used against enemies. It was designed to drive an adversary crazy, make them antsy, throw them off their game. "Good play, sorry it's not working, though. I know you're coming; you know it, too. Just give me a sign."

Turned out, he didn't have to wait long when he spotted movement up ahead on the ridge.

Then, he heard the ear-splitting howl of a wolf in agony. Good, they'd found the snares with the sharpened spears that had been set up to capture their enemies. He snarled smugly, "Welcome to the party."

Chapter Twenty-Seven

When the drone captured the fighting to the south, Brent paid careful attention to the monitors. That's where Quint, along with his men, were engaged. He knew Quint was strong and fast, almost as fast as he was, but still, Brent worried. With his golden pelt, Quint would be easy to spot, too easy. "Stay to the shadows," he whispered and hoped Quint heard his silent request; the bond they shared was certainly strong enough to form some kind of mental connection similar to what the vampires had.

Brent watched as the skirmishes continued. His packmates, Dorn and Jory, were fighting well, holding their own. And so was Quint. Pride engulfed him at how well each of them fought. Quint's instincts were sharp, sharper than most, thank God.

But where had these guys come from? Brent ran the tapes back. He wanted to see when the Red Claws had entered the park. Central Park South was usually bustling with human traffic, tourists all over the place; therefore, no one expected a major offensive from that direction.

He studied the tapes carefully, then it hit him. "Fuck. They were already here." The Red Claws must have visited the park sometime during the day and then hid themselves away so the patrols couldn't find them. The carousel and the rink had lots of alcoves they could hide in. So did The Dairy, where the Visitors' Center was.

And, if their enemies were hidden in the southern region, it was a good guess Renworth had his people strategically placed in all the other quadrants. He immediately alerted the Prime members, then something else on the monitor caught his attention.

Another lone wolf moving stealthily along the trail. Was it the same one as before? He didn't think so. This one moved differently, and the color of his pelt was streaked with silver.

"Oh, really, now who might you be?" Brent watched as the wolf crept farther away from the fighting and then peered up at the sky as if he knew cameras were mounted and wanted the attention. Brent adjusted the dial to focus more sharply on the wolf's features. When he stared into the wolf's eyes, the creature bowed his head once. "It seems I've been given an invitation." But an invitation to what? And by whom?

"Kael, take over." Brent removed his headset. "I'm going to step out for a while. I'll be back soon."

"Okay, but shouldn't you take your ear monitor with you?"

"No. I won't be gone that long."

When Brent reached the surface, he doffed his clothes and assumed his animal skin. Oh, how glorious it was to finally release his beast. Immediately, his senses felt enhanced. He could smell the different scents around him, see so much better, and hear the nuances of the woods, the birds overhead, the insects on the ground.

He padded in the direction he'd seen the lone wolf go off in. Perhaps he should have been worried he was being led into some sort of trap, but he didn't think so. The wolf's eyes betrayed intelligence, cunning, and...reserve.

He followed the trail farther away, his head raised for any type of danger. Not sensing any, he was about to continue onward, when seemingly out of nowhere, the wolf attacked, knocking him to the ground. The force of the hit was so strong they tumbled down an embankment.

Each rolled quickly to their feet and, teeth bared, circled one another. Their steps mirrored those of dancers, each one carefully measured, keeping pace with the other.

In size, they were about equal. But neither one charged the other. As the moonlight streamed through the trees, highlighting the pelt's streaks, Brent thought the wolf was magnificent.

Then, the other wolf did something unexpected. He started shifting to his human form. But there was something about the poised movements of the wolf that spoke of elegance, refinement, higher intellect. When the transition was complete, he stood, and a smirk crossed his face.

Well, I'll be damned. When Brent realized who the wolf was, he shifted, as well, until he stood and faced as his opponent. "You're about the last person I expected to see tonight."

"Dangerous times, my friend." His response was also barely above a whisper. "I didn't expect to be out here tonight. But Renworth ordered it so."

"Why?"

Victor Gren's features appeared darker as he moved farther into the shadows. "He wants you dead. Asked me to personally handle it."

"But, why?"

"Before Robin met with his untimely death, he informed Renworth it was you who had him interrogated and tortured."

"Well, he was half right. I did interrogate him for spying on us. But I didn't torture him."

The cadence of Victor's voice altered. "Who did?"

"There were others in the room; they did the honors."

"But you gave the command?"

Brent nodded once. "Previously, he attacked one of our younger members, gutted him badly. Our queen wanted answers."

"I'm sure she did. Unfortunately, the little shit was one of Renworth's favorites. Rumor had it Robin might have actually been one of his offspring, though it was never acknowledged."

"We lost one of our people to your clan. Dan died on the exam table, bled out before the doc could properly stitch him up."

"I'm afraid we'll both be seeing more of that." Gren's gaze shifted up to the ridge. "I won't be able to contact you, again, for some time. Renworth has become a little paranoid; he's having his closest people investigated."

"What caused the paranoia?"

"Renworth doesn't need a reason. He's suspected for some time he's had an informant in his midst. He had his lawyer, Cantrell, killed in the cage fights because she was photographed with your beta."

Brent tried to digest the information. Gavin had informed them he'd met with Cantrell and that she'd given him info on someone they needed to be wary of. "Renworth killed one of his own?"

Gren nodded. "Nothing compared to what he'd do to me, if he ever found out about our connection."

"He won't."

"You sound so sure."

"You've always been careful. So have I; he won't find out from me."

Gren turned from him. "I must go. Stay out of this battle, Brent. Live to fight another day."

Before he left, Brent asked, "Does Werehaven have an infiltrator?"

"Renworth is keeping his cards close to the vest and doesn't always confer with me. But I believe so; it's what I would do."

"One last thing." Brent knew they'd already spent too much time out in the open, but he wanted confirmation on something. "We have intel that there's a female warrior in your clan who is particularly deadly. I believe she's called Cobralady."

"There's a reason they call her Cobra. Her attacks are lightning quick." Gren disappeared farther up the embankment and into the shadows. "She's the one responsible for your packmate's death."

Brent would have liked to have spoken more with Gren but knew any further delay would be dangerous. He wanted to thank Gren for all his help and regretted not telling him that before he left.

Victor and he had once been friends, years ago, before they'd chosen separate clans. God, it seemed like several lifetimes ago. How an astutely educated man could serve Renworth was beyond Brent. Victor didn't belong with someone as cruel as the Were King, but for reasons unknown to him, Gren had pledged his obedience to the Red Claws.

When Victor first agreed to meet with him and help the Black Stars, Brent had asked him why he'd make such a bold and dangerous move. For certain, Gren had been correct in assuming the carnage Renworth would visit on him would be horrific if he ever found out about them. Victor had replied that he'd seen enough bloodshed in his life and considered sacrificing life for trivial matters *"distasteful"*. And, though he respected some of Renworth's business ventures, he didn't agree with all his methods.

Both of them knew wars should only be fought as a last resort. Life was God's greatest gift, something to be cherished and enjoyed. Not something to be surrendered because of one man's greed or delusions of greatness. If good people were to die, it had better be for something vital. Like defending their people, their home.

And, Brent would do whatever he could to make sure no one threatened what was most sacred.

***

After the fighting had continued on for hours, most of the wolves had shifted to their werewolf forms. Liz did, as well, knowing communication with their war room was crucial to their success. Brent had been keeping her updated on the progress of the different teams. She knew that, even with the men Jenks had sent her, they were still outnumbered, but nevertheless, they fought on.

Brent reported how Cyrus fought nobly against numerous Red Claws, sometimes two or three at a time, and each one defeated by his deadly claws. She'd made the right decision putting him in charge of defending Werehaven. Brent had also cited the many cases of heroism Gavin had showed on the northern field, quickly coming to the assistance of his fighters when they'd needed help.

Gavin was a strong believer in not leaving anyone behind. His unit was slowly being herded toward her section. As was Quint in the south. It seemed Renworth wanted them all in one place for his grand finale.

Renworth wanted to conquer. Liz wanted to defend what was theirs, make her ancestors proud. She gazed out over the bloody terrain and the fallen soldiers on both sides. Her heart ached at the unmitigated loss, but she couldn't afford the distraction and would find the time later to grieve.

She didn't need to vanquish the Red Claws, all she had to do was to keep fighting until the sun rose, which would be in a couple of hours.

At dawn, the fighting would subside because the gates would open to the early morning human joggers. If the city council ever learned the Weres had engaged in bloodshed in the park, they would forfeit their territories.

Neither the Red Claws nor the Black Stars wanted that to happen. Even if it was proven that her lands were the ones invaded and made war upon, the council members would not show any leniency their way. They took their business interests very seriously, and threat to the tourist industry would not be tolerated.

And so, they fought on.

***

Edgar Renworth, along with his elite enforcers, watched the fighting from high up on the western wall. His eyesight, even in human form, was excellent. He didn't even need the binoculars or the screens to see what he desired most. All was going according to plan. The wolves were getting tired from every barrage hurled their way. He'd been relentless in sending in wave after wave to challenge the Black Stars, effectively wearing their strength down.

He wasn't arrogant enough not to admire the fight they put up. There were several among the Black Stars he'd taken note of who had superlative techniques and combat maneuvers. As the reports and film Robin had provided revealed, they had been trained exceedingly well. Their commanders knew their stuff, and the men under them obeyed the orders with remarkable results.

But that was all about to change. He'd kept his best fighters out of the battle, wanting them fresh and psyched up to engage after his soldiers had exhausted the enemy.

Renworth turned to his elite and projected his voice loud enough for all to hear. "Tonight is a glorious night."

The enforcers raised their arms in salute and roared their approval.

He held up his hand for quiet. "Tonight, we take what we fought for. Blood has been shed and must be answered for. It's time to finish this conquest. Time to seize what should have been ours long ago. Tonight, we claim Central Park!"

The warriors stamped their feet against the stone wall and howled their anticipation of joining their brethren on the field. The sounds pleasing to his ears. Their excitement was rich in the air, their need to release the predator within raged on. He gestured for them to hear him. "My people, you have one directive, one that you will not fail me in. One that will solidify our aim and bring fruition to our goals."

When he was sure he had the attention of all his warriors—Curtis, the best fighter in the clan; 'Sin'clair, an extraordinarily lethal soldier; Ramos, dangerous with his speed; and also deadly, Bali, who knew well how to use deception in her battles—he addressed them. Then, he pointed in the direction of Werehaven. And smirked deviously when he gave his final directive. "Kill the queen."

Howling, they jumped down from the wall, shifting into their werewolf forms. When Victor went to join them, Renworth stuck his arm out. "Not you. You stay by my side."

"But you told me you wanted me to fight for you."

"And so, you shall," he grinned, "but not yet."

Chapter Twenty-Eight

Cyrus knew it was just a matter of time before Renworth decided to unleash hell on earth. He watched as the Were King's lead enforcers charged his way. At first, he thought all four would barrel down on him, but at the last moment, three of them veered off in different directions, each one on a separate trajectory to the north, south, and west. That left Renworth's fiercest warrior, Curtis, for Cyrus to deal with.

The muscular werewolf, whose eyes seemed to glow red, snarled as he began to circle Cyrus. "So, you're the queen's alpha. We've heard all about you. I bet with that white hair of yours, all the pretty ladies line up to get a taste of you."

Cyrus had read up on Curtis, knew he was one of Renworth's deadliest warriors. The guy enjoyed proving himself in the ring, strutting his stuff to all onlookers, packed a punch that could decimate an opponent if he wasn't smart enough to evade. And, if it was steroids making his eyes red, then his hits would be excruciating. Curtis wasn't one to rush a fight; he liked to play with his prey before he pounced.

But, then again, so did Cyrus. "And not one of them has ever complained."

"I'll bet."

Curtis sized him up pretty good, but when his eyes lingered between Cyrus' legs a little too long, Cyrus decided to play with the guy. "I hear you serve Renworth pretty well. I wonder if that includes sucking him off. The way you're staring at my dick makes me think you really enjoy it."

"The only thing I'm going to enjoy is ripping your fucking head from that neck of yours."

Cyrus never could refrain from poking at rattlesnakes. He blew him a kiss and winked his way. "Which head?"

A menacing growl was the only warning Cyrus got before Curtis lunged for him. Evading the blow, he danced around Curtis and struck him with a hit so powerful Curtis stumbled back. It had been some time since he'd fought against someone who was close to him in size, and he welcomed the challenge.

Curtis shook his head, as if he hadn't expected Cyrus to move as fast as he did. 'Roids gave you an initial power boost, but the long-term effects were damaging and threw your equilibrium off, as well as your reflexes. Cyrus hoped the latter was true of his opponent.

Curtis wiped the blood from his mouth and smirked. "First blood. Oh, I'm going to enjoy this."

"Let's bring on the hurt."

And, then the brawl began, each one trying to best the other with a series of punches that would have broken the ribs of men with less muscular frames. Claws slashed at one another as they fought, as if this would be the final match, each one refusing to back down.

Cyrus was able to wrap his arms around Curtis' midsection and threw him into the trunk of a tree. The ferocious sound of something cracking reverberated loudly, and Cyrus wasn't sure if it was the wood breaking or the bones in Curtis' back.

He got his answer when Curtis dusted himself off then charged him. More punches and kicks rang out around them, until Curtis got a hold on him, and they went crashing to the ground and rolled several feet away. Cyrus knew he couldn't afford to let Curtis get the upper hand. If he did, the beating Cyrus would take would be brutal.

The drugs he smelled on Curtis made his opponent frenzied with aggression. Cyrus had never fought anyone that hopped up and had one second for that realization to manifest before Curtis walloped him with a punch that made him see stars.

His reflexes quickly kicked in, and Cyrus threw the Red Claw off him. For some reason, he heard Wham's song, "Wake Me Up Before You Go," playing in his mind, laughed, and thought, *Oh, what the hell, go with it.*

***

Sweat pouring down his back and panting fiercely, Gavin thought it was like watching a fucking football game where one team decides to blitz the quarterback. But, in this case, the quarterback was Lizandra, and the opposing team were the Red Claws. Waves of enemy Weres were relentlessly blitzing them from all sides until nearly all of Liz's Prime members were consolidated in the mid-section of Central Park's Great Lawn.

After fighting off dozens and dozens of warriors, and now in his werewolf skin, Gavin was feeling the grueling effects of fatigue, but he shook it off. He was sure the rest of the Weres were running on fumes, as well, but still, they fought on.

When an aggressor charged him, he quickly deflected the attack. Another bolted into his side, and then, teeth and claws sank into flesh. The coppery smell of blood saturated the air around them. Gavin used martial arts moves Remare and Bas had taught him. Both were tough instructors, never showing any mercy, and now, Gavin was grateful for their arduous lessons. He grabbed hold of the neck of his opponent and twisted until he heard it crack. The enemy slid to the ground with no chance of ever rising.

Gavin looked up in time to see more warriors making their way toward Lizandra. Her brothers were doing a great job of keeping most of the attackers at bay, but they couldn't deflect all of them. Gavin moved toward her to keep her protected. No one was touching her. He would gladly lay down his life to save hers.

He kept his back to her as he said, "Fancy meeting you here."

"Where the fuck else would I be?!" Enraged, she threw a roundhouse kick against one of the werewolves that sent him flying, then quicky used a combination of uppercuts, jabs, and hooks against another that had him clutching his stomach as he rolled away.

He was glad she still had that spark of sass he loved so much. She was magnificent to watch, and he swore, as he'd done many times before, she had to be a descendant of the Amazons. Her fighting skills were amazing. The woman was fearless and resolute. Her grace under pressure unwavering and revered.

She glanced up at him. "How are we doing?"

Gavin wasn't sure she was inquiring about his bearing or that of their clan. "We're holding it together." She knew as well as he did that, as skilled as their warriors were, as hard as they fought with their hearts and souls, this was a battle they couldn't win. Sunrise was only an hour or so away, but at this rate, they would be lucky to be alive to actually see it.

The harsh reality of it was that they were greatly outnumbered, and even with the extra men Jenks had sent, it wasn't enough, not nearly enough.

When another adversary rushed them, Gavin intercepted him and used a series of twists and spins to knock him out cold. He quickly scanned the area around them to locate any other immediate threats.

"In case we don't make it—"

His heart pounding, he panted, his voice harsh, "Don't you fucking go there."

Her back was against his. "I know, but if we don't…"

Gavin didn't want to hear this. Accepting defeat was never easy for a soldier, especially when you knew you gave it all you had, fought with a vitality you didn't know you possessed, discovered stores of energy you never tapped into before. The clan believed in them, fought to the death with them; losing wasn't something he wanted to comprehend.

"I want you to know...I've always loved you. No one ever replaced you. You were always in my heart and always will be."

That was sounding too much like a goodbye. "I know. Think you can save your amorous words for when we're alone, again."

She rubbed up against his back. "Yeah, I can do that...my king."

Gavin wasn't sure he heard her correctly as another fighter flew in his direction. Gavin engaged him with fists of fury, each pounding into the other until Gavin landed the killing blow. Wiping the sweat from his forehead, he stepped closer to her and asked, "What did you say?"

She grinned his way. "You heard me. You didn't want to be beta." She sent another attacker flying to her side who then met the fists of her brother. "So, I thought you'd like being my king better. Of course, I'm still the ruling monarch, and you'd be more the King Consort, but we'd rule together."

Gavin wasn't sure how he had the strength to smile, but a big ole grin split his face. In a moment of frenzied insanity, in a world already stained with too much bloodshed, he grabbed her and kissed her like it was the last time he'd ever get the chance, and with the way things were going, there was a good chance that might very well be the case. But the sheer delight in hearing her impassioned moans infused him with newly inspired vigor.

Movement to the side quickly caught his attention. The bitch that had killed Dan was making her way toward them. Bali. No wonder they called her Cobralady. She slithered more like a snake than an actual werewolf. And she switched directions with a speed that was uncanny, almost unnatural.

Her hands and arms were painted red, evidence of her triumphs on the battlefield.

Gavin was about to engage her, but then, Tia appeared out of nowhere and landed on Bali's back, striking with awe-inspiring force. Infuriated, the Cobra twisted and threw her off, and each went at the other with a viciousness he'd only ever seen in female fighters. In all his time at Werehaven, he'd had his share of breaking up fights, mostly with men. But, when the women occasionally fought, he let someone else do the honors, knowing all too well how ferocious some females could get.

Tia and Bali continued to hiss and claw at each other, then Bali did a combination of acrobatic moves that bedazzled the eyes and kicked Tia to the ground, she was about to throw a killing blow when something whizzed by him.

In a series of moves resembling a gymnast's floor routine, Max bounded in and used both feet to kick Bali away from Tia, then Max did a couple of impressive side-flips, channeling her energy into a twisting move that caught the Cobra's neck in a chokehold between her thighs that squeezed the air from her.

"Holy shit," he muttered. "Someone sure ate their spinach today."

After Bali's lifeless body slid to the ground, Max looked up and winked at him. Gavin had wanted to be the one to avenge Dan's death, but this was even better. When Tia extended a hand to help Max up, they fist-bumped and then went after more enemy soldiers.

Fucking Amazons.

He loved each and every one of them.

Chapter Twenty-Nine

Brent watched as the battle raged on. In less than an hour, the sun would be up and put an end to all the carnage. He watched as Cyrus battled Curtis. From what he could see on the monitors, it was a pretty even fight. Both were huge werewolves, incredibly fast, but he thought Cyrus might have the advantage of thinking on his feet.

Any good soldier knew adaptability was key to surviving a perilous situation. It seemed like Curtis was the more aggressive, faster even, but his ability to use the resources at hand was slower.

He switched his gaze to the fighting around Lizandra. Fuck. They were throwing everything they had her way. She battled nobly, as did Gavin, who fought side by side with her, not letting any of the more vicious werewolves near her. They seemed to be holding their own. But for how much longer? Each side had to be feeling the effects of battle fatigue by now. How some of them were still standing was a testament to their beliefs.

"I should be out there," he muttered aloud. "They've been fighting for hours. I'm rested, more than able to fight. I haven't even thrown one punch tonight."

Brent flicked his eyes to where Quint was now fighting with the enforcer known as Sin and nearly had a heart attack. All the fighting had now moved to the Great Lawn. Renworth had them surrounded on all sides. This wasn't going to last much longer.

Quint was good, knew maneuvers Brent had taught him, but he didn't have the bloodlust Sin obviously had. Both were pommeling the other with rancorous blows, but Sin seemed to be possessed by the spirit of Achilles.

That did it. Brent made up his mind and ripped off his transmitter. "Take over, Kael. I'm going out there."

Kael swung toward him. "I can't let you do that."

"I didn't ask for permission. They need me out there."

"That might be true. But you heard Lizandra's directive. If it begins to look like they're gonna lose, you need to get Sasha and everyone else out of here."

Liz had requested he get the non-combatant Weres, the ones who couldn't fight, to safety through a series of secret tunnels only the Prime were familiar with.

His gaze shifted to Sasha, who was walking toward him. "You do that, if it does come to it. I'm going to try my hardest to make sure that doesn't happen."

"Go Brent," Sasha said. "I'll keep an eye on the monitors; I've already relieved the other technicians when they needed bathroom breaks. I *can* do more than just fetch water and food."

Knowing she had competent computer skills, he said, "Thanks, Sasha." With one last glance at Kael, he turned and left. As soon as he reached the surface, he shifted to his fastest form, that of a wolf, and flew over bushes, trails, benches, to get to his partner.

When another enemy werewolf tried to enter the fray along with Sin, Brent sent him flying and lunged up to tear the guy's throat out. Eyes blazing, he morphed into his werewolf form then turned his attention to Sin.

***

Feeling victory close at hand, Renworth used the binoculars to make sure he wasn't missing any of the action, then zeroed in on the new wolf who just entered the fighting between Sin and the golden wolf. Smiling smugly, he knew exactly who he was. He lowered the field glasses and turned to his second. "All right, Victor. Now's your chance. Kill the bastard who had Robin tortured." He pointed in the direction where Brent was fighting with Sin. "Remember, make him suffer first."

***

Liz felt the first pangs of regret as the enemy circled them, boxing them in and effectively cutting off any means of retreat. As she stared out at the field of battle and witnessed the bloodshed surrounding them, sorrow filled her heart. Loyal people had died tonight, hers and Renworth's. Others were lying on the ground in agony from their wounds. Blood soaked the earth in many areas.

Why had it come to this? Could this have been avoided? Should she have taken Renworth's offer? The Were King wasn't the only enemy to be fought this night, an even more challenging foe emerged: doubt. Doubt in her abilities, doubt in her decisions. No good ever came from second guessing yourself, she knew this, but she felt compelled to do just that.

Renworth's voice carried over the distance from the megaphone he used. It was a stab wound to her heart. "Surrender, Lizandra. You are surrounded, and there is no hope left for your clan. Admit defeat, and we'll allow your people to leave peacefully."

"Do you believe that?" she asked Gavin.

"Not a chance. The minute we surrender, they'll go after you. You're the only one with a rightful claim to these lands. He won't permit you to just walk away. He'll kill you first."

She knew that to be true, and lines from Tupac's poem, "In the Event of my Demise", a poem that had always haunted her, began reciting in the back of her mind, especially the line about dying for a principle you believed in.

People fought wars for all kinds of different reasons. But not her, she didn't fight for glory or ego, for someone else's lands. She fought for Werehaven and everything it stood for. It was more than a place for social gathering; it was a place of justice, of sanctuary for those who called it home. Lizandra fought for her clan, to protect them.

Wasn't that what good rulers did, protected their people?

Her gaze shifted over her exhausted soldiers who had fought admirably and with so much zeal, to the fallen in utter need of medical attention. She raised her head and was about to answer Renworth when the ground beneath her feet began to vibrate. "What is that?"

Gavin looked to the east where the sun was just beginning to rise. "I don't know. It almost feels like an earthquake, but we don't get them here in New York. At least not usually."

The sounds grew louder, and everyone started getting anxious, nervously gazing about, trying to figure it out. Gavin threw his arm around her in a protective move. And, unexpectedly, she heard music playing. Who the hell was playing music at a time like this? But, then, howls erupted in the distance. A symphony of wolfen magic, their voices in sync, crystal clear against the fading of the night.

Then, one wolf's voice echoed louder and more majestic than the others. A voice so pure, so powerful, it could bring tears to people's eyes. The crescendo reaching higher and higher until it sounded like angels singing.

A tear almost gathered in the corner of her eye. There was only one person who could hit notes that high and had the talent to sustain them.

Suddenly, a striking figure appeared high up on the rock formation. He was backlit by the rising sun, a corona making him appear otherworldly. His skin resplendently tanned and muscular, his ebony hair fell in waves around a face that was nothing short of stunning. His mesmerizing beauty held everyone in awe as he gazed out over them with eyes the color of shimmering sapphires. Power radiated from him, holding all who beheld him spellbound.

Then, two werewolves flanked him, and then another pair, and another until an army emerged around him. Dangerous males and females who looked like they were ready to take on the world and would cut down anyone who stood in their way.

"Orion." Liz's heart leapt up in her chest. The rock star was dressed in his stage persona with black leather pants and vest. He wore a crystal around his neck, similar to the one Miranda had given her. His sexual appeal was so profound, so intense, he attracted men, as well as women. Though, those who were well-acquainted with him knew his heart belonged to only one.

Gavin dropped his arm. "I'll be damned."

All the people around them seemed dumbfounded by Orion's unexpected appearance. His songs were played on all the media outlets, his fame well-known. People adored him, loved him and his music, were in awe of his talent and the sheer splendor of his music.

With ValCorp backing and producing his albums, Orion's career had skyrocketed with multiple songs on the Billboard Top Ten for months at a time. Even the Red Claws gave him a wide berth as he made his way toward her.

Orion bent one knee before her and smiled her way. "My queen."

"Rise, you idiot." She pulled him up, embraced him, and gratefully whispered, "Thank you."

He affectionately stroked her cheek. "You saved my life once, remember? Gave me a home, a place to belong to. Figured I'd return the favor."

"But how—"

"We were in Miami, taking a much-needed break from the tour when a little bird informed me you were having some sort of soiree. Figured I'd come up here and see for myself." He winked at her then turned and faced the Red Claws. When he spoke, his tone had dangerously darkened and resonated loudly. "My people and I are loyal to Queen Lizandra. You make war on her, you make war on me and mine. Is that the path you wish to follow?"

When the Red Claws, many of which were showing signs of exhaustion and battle fatigue, got an eyeful of just how many people, who had shifted into human form, Orion had brought with him, they backed away, receding in the direction of their departing king.

Liz wasn't sure the reason the Red Claws retreated was because they had no desire to attack Orion, who after sharing blood with his vampire lover, appeared more ethereal, more potent than ever, or because of the army he had with him. Either way, they were now a fading memory as the sun began to shine ever so brightly on the horizon.

"A wise decision." Orion smirked then faced Gavin. "How you doing, old man? Miss me?"

"I've told you before, I'm not that old." Gavin grabbed him in a bear hug. "I am so glad to see you, again."

Orion returned the gesture. "Once a Black Star, always a Black Star." He rubbed his stomach. "Got anything to eat around here? I'm starving and didn't get a chance to have any food, yet."

Grinning, Lawe came forward and threw his arm around Orion. "My man, you can have anything your little heart desires. I will make you the best breakfast you ever had."

As they walked back to Werehaven, their soldiers carrying the wounded and the fallen, Liz asked, "Who are all these people?"

"Friends of mine. Some are roadies, some part of the crew, others are friends of theirs. When I told them what I was planning to do, I didn't even have to ask for volunteers. They happily came with me."

"Whoever they are, they are most welcome."

Chapter Thirty

After they'd feasted on eggs and andouille sausage, Liz invited Orion to stay for part of the day, but he'd respectfully declined, citing he had a certain someone he wanted to get back to, but assured her, if she ever needed his help, again, he was only a text away. He even promised, when his tour was over, to hold a concert in the park and donate the proceeds to Werehaven and the families of the fallen.

Knowing that this war with Renworth would turn ugly, she'd called Doctor Gabriel, a vampire and friend of the clan, along with a colleague of his, Doctor Singh, who had worked on Weres before, to administer to the wounded. They had worked tirelessly in stitching up and treating the injured who were now recuperating comfortably at Werehaven.

Resting in the VIP lounge, in her favorite recliner, was Cyrus, who had suffered some cuts and bruises but seemed content enough with the four females surrounding him stroking his arms and legs. He saluted Liz and Gavin with his bottle of Lagavulin when they passed by. The other members of the Prime had retreated to their rooms to spend quality time with their loved ones.

Exhausted, Liz and Gavin barely finished their showers when they tumbled naked onto the bed. Neither one wanted to move a muscle but, rather, just bask in the knowledge that they had survived and were immensely grateful to still be breathing.

Gavin grasped her hand, his whiskey-colored eyes conveying his curiosity...and something else—hope, perhaps. "Did you mean what you said, out there on the battlefield?"

"About what?"

"You know, what you said about making me King Consort. Now that we're *not* facing certain death."

She turned her head his way. "Of course, I meant it. Have you ever known me not to mean what I say?"

His lopsided grin made the butterflies in her stomach take flight. "Uh, not really."

"We'll rule together, but Cyrus stays as alpha, he deserves that much. Brent relayed to me how he fought against Curtis. He really came through for us in defending Werehaven."

"I know." Gavin rubbed his brow. "So, who should we have as beta, then?"

She thought about it then reached across the night table for her phone.

A few minutes later, there was a knock at the door. She called out, "Enter," then added, "We're in here."

Brent slowly slid the bedroom door open to find her and Gavin lying on their stomachs facing him. "Should I come back later?"

"No need for that. I understand you disobeyed my orders and left the tech room to help in the fight."

Brent had the good grace to look chagrined. "I did."

"I should punish you for that, but since I understand your reasoning, I won't. I have something else in mind for you."

His eyes seemed to ask, "And, what is that?"

"What do you think of becoming beta?"

Brent looked shocked, like he couldn't believe what he just heard. "Are you suggesting I become—"

"You've proven your worth, time and time again. I can't think of anyone else who deserves it most. Besides, I respect a man who can think for himself, even if that means defying a directive to serve the greater good." When he just stood there, looking less than thrilled, she asked, "The job doesn't appeal to you?"

"Rumors abound that Gavin will be your King Consort…"

Apparently, she'd been overheard during the battle. Were hearing was acute, so she wasn't all that surprised. "Truth, not a rumor."

He nodded. "And, Cyrus is your alpha. Maybe you should have a female as beta, so there's balance."

"A female?" She hadn't thought of that. "Who?"

He shrugged. "There were many female warriors out there today, uh, yesterday, who proved themselves. You could choose any one of them."

Gavin asked, "You hesitate; does this mean you don't relish the idea of becoming beta?"

He sighed. "It's just that I have much work, considering the financial investments for Werehaven, so to take on even more responsibility, I'm afraid it would be detrimental to my current concerns."

Liz pondered his answers. "Very well. Take a few days to consider my offer. Then, we'll discuss it."

Brent nodded once then turned and left, closing the door behind him.

Liz exhaled. "Well, that was a surprise."

"Not really. Brent prefers being in the shadows. Lets others get the glory. That's just not him."

"I am disappointed. Who do you think we should choose, now?"

He rolled them over so that he was on top, his weight resting on his elbows, his body arousing hers. "We have plenty of time to discuss that. For now," he bent down and claimed her lips in a passionate kiss so hot her toes curled, "I can think of better things to do."

"I bet you can." Liz wrapped her arms around her love, her king. "You know, Jenks told me before we left Moon River that if we survived the war with Renworth, he'd marry us and give us a banquet we'd never forget, all at his expense."

"He did, huh?" Gavin flashed her a crooked grin. "I guess he wasn't expecting us to win."

"Maybe not. So, what should I tell him?"

His eyes glinted with glee. "Rethinking getting married, again, Liz?"

"It's possible." She grabbed his ass and pulled him closer. "If my king will give me an answer."

"I'd have thought you'd want a wedding at Werehaven."

She shrugged. "The where isn't the important part."

He slid his body seductively over hers, making her heart beat louder. "Oh, what is?"

"An answer in the affirmative."

"I asked you long ago to marry me, you said no then."

"I know." She stroked his brow. "I've seen the error of my ways. So, my answer now, is yes."

"Is it, now?" His breath tickled her ear. "Funny, I don't remember asking, again."

She growled. "No. I asked you, and you said..."

He purred, "Affirmative." Then, he ground his body temptingly along hers so that every inch of her was seriously stimulated. "I love you, Liz. I'm gonna take you higher, higher than you've ever been before. And, once I'm done with that," he kissed her, again, his tongue tangling with hers as searing pleasure coursed through her veins, "I'm going to do it, all over again, until our bodies are singing sacred arias."

Overcome with joyous ecstasy, she couldn't wait. "Bring on the music."

Epilogue

Three weeks later

Renworth stood in his room in his castle overlooking the Hudson. The night was still, hardly a breeze was coming off the water. He brought the glass of scotch to his lips and sipped. The war between clans had not gone according to plan. He should have won, his people had been primed for the fight, everything was going right, until the unanticipated happened.

He did not fault the loss as one of his own. No one could have predicted that the singer would show up, and with an army to boot. He snorted. The fallacies of war, he supposed. The unexpected frequently happened. Not all things were within his control; he had to accept that.

When a cool breeze finally caressed his face, he relished the feeling, knowing autumn was coming soon. The leaves with all their pretty colors would begin to fall.

He swallowed the rest of his drink as one of his assistants knocked and then stood in the doorway. "Your visitor has arrived. Should I send him in?"

"Yes, but give me one moment first."

"Of course."

Renworth assumed his seat behind his mahogany desk and swiveled, glad that his recently acquired ally at Werehaven could slip away long enough to pay him a visit. They had much to discuss, much to plan for.

His guest entered and parked himself in one of the chairs in front of him without waiting for permission. Renworth liked the confidence the guy had in himself and the self-assured smirk he wore reminded Renworth of his younger self. He had given a great deal of thought on how to seduce the man; money wouldn't do it, neither would career status, but in the end, he had chosen something that would appeal to his vanity.

Ah vanity, the deadliest of the seven deadly sins.

"You don't look too upset after your defeat at Werehaven."

"It's a temporary setback," Renworth replied. "Many lose battles who, eventually, go on to win wars."

"Is that right?"

Renworth poured his guest a tumbler of Lagavulin. "Definitely."

His guest sipped his drink. "And, what makes you so sure you can win a war against Werehaven?"

"Because I have an offer for you that I believe will be most appealing."

His smirk widened. "Oh, yeah, and what might that be?"

Renworth grinned, knowing he had a powerful ally before him. Together, they would be impossible to overcome. "How would you like to be king of the Black Stars...Cyrus?"

Coming Soon

Veil of Light
(Series Finale)

It's been three years since Miranda Crescent left New York City, sacrificing all that was precious, to become the *Elemental* she was always destined to be. But ambition comes with a price and much has changed since she's been gone. Learning about the brutal death of a loved one, Miranda vows vengeance on those responsible. A quest that will test the limits of her power and forever change the course of her life.

Meanwhile, Lord Valadon, *King of the Vampires*, has his hands full running his corporation, ValCorp. Since the loss of his greatest ally, and the disappearance of another, he must finally confront the group responsible for the deaths of his people, the dangerous HOL, and its leader, Stuart Blackmore, aka *The Regent*.

In this final installment of *The Seven Deadly Veils* series, old adversaries band together to fight the war that will determine who truly is the supreme power in New York City.

Diana Marik is the author of the Seven Deadly Veils Vampire Series. She grew up in New York City and has her MA in English Literature from Hofstra University. Before becoming an author, Diana worked as an educator, mental health therapist, yoga instructor and camp counselor.

Among Diana's passions, traveling is her favorite. One of her favorite places to visit is the American Southwest and her home away from home, New Orleans. When not writing, Diana loves discovering museums. In her leisure time, she enjoys going to the movies and hanging out with her friends.

Diana is currently at work on her latest novel in the Veilverse and would love to hear from her fans. She can be contacted at www.dianamarik.com.

Made in the USA
Middletown, DE
14 January 2022

58722188R00177